Brought Us Together

Brought Us Together

Jean De Vries

the Write Place

PUBLISHING + DESIGN

ISBN: 978-1-7345829-1-8

Library of Congress Control Number: 2020909940

Published in the United States of America by the Write Place, Inc.
For more information, please contact:

the Write Place, Inc.
809 W. 8th Street, Suite 2
Pella, Iowa 50219
www.thewriteplace.biz

Cover and interior design by Michelle Stam, the Write Place, Inc.
Cover photography by Megan Rochelle Photography.

Hymns quoted in this book:
"Softly and Tenderly" by Will L. Thompson (1880),
"What a Friend We Have in Jesus" by Joseph M. Scriven (1885),
"Abide with Me" by Henry F. Lyte (1847),
"He Leadeth Me" by Joseph H. Gilmore (1862), and
"His Eye Is on the Sparrow" by Civilla D. Martin (1905).

View other Write Place titles at www.thewriteplace.biz.

— Dedication —

This book is dedicated to my own beloved grandmas.

To Grandma Bea, who encouraged me to keep writing and whose love was a bright, shining light.

To Grandma Ella, who was so generous with her time and affection. There are so many pieces of her in this book—her laugh, her words, and even her cake pan.

Both women gave me unconditional love, and both gave me Jesus.

— Chapter One —

"Can I help ya?" Amy smiled at the woman searching over the dry bulk goods.

"Oh, um…yes. Do you sell yeast in bulk?" she asked a little nervously. Amy saw the way the woman's eyes slid gently over her dress and apron in polite curiosity. Over a decade of working with her family in their store, the Amish Country Market, made helping English customers as easy and comfortable as dealing with her Amish neighbors. Very little phased her anymore. She figured she had heard every question or comment—rude, curious, or otherwise—about her lifestyle.

Did she ever try driving a car? No.

Did she really wear dresses every single day? Yes.

Wasn't it oppressive to live with so many rules? No.

Did she have to get married young? No.

"Our yeast is over here. We carry two sizes. A one-pound package and a three-pound package," Amy said as she reached to the top shelf a foot above her head. Her fingers gently brushed the crinkling plastic packages with their simple but straightforward labels.

"Oh, wonderful! Such good prices, too! I like to bake my own bread," the woman replied, plucking the three-pound package off the shelf.

"Me, too." Amy smiled warmly.

The Englisher laughed and placed the package in her shopping basket.

Amy walked back to the front, tidying various items on her way. The aisles of shelves and rows of tables held a variety of items. Some had fresh produce from her family's own large garden. Some displayed hand-crafted items made by other Amish in the community. There were many tables of fabrics and sewing notions. And of course, a solid half of the store was dedicated to her brother's woodworking and handmade furniture. But one extra-large table right in front of the doors held a display of baked goods—artfully arranged cakes, cookies, breads, cinnamon rolls, muffins, and even pies.

The Amish customers would walk right past that table. But not the English customers. That was their first stop and favorite section of the market. Over the past several years, more and more of their customers were outsiders, or Englishers. After a lifetime owning and operating the market, Amy's parents, Daniel and Mary, were extremely comfortable dealing with them. Amy's life had never been quite as sheltered as some of her friends'.

As she turned away from straightening the shelves of homemade preserves, Amy noticed Sophie Esh standing at the checkout counter next to the glass double doors at the front of the store.

"And how is Sophie today?" Amy asked as she rounded the counter to stand opposite the elderly Amish woman.

"Ah, Amy Miller. I am *gut*! I ran out of embroidery floss for the tea towels I am working on for Lucas and Essie," she said as her blue-veined hands laid three small bundles of thread on the counter.

The mention of Lucas stopped Amy for a split second.

"I hope ya found the colors ya need," she said smoothly, proud of herself for keeping her voice from trembling.

"*Jah*, I surely did. God makes flowers in every shade of the rainbow, so I won't be picky," the gray-haired woman laughed.

Amy forced a sweet smile though her mind was suddenly elsewhere.

"You'll be at the wedding, too, I hope?" Sophie asked, lifting her wire-rimmed gaze to peer inquisitively at Amy's face.

Fortunately, Amy had anticipated Sophie's question. The dear old woman wasn't exactly known for minding her own business.

"I hope to be, as long as we can find others to manage the store," Amy replied with a gentle smile.

"Ah, that's *gut* to hear. I know he was an old beau of yers, and I'm glad to hear there are no sour grapes." Sophie nodded as she placed her change in a tiny leather coin purse.

Sour grapes? It was true Amy no longer pined for Lucas. She'd forgiven him for breaking off their relationship, even though she would never agree with his reasons. Time had lessened the pain of his rejection. But she still remembered the list of excuses he'd given her that night. How he'd said her family was on dangerous ground because they had welcomed an Englisher into their midst. Lucas Beiler's family had not exactly been supportive when Silas married Kirsten. And while nearly the entire community had eventually come around and welcomed Kirsten warmly, the Beilers still kept a distinct distance.

"There'll be someone else for ya. Lots of boys looking for a wife yet. Someone will notice ya sooner or later," Sophie's voice scratched.

Amy held back a flinch as Sophie's words found their mark. The woman hadn't meant to offend, she was sure. But there was that assumption—that she needed to find a husband.

That was something Amy had absolutely no intention of doing.

She was perfectly fine on her own, thank you very much. Just a few years ago, her mother had taken a semi-retirement from working at the store. Amy had seamlessly stepped in to take her place. Sure, her dad was most often in the back of the store—managing inventory, making repairs, and doing the heavy lifting. But it was Amy who, for all intents and purposes, ran the day-to-day operations in the storefront. She made a nice wage. She enjoyed her work. And her days were full. There really wasn't room for a husband in her life…or in her heart.

"*Gott segen eich*," Amy said with a nod as Sophie scooped up the bundles of thread.

"See ya Tuesday," Sophie chortled as she shuffled to the doors.

Tuesday. Amy sighed. Three days. She had three days to muster up the strength to sit through Lucas Beiler's wedding. Three days to endure the questioning looks from what felt like the entire Amish community.

— Chapter Two —

The scenery blurred by the windows of the passenger van. Nathaniel fought a wave of nausea as his seat in the back jostled wildly. He wasn't a stranger to riding in a vehicle. He'd done that nearly every day since he'd turned eighteen and started working at the RV factory. But those trips were less than fifteen minutes long. And he'd ridden in the front seat. This two-day road trip was way more than he could handle.

Relief surged through him as the driver pulled into the gas station. Gingerly, Nathaniel stepped over his sleeping siblings, who were curled and sprawled on their seats between him and the door. His back and neck cracked audibly as his feet hit the ground and he finally stretched his arms above his head.

"Almost there, *sohn*," his father said, slapping him gently on the back. "This will be a *gut* trip, I think."

Nathaniel could only nod. A glance through the back window of the van revealed his three sisters and four brothers all slumped over in their bench seats. The harsh fluorescent lights of the rest stop canopy overhead made his reflection more prominent than their faces. He looked haggard, beaten down, defeated.

The truth was he knew why they were here. Their farm back home was big enough for his dad, and maybe just one *sohn*. But with five boys in the family, there was not enough room for all of them. That simple fact had been the reason Nathaniel sought out work at the RV factory. What they needed was more land. And there simply wasn't more to be had in Middlefield, Ohio…or anywhere nearby. To find land in an Amish area they would have to travel at least as far away as Iowa. Bradford, Iowa, to be exact. Though his dad had yet to admit the truth. This trip was still being touted as an outing to a cousin's wedding and a chance for his mother to see her sister.

ﮗﮗﮗ

Amy stared ahead at the smiling face of the groom. Lucas was happy. That much was obvious. Essie was also happy. That was doubly obvious. She was a tiny slip of a girl, but she was almost bouncing on the balls of her feet with a giddy grin on her face. The couple gazed at one another, and for a moment Amy was happy for them. Truly happy.

"*Aendi* Amy!" The too-loud whisper came from the toddler clutching a fistful of Amy's navy-blue dress. Amy smiled down at her niece. Grace was three already, and her little brother, Benjamin, was nearly two. Kirsten sat jostling Benjamin as best she could. The service was nearly over, and it was clear the little ones had run out of *sit*.

Amy reached out for Grace and pulled her up into her lap. The little girl tucked her bonnet-covered head beneath Amy's chin and snuggled close. Amy sighed deeply, relishing the feel of the little one in her arms.

The little girl in her lap was quite possibly the reason Amy was sitting where she was and not standing at the front smiling into Lucas's face. When Kirsten had learned she was pregnant with Grace, Silas had shocked everyone and offered her a home and a family. Of course, Kirsten was not Amish at the time. The whole Miller family was pulled into a risky time while they waited to see if Kirsten would come to faith and seek baptism. Grace was born, and it wasn't long afterward that Kirsten did indeed see God's amazing care and provision. And Amy had fallen head over heels for Grace.

But the whole situation had cost Amy. It had cost her Lucas.

Given what she knew now, Amy wouldn't have traded Grace for anything. Of that much she was for sure and for certain.

"This is a big wedding!" Kirsten said in quiet surprise as they watched the people emptying out of the full house.

Amy turned and couldn't stop the giggle from trickling out.

Kirsten studied her face for a long moment before smiling crookedly. "This is normal size, isn't it?" she asked Amy finally.

Amy simply nodded. Even after more than three years as an Amish woman, Kirsten was still learning customs and practices Amy had grown up with in the New Order Amish community.

"I didn't realize the Beilers had such a large extended family," Kirsten murmured, almost to herself.

"*Jah.* Hannah moved here from Ohio to marry Joseph Beiler. She had thirteen *bruders* and *schwesders.*"

Kirsten's eyes widened, and Amy laughed.

"Big families are fairly common when Amish people marry in their teens," Amy whispered. Since Silas and Kirsten had married when she was only eighteen, the teasing comment hit the mark.

Kirsten's eyes shot to Amy's face, and Amy had to cover her mouth to try to hide her laughter. But when Kirsten snorted in her own effort to hold in a laugh, both women had to turn away from the others milling around in an effort to compose themselves.

Eventually, Amy was able to hand off Grace to her brother, Silas.

"Did ya sit *gut* for the wedding?" Silas smiled down at his daughter.

"*Jah.* But it was a long sit!" Grace said with wide eyes.

Silas laughed and bounced her in his arms. Amy left them and went to see if she could help set out the wedding meal.

The kitchen was packed with most of the women, all working busily to get the wedding meal served in the basement of the huge white farmhouse. Amy waited around the edge of the doorway. If a few women exited, there would be room for her to come in and lend a hand.

"Ach, Hannah, what a lovely wedding." Amy didn't recognize the voice but knew the stranger was talking to Lucas's mother, Hannah Beiler.

"Thank you, *schwesder!* It is so good to have ya here to celebrate with us!" Hannah enthused.

"I think yer Lucas has found a *gut* wife," the other woman said sincerely.

Hannah sighed, and there was no mistaking her relief. "Finally, he has, *jah*. It was a long road. He made some questionable choices some years ago, but we are mighty glad about the girl he ended up with."

Questionable choices. The words rang in Amy's ears. She hadn't meant to eavesdrop and overhear. And no one had actually mentioned her name. But she knew with certainty she was the questionable choice in Lucas's past that Hannah was referring to. He'd barely courted any other girls in the years between her and Essie.

"There was a girl a few years ago he was pretty serious about. But Joseph felt the family was not committed enough to the community, and he encouraged Lucas to look elsewhere. We worried she would pull him away from the church and the People too much."

Amy stood in stunned silence. Lucas had said all of that to her face several years ago—the night he broke it off with her. None of it was new information, but hearing it again was painful.

"Did she ever bend the knee for baptism?"

"Eventually," Hannah admitted, but her voice was heavy with recrimination.

"Sometimes *buwes* get a little lost, *jah*? My *sohn* doesn't seem in any hurry to settle down," the other woman sympathized.

"I heard that in yer letter..." Hannah's voice trailed off as Amy backed down the hallway. She'd overheard more than enough. With silent footsteps, she retreated toward the front door. The cool November air blasted her lungs but did nothing to help the lump in her throat or the tears pooling in her eyes.

She stumbled down the porch steps and rounded the corner of the house too quickly. She crashed into someone, excused herself, and hurried away to find a quiet corner where she could pull herself together.

⚬୧୧ ୨୨⚬

Nathaniel sucked in a few breaths after having the wind knocked out of him. With barely a word, the young woman had pushed off and dashed away. She was practically running, and without a coat in this cold weather. But the tears streaking down her face explained the urgency with which she hurried away.

He had no idea who she was, of course. He knew almost no one here even though he called several of them his cousins. It had been at least fifteen years since he'd been to Bradford. Lucas had been just a little kid then. And now he was a groom. Strange to think that now he was a husband, a married *mann*. He appeared to be completely delighted with his tiny bride. Lucas being only five-foot-nine made her look a bit taller than she really was. If Nathaniel had to guess, Essie was only five-foot-three. Fitting her next to him in a buggy wouldn't be any problem. They made a good match.

"Nathaniel, there's chocolate pie!" Zach squealed as he descended the stairs into the spacious basement.

But it wasn't the desserts that caught Nathaniel's attention. There was a massive boiler in one corner of the basement. No wood stoves trying to heat the whole house. He'd even spied a gas-powered refrigerator in the kitchen upstairs. His mom had said something about gas-powered washing machines being allowed here, too.

Nathaniel wasn't eager to move. He had a good life with a good set of friends in Middlefield. Not to mention Miriam. But there was no reason he couldn't get settled here, get away from the job he hated at the RV factory, and then go get her. Yes, he could build a life here and be content.

The enormous task of relocating the family to a new farm was daunting, but some of the conveniences allowed in this church district were pretty appealing. Their bishop back home was fair, but very strict.

Things seemed a little easier in Bradford.

— CHAPTER THREE —

"This has been a bitter cold winter," Daniel commented lightly.

Try as she might, Amy could not stop shivering as she sat nestled next to her father in their enclosed buggy.

"*Jah*, it sure has," she said through chattering teeth. "Though it hasn't slowed down traffic at the store."

"This is true," her dad agreed with a nod.

Lately, the two of them had their hands full as they tried to keep up. Business had boomed ever since Kirsten had suggested new signage along the highway. The market had become a tourist stop ever since.

"I saw the boxes in the back room yesterday. Looks like we have plenty of shelving to get done today," Amy said with raised eyebrows.

"*Jah*, we surely do," Daniel sighed. "It's getting to be a little more than I can handle lately."

"I know what ya mean. The day before yesterday I had such a long line of people at the checkout counter I couldn't help Fannie Stoltzfus with her fabric order."

"With yer *maam* working just a few mornings a week, maybe it's time we hire some extra help during the busy hours. What do ya think?" Daniel asked, turning his gaze to Amy.

His suggestion caught her off guard. It wasn't that he wanted to hire help that surprised her, but the way he was honestly asking for her input. For as long as she could remember, any decisions to be made about the store were handled by her parents. Together. The look in his eyes made her feel that he now valued her opinion. A rush of warmth filled her from within, suddenly melting away the bite in the air.

"I think that might be a good idea. Maybe someone from eleven o'clock to three or so?" Amy carefully suggested.

Daniel nodded and turned his gaze back out to the road.

"Mighty cold day to be moving," he said as they neared the farm that sat just between their home and the market.

"*Jah*. Too cold," Amy murmured.

Up ahead, a moving truck that had not been there last night sat next to a small white farmhouse.

"I wonder if Ollie's son is finally moving in," Daniel mused. Oliver Strapp had been one of their English neighbors for as long as Amy could remember. But about six months ago the widowed farmer had taken a bad fall and moved to a nursing home. Ollie was cantankerous and cranky and had a reputation for being difficult, but her dad had never had a problem with him. Indeed, Daniel seemed to be the only person Ollie really liked.

Almost as soon as Daniel had spoken, a large semi-trailer full of Amish buggies and farm machinery pulled onto the yard.

"I'm guessing Ollie's son isn't Amish, though," Amy said with a small smile.

"*Nee*. Ollie's son is not Amish. Those buggies are a bit different than ours, too. Must be someone new to our community. They got a big chunk of farmland, that's for sure and for certain. Course, judging by the size and number of buggies, they might need the space!" Daniel laughed as they passed by Ollie's old place.

Amy grinned and turned her eyes to the road ahead. They were almost at the market now. But her thoughts stayed on the new family moving in. Maybe they would have some girls her age. It sure would be nice to have some friends so close by. She had her sisters, of course—she loved Shelby Jo and Anna Mae dearly. Deborah, her brother Michael's wife, was a dear soul. Sarah, her brother David's wife, was a good mother but kept to herself. And strangely, even ex-English Kirsten, her brother

Silas's wife, had become a very trusted friend. But none of them were in her exact stage of life. It would be nice to have some single, adult *maed* so close by.

There were other single women in the church, but over the years Amy had lost touch with them. Aside from a few passing conversations on any given church day or at the market, she rarely talked with them. When she'd begun working full-time at the market three years ago, she'd also given up much of the social aspect of Amish life. But she still had Ella—her mentor. And for Amy, that was enough.

.୧ℓℬ.

"*Daed*, I think we have bitten off more than we can chew," Amy said exasperatedly as she stood in the back room.

The bell above the glass double doors jangled loudly, causing Amy to drop her hand from her forehead in surprise.

"*Jah*, I think ya might be right, *dochder*. I'll call yer *bruder* to see if he can come out and help," Daniel said as he bent over yet another box of jams and preserves. It never ceased to surprise Amy just how many jars they sold in a day. It was a favorite among the English customers especially.

For the next hour, Amy walked quickly from the checkout counter to help customers scattered throughout the store. Her shoulders sagged in relief when she turned to find two of her brothers standing in the doorway, their tall frames blocking out nearly all the light.

Silas, blond and bearded, and Caleb, blond and lanky, stood surveying the busy store.

"Oh, I am mighty glad to see the two of ya," Amy breathed with a smile.

Silas returned her smile and nodded. He never had a lot to say.

"*Jah*, we saw ya napping in the corner," Caleb teased with a wink. His bright eyes bounced around the room, taking in the shoppers. His eyes paused on a group of Amish girls near the bulk goods.

"I'm sure *Daed* has plenty to keep ya busy," Amy said with a quirked eyebrow.

Caleb, all of seventeen years old, grinned mischievously. He obviously didn't care that he had been caught looking.

"Hey, I'm just following in my big *bruder's* footsteps and shopping for a wife at the market."

Silas, who had indeed met his wife at the market, grinned and shook his head. Without a word, he walked out the door and Caleb followed. Minutes later the two of them carried in a large dining room table.

"Well, that's different," Amy said, tilting her head as she studied it.

"It's Silas's first live edge table," Caleb announced, placing his hands on his hips and surveying the piece.

"Um...yeah. Okay," Amy stammered. The long side edges were rough and almost looked unfinished—like they were still wearing the bark of the tree. The top was a glorious light golden color that Silas had polished to a high glossy shine. It was rustic, but strangely perfect, too.

"Kirsten made him do it," Caleb whispered loudly.

Amy laughed as Silas's eyes snapped to Caleb's.

"He doesn't like it," Caleb whispered noisily again.

Silas shook his head and shrugged. "Doesn't look quite finished, but my wife seems to think it's all the rage right now. Guess we'll see if it sells."

"She's been right before," Amy admitted as she chewed her lip. It surely wasn't Amy's style. She already knew what table she would want Silas to build for her someday, and it definitely wasn't this one. But Kirsten certainly had a better feel for the outside world than they did.

"I'll get the benches," Caleb said as he turned on his heel and sauntered out the door.

Minutes later, two matching benches were placed along either side. A complete set.

"Kirsten made another batch of soap," Silas said as he placed a small basket on the counter.

"Oh, that's *gut*! We were almost sold out." Amy grabbed a small, white paper bundle out of the basket. Kirsten had an eye for packaging, that was sure. Her soaps were always wrapped in white paper, tied with twine, and clearly labeled. Amy brought the bar to her nose and inhaled. It did indeed smell like a cinnamon roll, just as the label indicated.

"Any cinnamon bread left?" Silas asked, his eyes scanning the baked goods table.

"*Nee.* That never lasts past noon," Amy said with a flick of her wrist. "I'll bring some over later though." Kirsten loved cinnamon bread.

Silas nodded and left without a word. Caleb had already been put to work stocking shelves with Daniel.

Amy breathed a small sigh of relief that there was another pair of hands to help. Yes, hiring someone would be a good idea. Of course, finding another Amish person willing to work in this particular setting wasn't always easy. She knew many Amish who would like a part-time job, but many were shy and quiet and not altogether comfortable socializing with Englishers. It would need to be someone friendly.

At that precise moment, Sally Yoder walked in the door.

"*Guder nammidaag,* Amy," the young woman said with a huge smile on her face.

"Good afternoon, Sally," Amy returned, an idea slowly forming in her mind.

"I have been busy baking up a storm this week and I ran plumb out of sugar. Can ya believe that? I didn't really want to travel out on such a terrible cold day, but I still need to bake a few pies for supper, so here I am!" Sally gushed. Amy wasn't sure she had taken a breath in that entire speech.

"Goodness, look at all yer customers! I think you are busier every time I come in! Business has been *gut, jah?*" Sally continued, not waiting for a response.

Amy smiled broadly. "*Jah,* business has been *gut.*"

And now she knew just the right person to step in and help out.

⋅᠔᠐᠙᠐᠕⋅

Nathaniel tugged the black stocking hat over his ears and slipped his arms into his coat sleeves. They'd managed to get the semi-trailer unloaded quickly and sent on its way before lunch. The buggies and machinery and tools were all scattered about the farmyard. But they would have to wait.

With a firm pull on the handle, the big door of the moving truck lifted.

Gideon, his fourteen-year-old brother, whistled low. "Where's it all gonna go?"

Nathaniel had no answer for him. Their house in Middlefield had five bedrooms, a large living room, a parlor, a massive kitchen, and a spacious dining room. Not to mention a wide-open basement where they hosted Sunday meetings. The two-story farmhouse that would now be home had only three bedrooms, one bathroom, a small living room, a smaller dining room, and a tiny kitchen. There would be no Sunday hosting in the small basement.

Even though they lived simply with far less furniture and belongings than the outside world, finding a place for the contents of this trailer full of furniture was going to be difficult. As if fitting just their family into the house wasn't enough of a challenge.

"Let's just get started," Nathaniel sighed as he jumped up into the back of the truck.

"At least there's no *schnee*," Gideon grunted as he lifted his end of a corner cabinet and followed Nathaniel down the small sidewalk to the house.

The frozen bare ground did make it easier to get unloaded. That much was true. But the cold wasn't helping any.

Inside, all his siblings had been put to work, even three-year-old Matthew and six-year-old Zachary. His sisters were washing walls and cabinets. His mother was directing both the cleaning and the furniture unloading with calm, quiet confidence. It was work, but it was noisy and exuberant work.

They'd left a big house on a small farm in Ohio. Here there would be just the opposite—a small house on a big farm in Iowa. Though even now his father was outside measuring for an addition they would be starting as soon as possible. Two more bedrooms upstairs and a larger kitchen and dining room downstairs. Then they could rearrange the existing rooms to make a larger living room.

"What do ya think, *sohn*?" his father called as Nathaniel stepped back outside. His arm swept across the wide expanse of land that surrounded their farmyard. Nathaniel's eyes took in the acres and acres of black dirt, dotted with the remaining snow, that stretched all around. How they would ever get it all planted, he wasn't sure.

It would take a lot of work, but Nathaniel never complained about work. And just about anything was better than the factory he left behind in Middlefield.

"More space, *jah*?" his dad asked him, with furrowed brow. Nathaniel could see the wrinkles around his father's eyes were etched with a hint of worry and uncertainty.

"*Jah*," Nathaniel agreed. "Lots of space, *Daed*."

His father's expression eased into a joyful, expectant grin. "No more factory work for you!" he cheered.

Nathaniel nodded in agreement. That, at least, was a good thing.

— Chapter Four —

Amy twisted the knob on the door and walked in, quickly closing the door behind her and stamping the snow off her shoes in the entryway.

"It's a cold one again," called the scratchy voice from the kitchen.

"*Jah*," Amy agreed as she turned to smile at Ella. She watched as her elderly friend tottered down the galley kitchen, in her familiar wobbly walk, toward the door where Amy still stood. Ella's bright white hair blended almost perfectly with her white cap.

Amy quickly shrugged out of her black wool coat and stepped out of her shoes. There was no need to leave puddles of melted snow on the floor. One slip and Ella would no longer be able to live in her own home. The thought pierced Amy's heart.

When she turned around Ella stood nearby, arms outstretched, ready for a hug. Gently but firmly, Amy wrapped her arms around the frail woman and held her for a moment. Ella was several inches shorter and quite a bit rounder, but her hugs were strong.

"I'm in the mood for cream cheese muffins today," Ella said as they parted and started making their way to the kitchen.

"Sounds *appleditlich*," Amy agreed. Everything Ella made was delicious. For years, Tuesday mornings had belonged to Amy and Ella. Amy had started her visits when Ella's husband, Hank, had been diagnosed with Alzheimer's. Amy had intended to do some simple housework to help her two elderly neighbors out. Since they lived just a few miles away, it was no trouble and it gave Amy something to do on her days off.

Over the span of twelve months, Hank's mental condition had deteriorated. Toward the end, as he would sit at the kitchen table he had built in the home they had lived in for at least fifty years, he would turn to Ella and say, "I think it's time we go home now, don't you?"

For the first few months, Ella would shake her head and say with some gentle exasperation, "But Hank, we are home! This is where we live."

Hank's bushy eyebrows would bunch together as he furrowed his brow in confusion. Hank was never the talkative type, but Amy felt like he grew more and more silent all the time.

Then one day, as they sat together having an afternoon coffee time, Hank had again suggested they go home. Ella had simply said, "*Jah*, we'll go soon, Hank." Amy had blinked back tears. Ella's gentle resignation was beautiful and heartbreaking, all at the same time.

When Hank passed away, Ella had been sad in a quiet way. Occasionally, Amy would see her wipe a finger beneath her eye. But Ella also seemed very peaceful.

"He's in a much better place," she murmured whenever Hank came up in their conversations.

That had been two years ago. Ella looked every one of her ninety-three years. And yet, there was a feistiness in her that Amy loved, too. Spending Tuesday mornings with Ella was one of the greatest joys in Amy's life. Both for the baking and the talking they would do.

"Okay, where shall we start?" Amy asked as she pulled the large green melamine mixing bowl out of the cupboard.

"First put in some flour," Ella instructed as she stood next to her, both hands on the counter.

"Okay. Any idea how much?" Amy grinned. This was typical. Not a one of Ella's amazing recipes was written down anywhere. Ella never spoke in specific measurements. After nine decades of baking, the dear old woman just knew what the right amount was by eye or by feel or by taste. She followed no recipe—just the memory of baking things hundreds of times.

But over the past few years, Amy had been slowly learning all the wonderful recipes that lived inside only Ella's head. Ella would give instructions. A little more of this. Not so much of that. Maybe don't mix it quite so much. Amy would studiously follow every direction. When she got home, she'd pull out a special notebook and write down as many details as she could remember.

Ella knew about the notebook, of course. She often sampled bits of her own recipes that Amy had made at home. And even when Amy had gotten it wrong, Ella was gentle with corrections and generous with her praise.

"*Jah*, you're almost there!" she would cheer.

Amy took those wonderful baked items, the ones that were almost as good as Ella's, and sold them in small batches at the store. Chocolate chips bars. Crème de menthe brownies. Snickerdoodle muffins. Sugar cookies. All Ella's personal recipes and all of Amy's best-sellers. Only the cinnamon bread recipe came from Amy's mother.

"Some baking soda now, I think," Ella said quietly as she handed Amy a plain old kitchen spoon. This made the trick even harder. Ella had one set of measuring cups and spoons, but never used them. They were as foreign to her as motorized vehicles. She didn't mind when other people brought them out, but she sure didn't need them. Ella had grown up in a time where such things weren't necessary or even available. And like many elderly people, she just never adapted with the times. It wasn't the Amish way to change as the world advanced.

Amy scooped a bit of baking soda onto the spoon, guessing she had about a teaspoon's worth.

"Looks about right," Ella said, nodding her approval.

Amy dumped it in with the flour, committing the measurement to memory.

"Now, we start these out hotter and then turn it down after a bit," Ella said as she turned to the oven behind them.

Forty minutes later, Amy's stomach rumbled in anticipation of the delectable treat sitting in front of her. This would be a most decadent breakfast. Ella brought the coffee pot to the table and set it down on a crocheted potholder after she'd filled their mugs.

"They smell amazing," Amy said as she closed her eyes and inhaled deeply.

"*Jah*, they always brought my kids running to the table in the morning." Ella smiled. All seven of Ella's children were still living, some of them quite close by. But they had their own children, grandchildren, and even great-grandchildren. None of them visited more than once a week.

Amy slid her fork carefully down through the crumbled topping, through the cream cheese layer, and into the cakey muffin, watching the steam escape. The first bite was indescribable. Amy closed her eyes and let the flavors linger on her tongue.

"Ella. This is way beyond breakfast. This is like a dessert!" Amy enthused with wide eyes.

Just as Amy had suspected, her praise made Ella laugh. Ella had the best laugh. She'd squint her eyes and wheezily suck in short, squeaky breaths of air.

As they ate, they talked. Amy told Ella about the new neighbors and the many buggies she had seen yesterday. Their yard stretched along Ella's own property. Ella told Amy about the visit with her most recent great-great-grandchild. And as always, Ella loved to hear Amy's stories from the market. Ella didn't get out much anymore. Amy did all her grocery shopping for her and delivered it every Tuesday. But the stories Amy brought to Ella were one small way of bringing a piece of the world to her. And judging by Ella's questions and inquisitive expression, that little piece of the world still mattered to her.

All too soon, three hours had passed, and it was time for Amy to go home and bake more treats to take to the market tomorrow.

She slid her arms into the coat sleeves and fastened the buttons.

Ella shuffled into the room behind her, and when Amy turned around she found Ella, as always, reaching for her. Amy stepped close and steadied the old woman with her own grasp. Gently, Ella pressed her forehead against Amy's. This was routine, though it was anything but normal. For several long moments Ella would simply hold firmly to Amy, press her head against her young friend, and hang on. At times, Amy wondered if Ella was praying. But other times Ella would speak of how much she appreciated Amy coming to spend time with her, or about how she missed Hank, or about what a good life she'd had. And no matter what Ella would say, Amy would feel tears welling in her own eyes. This fragile but faithful old woman had become dearer to Amy than she could say. Their shared love of baking was a great connection. But there was more to it, Amy was sure, for both of them. Ella was a beloved friend. With a last gentle squeeze, they parted. Amy stepped out the door, hearing Ella call out behind her to be careful not to slip on the ice.

⋅ఴ⋅ఴ⋅

"It will be several months before we can get in the field," Nathaniel's dad said as they sat gathered around the supper table. Given the lack of space in the house, the large dining table had been placed in what had been the living room. The small space previously used for meals now housed several rocking chairs. The couches had been somehow crammed into his parents' bedroom. All five boys were sharing one room, all four girls in the other. The house seemed to literally be bursting at the seams. Nathaniel loved being a part of such a large family, but even this seemed a bit too cramped. Sharing a bed with his two youngest brothers had not made for the best sleep, either.

"I was thinking of looking for some work. At least something to do until the ground thaws," Nathaniel confessed.

"Jah, I think that's a *gut* idea, *sohn*. Not sure what there is to be found for work around here. Might be a factory in town that would take you on."

Nathaniel suppressed a shudder and pinched his lips together. He had hated his work at the factory in Middlefield. The foreman had been intense. And even though Nathaniel appreciated hard work, he hadn't appreciated the pace demanded of them. He and his friends had literally run as they assembled the giant RVs. The work was not especially challenging, and the pay was good. The workdays went by quickly. But he'd been glad to give his notice when their move was set in stone.

"I'm sure I'll find something," Nathaniel assured his family. He had no intention of applying for factory work, though. Not unless it was absolutely necessary. But neither was he sure what else there was to do.

⁗⁗

Amy spread the last bit of dough into the pan. She sprinkled the crumbled topping over the coffee cake and set it aside to bake after supper.

With a sigh she stood and surveyed the quiet, sunlit kitchen. Tuesday afternoons at home were blissfully quiet. Her mom and dad managed the market on their own, just as they had for so many years. That left Amy at home to do whatever she wanted with her day. She could sew or clean or read—all of which she enjoyed. But she always baked for the market.

Pies. Cookies. Coffee cakes. Cinnamon bread. Bars.

Her mom still made dinner rolls and other breads. But the rest of the baking was Amy's—her love and her hobby. A pastime that paid off more and more as their customer base became increasingly English.

The anonymity of craftsmen was one of the things Amy loved the most about their business. She and her parents knew who provided what products to sell, of course, and they would get a healthy portion of the sale. But the Amish shunned anything prideful, and a seller would never put their name directly on an item just to receive recognition.

The clip-clopping rattle of the buggy sounded faintly through the window just as Amy pulled the heavy pan of lasagna from the oven.

"I wouldn't do that if I were you," Amy said over her shoulder. She turned to see exactly what she expected: Caleb with his hand frozen guiltily above the pan of frosted crème de menthe brownies. His gaze followed the slow swing of the wooden spoon as she smacked it against her own palm.

"Fine," he muttered standing up straight. Then, quick as a flash, he grabbed a cookie off the cooling rack and popped the whole thing into his mouth.

Amy's jaw dropped in disbelief. "Caleb!" she said in exasperation.

"What?" he mumbled over his mouthful, as he folded his long frame into his seat between the table and the long bank of windows.

"What? You'll ruin yer supper, that's what!" Amy huffed.

Caleb grinned as he chewed. "Since when have ya known me to *not* finish my supper?"

Amy shook her head. "I don't know how you are as thin as you are with the way you eat."

"And I don't know how ya stand there baking all day and don't sample everything," he replied.

Amy smiled as she slid the heavy lasagna onto the potholder in the middle of the table. Caleb's eyes followed and stayed fixed on it as it sat steaming in front of him.

Their parents came in at that moment, a frosty blast of cold air following them in.

"Ach! Amy, smells mighty good in here!" Mary said as she shed her woolen coat. "My you've been busy, *dochder*!" she added as she scanned the plentiful baked goods covering the counters, windowsills, and shelves.

"I'm glad you're home. I was beginning to wonder what was keeping ya," Amy said inquisitively. If something had happened at the market, she wanted to know about it. She'd become very creative in finding ways of quizzing her parents for details of their day. *Were you busy today? Did you sell out of Eli's homemade cheese? Should I place a fabric order tomorrow?* Those simple questions nearly always sparked more conversation than if she just asked how their day had been.

"*Jah*, I'm sure ya were wondering. We stopped to introduce ourselves to the new neighbors on our way home," Mary answered.

There was something in her mother's voice that made Amy pause her cutting the lasagna to look at her face.

"That's nice," Amy hedged. "Is it a big family?"

"*Jah*, a big family from a big family," Daniel said as he moved to his chair at the head of the table. "Jonas and Leah Shetler and their eight *kinner*. Moved here from Middlefield since they needed more farmland than they could find in their community."

"Any *maed*?" Caleb asked with a funny smile.

Daniel slowly swung his gaze to his youngest son and simply shook his head in amusement. "They have one adult *sohn* and a couple of *dochders* about yer age."

Caleb wiggled his eyebrows in a goofy expression, making Amy snort. A small spark of curiosity about the girls lit in her mind. If they were about Caleb's age, they might be three or four years younger than she. Even so, they might become good friends.

"I took them some of yer cinnamon bread," Mary said as she sank into her own chair at the opposite end of the table from her husband.

"Oh, *gut*." Amy nodded her approval.

"I'll make sure to pay yer account at the store for them," Mary added.

"*Nee*, ya don't need to do that, *Maam*. I'm happy to give baked goods to *new neighbors*," Amy replied, her eyes landing pointedly on Caleb with her last words.

"This looks gut, *schwesder*," Caleb said with a sly grin and a nod at the lasagna. "What's for dessert?"

— CHAPTER FIVE —

"These look *wunderbaar*!" Sally gushed as Amy laid out the crème de menthe brownies she had packaged so neatly last night. Amazingly, the whole pan had been spared from Caleb's sneaky ways. "Are all these baked goods yer handiwork, Amy?"

Amy paused. She would not lie to Sally, but she also didn't want to sound prideful.

"Only some of them," she finally answered. It was true. The breads and rolls were something her mother and Shelby did together. Anna Mae loved to crochet handkerchiefs.

"I love working here, but these goodies are awfully tempting," Sally giggled. Amy smiled and nodded. Yet another reason Amy was glad Caleb spent his time working with Silas in his new woodshop. If he spent more time at the market, he'd clean her out. Last night she had finally resorted to hiding the pans of bars in her room in hopes he would not find them there.

"I'm going to go in back to see if I can help *Daed* unload the truck," Amy said with a glance behind her out the glass doors. A large delivery truck sat backed up to the loading dock.

"*Jah*, that sounds just fine. I'll manage things up here. I'm sure we'll be busy today with all the new goods coming in!" Sally agreed.

Amy walked away before Sally could say anything further. She sure was a good worker and so friendly. A good hire. Everyone seemed to love Sally. She knew the name of every Amish person, old and young alike, who entered the store. Amy had seen the beaming smiles on the faces of the Englishers, too, after they had experienced a conversation explosion from Sally. Working with her called for a bit of care, though, lest you got stuck in one of her spirited and long-winded speeches.

Amy made her way through the double swinging wooden doors to the back room of the store. There were wooden shelves stacked high with extra products just waiting to be put on the shelves in the front. A cool gust of air hit her from where the overhead doors to the loading dock were wide open. The sound of the pallet jack bumping and clanking let her know where she would find her father.

But coming around the corner she saw not the grayish-white beard of her father, but the smooth-shaven jaw of a man.

"Oh, hullo," Amy said, startled.

At the sound of her voice, the man lifted his head. When the brim of his hat came up, Amy found herself locked in the gaze of a tall, young Amish man. He was probably only an inch or two shorter than Silas's six-foot-three. But all Amy really noticed were his eyes—warm brown, but not like any she had ever seen before. They were several shades lighter than his dark hair.

"Hullo," he answered as he continued to maneuver the pallet jack off the truck into the loading space. With an ease that surprised her, he set it in place and approached her.

"I'm Nathaniel Shetler," he said as he held out a long-fingered hand.

She stared down at it for several moments before placing her own pale, slender fingers in his.

"My name is Amy," she said quietly. She was not one to be shy. Reserved maybe, but never shy. She felt his hand squeeze hers just a bit too tightly.

"I was just, uh, unloading this truck," he said as he quickly released her. She stared at him for a moment and then back at the pallets he had pulled off the truck.

"Oh." It was all she could manage.

He quickly turned away and lifted a case of bagged sugar. She knew from experience that those boxes were too heavy for her to move. Sometimes Caleb or Silas would lift one and carry it to the storefront for her. But even her dad opened the box and took out each package individually. Judging by Nathaniel Shetler's wide shoulders, he was no stranger to lifting heavy objects.

He set the box down on the bottom shelf precisely in place and turned to grab another. His eyes landed on her once again, and Amy quickly dropped her gaze, knowing she had just been caught staring.

⋅๑๑ ๑๑⋅

Nathaniel could feel his arms trembling, but it couldn't have been from the weight of the boxes. He'd thrown heavier things around on the farm countless times. Not to mention all the loading and unloading he had done during the move. But for some reason, the girl standing there set him on edge.

Blond hair glowed soft and thick on either side of her bonnet. Bright blue eyes had stared up into his. Taller than his sisters, but several inches shorter than him and very thin. She stood tall and straight. And pretty. Very pretty. Her wavering voice had contrasted with the intensity he'd seen in her face.

"I see you've met one another," Daniel called as the back door banged shut behind him. With a practiced tug on the strap, Daniel slid the door of the truck closed, latched it, and then waved as the driver pulled away. With another solid yank, the overhead door sank back into place, blocking out the sunlight and the cold winter air.

Nathaniel looked back at Amy to find her brow furrowed as she studied the older man.

"I hired Nathaniel to help out in the back and keep the store shelves stocked and things running smoothly," Daniel explained to the young woman. Even after the explanation she stood there in utter silence.

Amy merely nodded, but her lips were pressed together as if she were trying not to say something.

"I was coming back to see if ya needed some help, but I see ya don't," she replied.

"I got a fresh batch of cheese in this morning. Is there room up front in the cooler?" Daniel asked. Apparently, Amy had a sound knowledge of the inventory.

"*Jah*, there is plenty of room," she answered, sounding suddenly more assertive and self-assured.

"*Gut*, I'll bring some right out." Daniel turned toward the large walk-in cooler situated along the far wall.

Amy watched him walk away for a few moments before her eyes caught on Nathaniel. He quickly picked up another box—anything to stop the strange tingling that still lingered in the hand that had held hers. Without another word, she turned and walked out of the back storeroom to the store front.

⋅⋅⋅

Daniel was a hard worker, but Nathaniel could soon understand why he had asked if he was interested in a part-time job. There was no end to the heavy lifting, the restocking of shelves, and the maintenance of the store.

"Nathaniel! I'd like ya to meet Abe Stoltzfus," Daniel called loudly across the stock room. Nathaniel quickly set down the box of apple butter he'd been lifting and made his way to Daniel's side, where there stood a young man not much older than himself.

"Abe's wife, Johanna, makes some of our best-selling raspberry jam," Daniel said with a warm smile.

"She's mighty glad it has been selling so well," Abe said. "We'll have to plant more raspberry bushes this spring, I think."

Nathaniel took the heavy box full of glass jars that sat beside Abe. With as much care as he could muster, he carefully set them on the worktable nearby. He remembered the way his sister, Becca, had cried in dismay when their brother Jacob, only nine years old at the time, had dropped one of her full jars of strawberry jam. Each jar represented hours of work. The value sitting in this box could hardly be matched by a price sticker, that much he knew. He didn't allow himself to breathe normally until he had entered the jars into the inventory log, carefully priced each one, and placed them gingerly on the shelf.

"Excuse me?" came a timid voice above him.

Nathaniel sat back on his heels and peered up at a very well-dressed English woman. Her hair was a flaming red, but judging by the gray hair of her husband the couple was a little older than his parents. Their clothing looked expensive, and her perfume nearly made Nathaniel's eyes water.

"Can you tell me how much that quilt is?" she asked as she pointed a deep red manicured nail at one of the many quilts hanging along the wall. His gaze followed her finger to a crisp white quilt hanging well out of reach.

"I'll find out," he answered with a nod. His long legs carried him to the back room quickly, but a brief scan told him Daniel was nowhere to be found.

"Can I help ya with something?"

Nathaniel turned to find Amy studying him quizzically.

"Do ya know where Daniel is?" he asked, continuing to scan the back room as if the older man would suddenly appear.

"Why?"

His gaze swung back to her, and this time he studied her curiously. What a strange thing to ask.

"There's a customer asking about the white quilt out front," Nathaniel replied, a little more curtly than he meant to.

"Oh!" At that, Amy's face brightened. She spun on her heels and he followed her back to the front of the store. With a jerk of his head, he indicated the English customer who had asked him.

"Hullo! I heard ya were inquiring about the quilt?"

"Yes, it's just stunning. I was wondering how much it is?" the woman said as she continued to stare up at the swathe of white.

"It's $1,200," Amy answered calmly.

Nathaniel nearly choked in shock. He knew quilts could go for amazing prices, but he'd never heard of one selling for that much.

The price didn't seem to surprise the Englisher.

"Does it come with matching shams?" she queried.

"No, I'm afraid not. I'm sure ya could get some made to match. I could give ya the name of a friend of mine who does custom quilts," Amy seamlessly offered.

"Did your friend make this quilt?" the woman turned to study Amy's face.

Amy sighed as she stared up at the quilt. "No. This quilt was given to us anonymously. All the proceeds will go to our community fund."

"I'll take it," the woman said almost instantly.

Amy nodded once and turned to Nathaniel. "Could ya get the ladder from the back?"

Nathaniel turned at once, still shocked at the sale Amy had made before his very eyes. He returned quickly with the ladder, leaning it against the wall next to the quilt.

"It's easiest if ya just go up and lift the whole bar and quilt down together. I'll take it off and you can put the bar back when I'm done," she instructed.

Nathaniel climbed the ladder and studied the wooden bar held by matching brackets. With careful balance and a firm grip, he grabbed the bar and climbed cautiously down to where Amy stood, ready to collect the bottom so the quilt wouldn't touch the floor. The two of them carried it over to the clean fabric table where Amy set to work gently unfastening and then precisely folding it. She wrapped the quilt carefully in a large sheet of paper and tied it gently with string.

"Do you take credit cards?" the woman asked as she followed Amy to the counter.

"We do," Amy answered as Nathaniel climbed the ladder to replace the empty wooden bar. The whole space looked strange without the pristine quilt hanging on the wall and adding that touch of Amish décor.

A simple swipe of their plastic card through the little machine and then the couple walked out the door carrying the large, precious bundle to their SUV.

Nathaniel stood at the bottom of the ladder and watched Amy as she watched them get in their vehicle and drive away.

"Did ya make it?" he heard himself asking.

Her eyes darted to him. "No," she insisted. "It was anonymous."

"You really don't know who made it?" he pressed.

"No, I have no idea. We only had that quilt for a week."

"But why would someone do that? Why not get something for the hours of hard work?" Nathaniel wondered.

Amy shrugged and gazed back out the glass doors.

"You don't seem happy about the sale," he observed.

From her profile, he could see her slightly twisted smile. "I am happy the community fund will receive this wonderful gift. But I'm a little sad to see it go. It was just so pretty to look at."

"Maybe there'll be another one," Nathaniel offered as he pulled the ladder away from the empty wall.

Amy shrugged. "Maybe. But sometimes beautiful things only come around once."

Something in her expression, stoic though it was, hinted at a deeper hurt.

ஒ௨௨

"You sold it?" Caleb demanded incredulously, bringing conversation to a halt around the lantern-lit table.

Amy looked up from her plate and considered him wryly.

"Of course I sold it. We do run a store where people *buy* things," she answered with a sassy tilt of her head.

"Yeah, I know. But maybe ya should have priced it higher or something," Caleb insisted.

"I priced it higher than any other quilt we have ever priced. Twelve hundred dollars is more than fair." Amy shook her head.

"It will be a wonderful gift to the community fund," Daniel agreed without looking up from the mashed potatoes he was piling on his fork.

"Maybe there'll be another one," Anna Mae said quietly.

Amy started at the repeat of Nathaniel's reassurance. Why would anyone think there would be another one? That one had been so unspeakably beautiful she couldn't imagine there would be anything ever as lovely again. The hours that had gone into it by that one person—well, there weren't many Amish women who could devote that kind of time to quilting. Surely it would be years before the mystery donor could manage to make another.

"It will likely be a long time before another can be made," Mary echoed Amy's thoughts. "The stitching on that piece was unlike any I have ever seen. Even Deborah was amazed, and she is a wonderful seamstress."

"Since when are you such a quilt enthusiast anyway?" Amy asked her brother curiously.

Caleb shrugged. "I dunno. I just liked it."

Amy couldn't fault him there. The stark white fabric against the wood walls had brightened up the whole store. It was eye-catching. Nearly everyone who walked in would stop and gaze at it. She'd been stunned to find it sitting outside the back door, wrapped carefully and placed in a box with a note instructing where the funds should go. A part of her had been tempted to simply buy it for herself. But it was almost too beautiful to own. Even though she was sure the woman who had bought it would care for it and enjoy it immensely, she truly was sad to see it go.

— CHAPTER SIX —

Nathaniel stooped and carefully combed through his wet hair as the first rays of morning light brightened the room. There was only space for one very small mirror, and his father had hung it low on the wall so his little *bruders* would be able to see into it too. Easier for him to bend down than for them to stand on a chair. Besides, there wasn't room for even a chair in this cramped place that now housed five boys. A bunk bed on one side of the small window and a double bed on the other occupied most of the floor. It was just the way things would have to be until spring arrived and his Uncle Joseph could start construction of the addition.

"Are ya working again today?" asked Matthew. At all of three years old, his little curly brown head came up just past Nathaniel's knee.

"*Jah*, I'll be working every afternoon." Nathaniel grinned as he knelt down and looked the littlest member of the family in the eye.

"*All* of them?" Matthew said with wide eyes.

"I'll be home on Saturdays and Sundays." Nathaniel eased the blow with a gentle tug on one of Matthew's suspenders.

"Is it because that man with the white beard made you?"

Nathaniel fought back a laugh as he shook his head. "*Nee*. No one made me work at the market, Matt. I needed a job and he offered me one."

"You used to work at the other place."

"*Jah*, I used to work at the RV factory. I like the market better." It was true. He'd never enjoyed the factory. Working at the market was much different. He was still kept busy, but there was no reason to rush. And Daniel seemed to encourage conversation with customers. Nathaniel found it fascinating.

That said, he had noticed a few areas where things might be improved. The back room didn't seem to have a logically organized system, and Daniel had basically given him free rein to do whatever he wanted with it. If he could rearrange back there, it might make it easier to keep on top of the inventory. Ideas began filtering through Nathaniel's mind as he stood, pulled his own suspenders over his shoulders, and scooped Matt up in one arm.

⋅⊙ℰ ℱ⊙⋅

The firm, quick footsteps behind him could really only belong to one person. Nathaniel straightened and turned around to find Amy's piercing blue eyes searching the shelves where he had been working for the past several hours. He watched her as she scanned the newly reordered stock room.

"You rearranged the shelves," she said flatly, after a long moment.

"*Jah*. Makes more sense this way, don't ya think?" he asked. It couldn't hurt to get her opinion. As far as he could tell, she worked at the market full-time. That could be why she seemed to have such a sense of ownership over the place and why Daniel seemed to defer to her.

Her perfectly white teeth sank into her bottom lip as she considered his hours of work.

"See, the baking supplies, like flour, sugar, and yeast are all grouped here. The jams and jellies are here with the nut butter and honey. All the dried beans are here," Nathaniel explained as he swept his arm across groupings of items.

Amy winced. "It was all alphabetical before. This seems chaotic to me," she sighed with a frustrated shake of her head.

Alphabetical? He hadn't noticed that. Even so, this made more sense to him.

"I'm not a great speller, so this might work better," he said with a crooked smile.

Her eyes shifted to him and pinned him to the spot where he stood. Clearly, Amy didn't find any humor in the situation.

"It might work better for you, but you aren't the only one working here," she said with a disapproving shake of her head.

"You could give it a chance. Since I'm the one stocking the shelves, it affects me the most anyway."

"Maybe changing things around in yer first week on the job isn't the best idea."

"Sometimes when people work in a place for a long time they get stuck in a rut and a little change can help improve things."

It was then that her lips pressed together in a thin line. Her cheeks flushed pink, and he swore he could see her bristling. Maybe he had crossed a line, but it was rude of her to not even give his idea a chance.

"We wouldn't want anyone to get stuck in a rut. Especially not in a business that has been thriving for the last decade," she replied tersely.

Okay, so she had been employed here for a while. That could explain her reluctance to change up the back room. But her domain seemed to be the storefront. Why would she care so much about the stock shelves?

She spun on her heels and breezed through the metal swinging door. He'd found one way in which the work at the RV factory had been easier. There hadn't been any women and certainly no room for any opinions other than those of his supervisor. Several hours later, Nathaniel heard Daniel boisterously greeting customers and neighbors. This was as good a time as any to talk to him about some of Nathaniel's other good ideas.

෧ඁ෪

"You can't really be considering this," Amy gasped as Daniel tugged thoughtfully on his beard.

"Hm…" he murmured as he surveyed the area where Nathaniel had just suggested moving the baked goods table.

"If we move these shelves aside, there will be enough space to put the baked goods here. If ya have them too close to the front doors, customers won't get past that one table. If ya set it over here, they can still see it, but it will draw them farther into the store. They might be tempted to wander around some of the other aisles," Nathaniel reasoned with Daniel.

"But this is the stuff that sells the best. We want that right up front," Amy pleaded.

"It might work," Daniel finally allowed.

Nathaniel's heart leapt. His argument had won over Amy's and he felt vindicated.

"Or it might not!" Amy insisted, clearly not ready to admit defeat.

"We could try it out for a while and see how it goes."

"But…"

"Just give it a chance, *jah*?" Daniel said gently as he faced Amy.

Nathaniel could only see Amy's eyes as they searched Daniel's face.

"But *Daed*…"

"Let's just try it, *dochder*. He might be right."

Daed? Dochder? Nathaniel felt his stomach turn and his knees weaken a bit. Daniel was Amy's father? How had he missed that? Neither of them had ever said. Suddenly his victory seemed less sweet. He'd obviously made her angry with his rearranging of the stock room. And now he'd begun rearranging her domain. And most likely, it wasn't a good idea to upset the boss's *dochder*. Had he known he would have handled his arguments with more care and gentleness. He'd have been more considerate. Then again, he should have been more considerate regardless of who she was. Nathaniel had a fierce competitive streak, that much he knew. Somehow that thin spitfire of a young woman had challenged him, and he'd become determined to defeat her.

"Can ya make the changes Friday after we close?" Daniel's voice jarred Nathaniel from his self-recrimination.

"*Jah*," Nathaniel choked out.

With one last forlorn glance at the baked goods table, Amy turned away and walked over to a group of customers who were wandering near the wooden toys.

"This is her area," Daniel said by way of explanation.

Nathaniel felt his stomach drop even lower.

"We'll give it a try and see how it goes, *jah*?" Daniel clapped the younger man on the shoulder.

Nathaniel could only nod.

༺ ☙❧ ༻

Mary stood facing the slightly altered storefront.

"Well, this is different!" she said without a hint of annoyance.

Amy stood behind her mother and rolled her eyes. Of all the things Nathaniel could have suggested to her dad, he'd had to go and mess with the baked goods table. *Her* table full of *her* baked goods. Having things in a different place felt wrong. Amy rubbed at the bruise on her hip where she'd run into the moved shelves early this morning when she was sweeping.

Amy carefully set out the brownies, sweet bread, apple fry pies, whoopie pies, and sugar cookies she had made last night.

"Those look *appleditlich*!" her mom cried as she straightened the loaves of honey wheat bread.

"Which ones?" Amy asked, surveying the display.

"All of them," Mary whispered noisily.

Amy offered a lopsided smile. They were so far back from the front doors now. Customers probably wouldn't even notice them. With a sigh, she turned and made her way to the stacks of embroidered dish towels made by several women in their community. Amy had never really developed a love of sewing or quilting, but she could at least appreciate the beauty of the finished product.

Mary flipped the sign on the front door to open and unlocked the double glass doors.

"I'll be glad to see this cold snap end," she said with a sigh as she gazed outside.

Amy nodded as she opened the accounts book at the checkout counter. Kirsten had taken over the bookkeeping for the market in the last year. Silas hadn't been wrong when he'd claimed his wife was good with numbers. Her parents had kept good records, but it paled in comparison to Kirsten's careful and detailed work. She even handled the dreaded annual trip to the tax preparation office. Sometime yet today Amy would run the week's books over to her sister-in-law.

"*Wilkum*!" she heard her mother call as the bell on the door rattled and a draft blew in. "Here on yer day off, Nathaniel?"

Amy's head snapped up. What was *he* doing here? If he was here with more new ideas, she was going to lose it. But when she saw a woman about her mother's age and two younger women around her age, she breathed a sigh of relief.

"*Jah. Maam* and *mei schwesders* wanted to have a look around," he said.

"*Wunderbaar*! Come in!" Mary said cheerfully. Amy's mother had always had a special way with all their customers—Amish and English alike. She had a sense for when someone needed help and when they were only browsing. She could converse with anyone with a special ease.

Amy started when Nathaniel's eyes fell on her. She dropped her gaze back down to the accounts book, staring at it but not absorbing any of the information on the page before her.

"How's the table?" he asked, his voice quiet and unexpectedly close.

Why couldn't he just go shop with his *familye*? Did he have to torment her? But when she looked up, she didn't see a haughty smile. Instead, he seemed solicitous. As though he really wanted to know what she thought. Well, she would tell him just exactly what she thought.

"Far from the door," she answered.

Nathaniel nodded. "That's the idea. Draw the shoppers all the way in."

"Hopefully they see it then," Amy replied, scanning the full table. She'd meant to put a little bite in her words, but they came out uncertain and worried—just exactly as she felt.

"I appreciate ya giving it a try, just to see what happens."

She looked back to find his warm, honey-colored eyes fixed on her again. Still no gloating or bragging anywhere in his features.

She merely nodded in reply.

A young woman, several inches shorter than Nathaniel's tall frame, appeared at his side.

"This would be Becca, my oldest sister. She's eighteen," Nathaniel said with a tip of his head but without looking even once at the younger woman.

"Pleasure to meet ya," the dark-haired girl said with a nod.

"It will be nice to have ya living nearby," Amy returned politely. Which was true. It *would* be nice to have some girls living nearby.

"*Denki*! May I ask where ya got the fabric for yer dress?"

Amy looked down at her bright turquoise dress. She'd made it herself, of course. Becca was certainly observant. Amy guessed the Shetlers came from an Amish community that was far more restrictive than her own. Most didn't allow quite so many colors to their members. And even though there was plenty of variation in Amy's church district, she knew this particular dress stood out.

"Of course. We have some right over here. I special ordered it a few months ago," Amy explained as she stepped around the counter.

"The color is beautiful. It looks particularly lovely with yer hair and eyes." Becca smiled as she followed Amy to the fabric aisle.

"*Denki*," Amy flushed. Compliments weren't something she was accustomed to.

"You'll have to fill me in on some of the basic rules here. It's a bit different from where we came from," Becca said quietly with raised eyebrows.

"*Jah*, I'd be happy to."

For quite a while, Amy enjoyed helping Nathaniel's mother and sisters find fabric for some new dresses, curtains for their house, and black fabric for several pairs of slacks. When she looked up, the store was busy with many customers, all wandering the various aisles. Nathaniel was nowhere to be found.

"Excuse me, miss," called a middle-aged man standing next to Silas's live edge dining set.

Amy smiled and made her way to him. "How can I help ya?"

"Well, I was in a furniture store the other day and they had several items they claimed were made by Amish craftsmen. And I just wasn't sure. Are your pieces authentically Amish-made?" he asked as he scanned the selection.

"Yes, sir, they are," she answered with confidence.

"Are you sure about that? Do you know the craftsman?"

"Y-yes, he's my brother," she stammered at his insistence.

"Really? That's fascinating. Which pieces are his exactly?" the man asked as he turned his gaze back to the tables, rockers, benches, and bedroom sets all neatly arranged.

"Well...all of them," she said with a tilt of her head.

"All of them? That's quite impressive. He's very talented."

"He is."

"I'll take it then—this set here." He waved at the expensive set almost as an afterthought.

"Great," Amy responded as calmly as possible. Wait until Silas heard about this. Kirsten would love it.

Just as she finished hand-writing the man's receipt, her father appeared and introduced himself. The two sauntered over to the table, deep in conversation over the details of the woodworking. Amy looked up to see Nathaniel's family milling around, but still no sign of him in the storefront. They sure could use his help just to carry the table out. No need to make the customer haul it himself.

It was then she heard the scrape of the snow shovel outside on the wooden deck that surrounded much of the store. Quickly she pushed open the glass door and stepped through. Too late, she noticed the rubber mat that always sat outside the front doors was missing. One shoe slipped out from beneath her, and she felt herself begin to flail.

"Whoa. I got ya."

Impossibly strong arms suddenly wrapped around her and she stilled. Her arms, pinned between them, rested lightly on Nathaniel's solid chest. He was holding her so tightly that every inch of her was pressed up against him. She had never once been held like this. Surely that was why she couldn't look away from the golden-brown eyes staring down at her so intently. She couldn't move, but clearly that was because she was afraid of slipping on the slick wooden deck.

"Are ya okay?" Nathaniel's voice finally rumbled, close to her ear. She could even feel it in his chest.

Amy puffed for air like she had run a mile but managed to nod.

"I moved the mat to clean off the deck a little better. But you..."

Amy sucked in another breath and just stared up at him.

His grip loosened just slightly, and she felt his hands slide along her waist. A shiver ran up her spine.

"It's cold out here. We should get ya inside," he said, and she watched his Adam's apple move as he swallowed.

Was it cold? She hadn't noticed. But as Nathaniel pulled his arms away, Amy had to force herself to pull her hands from his chest.

"I was looking for ya," she said awkwardly.

"Oh?"

"I was wondering if ya could help *Daed* carry some furniture that a gentleman just bought."

Nathaniel nodded. "Sure."

Amy stepped back toward the doors but jumped as she felt Nathaniel's hand cup her elbow. His hand didn't leave her arm until she had taken several steps into the store.

She watched in a daze as he stomped the snow off his boots onto the rug and then made his way over to the table and bench set. Nathaniel hefted one side of the table effortlessly as Daniel carried the other and backed it out of the store to the man's waiting truck. Mary held the door as Nathaniel then carried each bench on his own out the door.

"You're sure you're okay?" he said several minutes later, when his mother and sisters exited with their purchases.

"Fine," Amy squeaked. "Why?"

"You've been rubbing yer elbow." His gaze flicked down to her arm.

Amy was annoyed to find he was right. Instantly, she yanked her hand off her arm and tucked both behind her back.

"I'm fine," she said again. She tried to shake her head and clear the warm flush from her cheeks but was certain it didn't work.

"*Gut.* I'll see ya tomorrow," he replied.

"Tomorrow?" *What day was tomorrow?* She couldn't remember.

"At church," Nathaniel answered with the slightest hint of a lopsided smile.

"Of course." Amy nodded, mentally shaking herself.

— CHAPTER SEVEN —

The squeal was her first warning that the three-year-old bundle of energy was headed her way. Amy quickly set down the basket she was carrying so she could catch the little one barreling toward her. But Grace's feet got tangled together, and the little one went down with a smack on the wood floor just feet away from Amy's waiting arms.

"Oh, Grace," Amy crooned as she bent to pick up the whimpering little girl. Grace curled her face into Amy's neck and sobbed. "I've got ya now, sweet girl," she calmed her niece, rubbing her back in small circles.

Kirsten stood at her kitchen stove, stirring a pot of cheeseburger chowder with one hand while she watched Amy soothe her daughter. Another set of hurried, slapping footsteps sounded, and Amy soon felt small arms wrap around her leg.

"Hi Ben," she said as she smiled down at the blond boy beaming up at her. "You got a haircut since I saw ya yesterday." Amy ran her fingers through his soft curls.

"*Jah*. Got all three of them done this morning. First Caleb, then Silas, then Ben," Kirsten said with a smile as she set the spoon on the counter. "He still hates it, but he tolerates it better when he can sit on *Daed*'s lap."

Amy laughed at Kirsten's expression and then tickled Grace's tummy. Grace giggled and squirmed, so Amy set her down, the nasty fall forgotten.

"Please tell me you'll stay for supper. I made way more soup than we can eat," Kirsten pleaded.

"Sure," Amy agreed. "I brought ya the books and some cinnamon bread that didn't sell."

"I'd wager it didn't sell because you set it aside for me. But thank—I mean, *denki*."

"*Yer wilkum*."

"How did it go today?" Kirsten asked as she took the bread to the huge kitchen island. Kirsten had designed her kitchen and Silas had crafted it exactly as she asked without a single complaint. As such it didn't resemble many of the other Amish kitchens Amy knew. The cabinets were painted a soft gray. The countertops were hand-made butcher block instead of laminate. All of the walls were painted a gentle white. And the floors gleamed dark and shiny beneath the giant rag rug that their sister-in-law Sarah had made. It was all stunningly beautiful. Though Amy suspected that was because Silas had spent a great deal of time making it as perfect as he could. And when Silas set out to make something beautiful, he never failed.

"It all went *gut*," Amy answered as she followed her sister-in-law into the cheerful space.

"Did you sell out of your baked goods?"

Amy twisted her mouth to the side. "*Jah*," she answered with just a little annoyance.

"What's that look for? I thought you'd be happy about that," Kirsten laughed.

Amy sighed and shook her head. How could she explain that she was thrilled to sell out of all of her baked goods but annoyed that Nathaniel's plan had worked? People had walked in and perused the table of baked goods, then wandered up and down all the other aisles much more than they normally would have.

Amy shrugged. "I'm glad it sold."

Two large thumping footsteps sounded before the door swung open and Silas stepped in. Grace and Ben sprinted toward him and he caught them both easily, one on each arm.

"You have snowflakes in yer beard!" Grace giggled.

Silas gave her a grin before he leaned in and kissed her neck and cheek, making the little girl squeal with laughter. Then he turned to Ben and did the same.

"Supper is ready. Time to wash up," Kirsten said as she turned to the stove and ladled the soup into bowls.

"I have news for ya," Amy said in a singsong after the prayers had been said and the kids started digging into their meal.

"Oh?" Kirsten asked.

"We sold something of yers today," Amy said to Silas.

He paused and considered her.

"Did you sell the live edge table?" Kirsten gasped.

"*Jah*, we did!" Amy laughed while Silas heaved a silent sigh.

"You'll have to make another one." Kirsten winked at her husband.

"I'm very busy with a mahogany pedestal extension table with walnut inlays right now," Silas murmured as he bent over his soup.

"Sounds like hard work! After you're done with that, you'll be ready for an easier project," Kirsten teased.

Silas tilted his head, reluctantly acknowledging the truth of her statement.

"*Daed*, I fell today!"

Silas turned his attention to his daughter. Grace's eyes were wide as she looked up the table at her father.

"Where did ya fall?" Silas asked with the seriousness Grace apparently desired.

"By the door! *Aendi* Amy picked me up," Grace answered.

"I almost fell today too, Grace," Amy said.

"Where?" Grace's eyes got even bigger.

"On the deck at the market. I stepped out the door and slipped."

"Did ya get hurt?" Grace pressed.

"No. Someone caught me before I fell all the way down." Amy regretted admitting as much almost as soon as the words left her mouth.

"Who caught ya?" Silas asked. Amy seldom saw him look so strangely curious.

She swallowed. "Nathaniel," she answered as nonchalantly as possible.

"You fell at the market…and Nathaniel caught you," Kirsten repeated, glancing across the table at Silas.

Amy's eyes bounced between Silas and Kirsten, who were now both staring at her, their expressions ridiculously amused.

"*Jah*," she said slowly. "Is there something funny about that?"

"No, not a bit!" Kirsten shook her head, her voice unnaturally high.

Silas bent his head and quickly shoved a spoonful of soup into his mouth.

"You two are something else," Amy sighed.

෧෧෧

He was going to pay dearly for his actions. With such snowy cold weather, there was little to do at home on Saturday morning. So when his mother and sisters had suggested a trip to the market to see where he worked, Nathaniel had readily agreed. Besides, he'd wanted to see if Amy was still angry about the baked goods table.

But he hadn't planned on the way her eyes had flashed when he'd asked about the table. Her slightly sassy remark about it being far from the door had amused him. And he'd found a strange sort of pleasure in the angry flush that had crept over her face.

He hadn't planned on her wearing that turquoise dress, either. Her eyes matched it almost perfectly. When Becca had asked her about it, Amy's hand had smoothed down over her waist and the room had become suddenly over-warm. He'd escaped outside to cool off. Clearing away the bits of remaining snow off the deck had been a convenient excuse to stay outside—away from Amy.

Nathaniel rolled over on his half of the double bed. His *bruders* had all been snoring soundly for hours now. Sleep evaded him, but he closed his eyes knowing what was coming next.

He hadn't planned on Amy stepping outside or coming to look for him. Why did it feel so good to know she'd been looking for him?

He hadn't planned on her slipping and falling.

He hadn't planned on catching her and holding her tightly to him. He could still feel her gentle form tucked in against him, could still feel her hands braced against his chest. He'd held her longer than necessary. That much he was sure of as he considered and reconsidered the moment for the millionth time that day.

What was worse, he hadn't planned on being so affected by such a simple thing. She had slipped on the snow and he had caught her and helped her inside. That sounded so straightforward. But it hadn't been. His arms had trembled when he'd tried to lift his end of that table. His knees had felt the slightest bit weak when he'd hefted the bench in his arms and carried it past her.

He certainly hadn't planned on seeing her standing there and watching him, rubbing the place where he'd held her elbow. He'd worried she had been hurt, but her nervous reaction told him she wasn't in pain. She'd felt something too.

Nathaniel had absolutely no plans to fall for any of the girls in Bradford. As far as he was concerned, he had met his match in Middlefield. Miriam. She was the one. It had only taken driving her home three times after Singing to know she was his match. They'd never spoken about marriage, but they had an understanding. One with which Nathaniel felt very comfortable. He was in Bradford to make a better life for himself—a life that would allow him to support a wife and a family. And Miriam would make a *gut* wife. He'd never doubted that.

So why was Amy the one who filled his thoughts tonight? She was so stubborn and bossy. Miriam was quiet and meek. Amy was fierce and intense. Miriam was calm and shy. The two girls were polar opposites. Maybe that was what disturbed him so. Nathaniel sighed deeply. It was no use pretending he hadn't enjoyed those few seconds with Amy in his arms.

— CHAPTER EIGHT —

Eventually, life here would feel less foreign. But Nathaniel struggled to just relax and listen during the church service. The songs were sung a bit faster. The preaching seemed a bit more exuberant. Much of the service was even in English. And the men's haircuts were all far more English than his own.

Flanked by Gideon and Lucas, Nathaniel tried again to pay close attention to the deacon preaching at the front.

It wasn't until the service ended and everyone stood up to leave that Nathaniel spotted Amy. Gone was the turquoise dress. Instead she wore a brilliant maroon dress. A color strictly forbidden in Middlefield.

"I was surprised to learn ya were working at the market," Lucas said from behind him.

Nathaniel shifted his gaze.

"I thought ya moved here to farm."

Nathaniel saw the confused frown on his cousin's face and shrugged.

"*Jah*. But there ain't much farming to do right now."

"That's true," Lucas laughed. "So how's it going? Working at the market, I mean?"

"*Gut*. Better than building RVs," Nathaniel replied. The answer felt a little dishonest. He had hated working at the RV factory. Working at the market was *far* more interesting and enjoyable.

"I can see that. Just so ya know, the Millers are nice, but we haven't always seen eye to eye on things."

"We?"

"Our family. Long time ago, Amy and I used to go together. But then they let that Englisher into their family and I called it off with Amy," Lucas said quietly.

"How long ago?" Nathaniel asked. For some reason, the idea of Amy and Lucas together didn't seem right. He couldn't picture it, couldn't imagine it.

Lucas shrugged. "Oh, four years or so."

Nathaniel filed out with the rest of the men, his mind racing. He knew who Lucas meant when he said "that Englisher." He'd met Silas and Kirsten and their children just days ago when they'd stopped by one morning. His whole family had been surprised to hear of Kirsten's transition to becoming Amish. That wasn't something he'd ever seen anyone else do. Silas seemed very quiet, but also very wise. Given the amazing furniture he was selling at the market, he had a special talent. Lucas seemed to imply there was some kind of threat in Kirsten joining their community. But she and her family seemed the most unthreatening people Nathaniel could imagine.

Maybe he could understand a bit of initial hesitation. But certainly nothing that would still linger.

Lucas had broken it off with Amy? The image of Amy dashing out of the house after Lucas and Essie's marriage flashed through his mind. Obviously, she still felt pain. Maybe she was having trouble letting go, even now.

His head lifted and he searched the yard until he found Amy, balancing a little girl on her hip. Silas and Kirsten's daughter clung to Amy's neck as the two women talked.

Her eyes suddenly met his and Nathaniel sucked in a breath. With a lift of his hand, he waved at her. A mysterious expression crossed her features before she simply nodded and turned away.

Tomorrow could prove to be awkward.

⚬❦❧⚬

Amy's arms worked the batter, slowly mixing in the chocolate chips she had dumped in a moment ago. Mixing ingredients by hand was laborious in its own way, but it was the way Ella had taught her. And somehow it always turned out better than when she used an appliance. Baking was therapy. Her chance to take a messy pile of ingredients and make something wonderful—something everyone enjoyed.

"You're building up quite an inventory for a Monday morning," Caleb said as he peeked over her shoulder.

Behind her sat two pans of cream cheese bars, a batch of whoopie pies, and another two pans of crème de menthe brownies.

"Are ya planning to feed the entire district?" he pressed.

"The cookies are for us," she answered as she worked the dough.

"But I'm going to Singing," Caleb pouted as he looked down at his watch.

"There will likely be several of the six dozen left when ya get home."

"I'm relieved to hear that!" Caleb heaved a dramatic sigh.

Amy laughed and shook her head. "Behave yerself."

"Honestly, would I behave any other way than as myself?" Caleb asked, pressing a hand to his chest and faking a wounded expression.

"That's precisely what I am worried about."

"I'd invite ya along, but then ya wouldn't be here to make me fresh cookies...so carry on."

Caleb turned to go with a wave of his hand. The door shut behind him and soon the quiet jingle of the buggy cruised by the bank of windows that stretched beside the long table and looked out onto the yard between the house and the barn.

"Was that yer *bruder* I heard leaving?" Daniel asked as he came into the kitchen.

"*Jah*. Going to the Singing," Amy sighed as she set the bowl down with a heavy *thunk*.

Daniel wouldn't be surprised Amy hadn't gone along. Years ago, Amy had loved the biweekly Singings. But after Lucas, things had changed. She had tried to keep going, but the looks of pity or judgment she got were more than she could handle. And as time wore on, she realized she really didn't want a front row seat as he moved on with his life. She'd intended to only take a break and resume attending one day. But after a while, it just seemed strange to go back. Although now Lucas wouldn't be there because he was happily married.

She hadn't known until today that Lucas's mom, Hannah, and Nathaniel's mom, Leah, were sisters. She hadn't known Nathaniel was a cousin to Lucas. Kirsten, of all people, had told her.

"Did ya know Nathaniel was a cousin to the Beilers?" Amy asked her father. Her own voice almost surprised her. She hadn't considered even asking him about it, but she'd spoken the thought out loud now and there was no taking it back.

Daniel turned to her then. "*Jah*. Why do ya ask?"

Amy shrugged. He had known and still hired him? He must not have realized how deeply she had been wounded by Lucas and his family. He must not know they had single-handedly ruined any chance she had at finding someone to spend her life with.

Her dad sighed. "This family doesn't discriminate against other Amish families. Yer mother and I have always been considered different because of the market. We socialize and welcome Englishers into our place of business and sometimes even into our home. We live in the world though we are not of the world. We live differently than the English, but we don't shut them out. The Beilers have struggled to accept that about us. But what would be gained if I shut out the Beilers? They are part of my church family, and I won't treat them differently than I treat others. Perhaps the same courtesy won't be extended my way. Perhaps it will.

"There's a lot in the past, Amy. But I would remind ya that Nathaniel is not Lucas. And so far, he has proven he is not opposed to having us as coworkers and neighbors. Let it be so."

Daniel selected a whoopie pie and walked out of the kitchen, stopping only to let his hand rest gently on Amy's shoulder for a long moment.

Maybe he was right. Maybe Nathaniel had heard it all from his cousin already and still chose to work with them. Maybe he was clueless. Either way, it was still too close for comfort.

"Well, that was fun," Becca declared as the buggy pulled off the King family's yard.

Nathaniel gave a slight nod as the buggy swayed onto the road.

"It's too bad Rachel wasn't feeling well. She would have enjoyed that," Becca continued. "I met so many people today, my brain is full." She sighed and brushed her hand over her forehead.

"*Jah*, it's a lot to take in," Nathaniel agreed tiredly.

"There's just so much that's different and new and unfamiliar. Even the *buwes* cut their hair differently."

"About that…"

"*Jah*, I think I better get you *buwes* trimmed up tomorrow," Becca agreed.

"Before I have to go to work would be nice."

"Sure. Morning is better for me anyway. Speaking of yer work, I wonder why Amy Miller wasn't there tonight?" Becca mused.

Nathaniel had noticed.

"I don't think she goes to Singings very often." Caleb had said as much when he'd introduced himself before the Singing began.

"Well that's too bad. I missed getting to chat with her more. She seemed to always be on the other side of the yard after church today."

Nathaniel nodded again. Best not to admit how much he had noticed or not noticed Amy's presence today. He wasn't supposed to be keeping track of her.

— Chapter Nine —

Amy's stomach rumbled loudly. All morning people had been stopping in and buying up most of the baked items she had made yesterday. Only one package of whoopie pies remained, and it seemed to be calling her name. She liked eating sweets of course. That's how her love of baking had begun. But she also knew the sugar rush would fade, leaving her feeling sluggish and tired the rest of the afternoon. Not a good idea when her dad was spending much of today at home with Caleb, repairing a broken fence. But Nathaniel would be here.

Why wasn't that thought more comforting?

Between Amy, Sally, and Nathaniel, they could certainly manage the market on a Monday afternoon. Sally was easy. She kept herself busy visiting with customers, straightening items on the shelves, and dusting the furniture items on display. Nathaniel was another story. Would Amy have to give him assignments? If she didn't, he might just rearrange the entire stock room, and she couldn't take much more of his so-called improvements.

Amy's stomach growled again as she stood behind the checkout counter and glanced down at her watch.

"*Guder nammidaag.*"

Amy jumped at the sound of Nathaniel's voice. Her eyes snapped up and she placed a hand on her racing heart.

"Goodness, ya startled me," she gasped.

"Sorry about that," he said with a what looked more like a grimace than a grin.

"I'm glad you're here. I was going to take a lunch break. Would you and Sally be able to manage the front while I grab a bite to eat in the back?" Amy stood a bit straighter, feeling good about her suggestion. At least while she ate, he would be kept busy.

"*Jah*, I can do that."

Nathaniel pulled off his hat and ran his fingers through his hair. Hair that was now much shorter in the back and on the sides—freshly cut to match the other men in their district. Amy could feel her pulse in her throat.

"Yer haircut looks nice." The words came out before Amy could stop them. Her face flamed instantly. Why had she said that? She hadn't intended to say anything personal whatsoever to him the entire day. She certainly hadn't planned to pay him a compliment.

"*Denki*," Nathaniel responded, looking almost as startled as she felt.

"I'm going to eat lunch," Amy called over her shoulder as she hurried away to the stock room.

ༀ ༀ

"Those are the biggest snowflakes I have ever seen," gushed Sally as she stared out the window.

Indeed, the flakes were the size of silver dollars, floating gently down from the sky to join the light layer of snow that already covered the ground.

"So much prettier than the icy pellets we had last week." Sally looked over her shoulder to where Amy stood staring out at the dreamy winter scene.

Those icy pellets were the ones Nathaniel had taken such care to scrape off the deck. They were indirectly responsible for the incident—that embarrassing moment where Amy had fallen directly into his arms. He spent every day hauling and stacking boxes. She shouldn't have been so surprised by the strength she'd felt in his arms. But he was so solid and steady—not even a tremor when she had been shaking like a leaf.

"Are ya okay? You seem...confused," Sally said, breaking into Amy's daydreams.

"Oh...*jah*. I'm fine," Amy stammered. Nathaniel was always an unexpected distraction.

"Did Mrs. Zook find the fabric she was needing?" Amy inquired, desperately hoping Sally would redirect her thoughts.

"*Jah*, she surely did. She was needing several yards of blue cotton. I think she mentioned making shirts for her twin *buwes*. And then she said she might just make a dress for Emmie, too. I really do like it when families match, don't you? Makes them seem so unified and pleasing to the eye."

Movement caught the corner of Amy's eye, and she turned to see Nathaniel strolling with long easy steps past the shelves to the window where the girls were standing.

"I'm going to go scoop off some of that *schnee*," he said as he pulled his arms through the sleeves of his thick black coat. With gloved fingers, he pulled his stocking cap low on his head, stopping just above his eyebrows. Something about the dark cap framing his face made his eyes glow as he looked out the window.

He stepped away toward the door, then stopped and turned.

"I'll be pulling the rug away from the door, so you *maed* just stay put," he warned, his eyes practically boring holes into Amy.

She huffed. Did he think she wanted a repeat of what happened last time? Certainly not! Evidently, he didn't want to revisit the experience either—not with the intense way he was looking at her. By no means would she ever go out on the deck while he was scooping *schnee* again. Not even if the building was on fire. Well, maybe then.

The market was empty now that the snow had picked up. At least there was no wind, but drifts were beginning to form in the parking lot.

Sally was still staring out the window when Nathaniel came back inside, stomping his boots firmly on the rug inside the door.

"I scraped it all clean three times, but it will need it again soon," he said as he pulled his gloves off. With a yank he tugged his hat off and ran his fingers through his hair.

Amy whirled, turning her back to him and focusing on the shelf she had been dusting.

"Maybe Sally should get home before it gets too much thicker?"

Amy's eyes snapped to his face. Was he trying to tell her what to do? Still, try as she might, she couldn't find a single thing wrong with his suggestion. Other than the fact that he had made it before she could make it herself.

"Of course," Amy said as authoritatively as she could. "We aren't busy anyway. We'll likely close a bit earlier today."

"Oh, that would be a great relief to me! *Mei bruder* was planning to pick me up at three o'clock, but he's only been driving buggy for a year and never in a storm like this! I would have driven myself, but *mei familye* needed the buggy today for running errands in town. They were going to the Walmart. We buy lots of our groceries there. Nothing ya could buy here, of course, but just some of the other things we like. Like Pop-Tarts. Do ya like Pop-Tarts? We have them once a week and it's a big treat."

"I'd be happy to take ya home, Sally," Nathaniel offered smoothly, even though he was now grinning in amusement.

"*Denki*! That would be *wunderbaar*! Let me go get *mei* things. I don't live far, but it would be nice to be home if this *schnee* is going to keep up. We like to play games and drink hot chocolate on snowy days," Sally's voice continued as she stepped through the doors to the back room.

Nathaniel shook his head and smiled down at his boots before looking back up at Amy.

"I'll just run her home and be back in a bit."

"That's not necessary. You can just drop her off and then get home yerself."

"*Nee.* I'll be back. I want to clean up a few things in the back and then scoop once more before we leave for the day," he insisted.

Amy opened her mouth to argue, but stopped when he said, "It will make less work for yer *daed* tomorrow morning."

She closed her mouth, unable to disagree with that.

"Okay."

"I think I hear Sally coming," Nathaniel said with a funny grin. Sure enough, seconds later Sally re-entered the front.

"I'm ready to *geh*," Sally announced with a gleeful smile. Sally didn't have a beau, and as far as Amy knew she rarely rode home from Singing with a *buwe*.

"Well, let's get old Susie ready to *geh* then," Nathaniel said, returning her smile.

The two of them walked back to the stock room and out the back door, where the horses were kept in a small shed. In no time, Amy saw the buggy come rolling by the glass doors that looked out over the deck and across the small parking lot. Sally sat tucked in, warm and cozy, next to Nathaniel. There was no mistaking the beaming smile on Sally's face as they slipped noiselessly away.

— Chapter Ten —

Amy slid the pan of cream cheese muffins into the oven just as the yard lit up with the first glow of dawn. She would need to get an early start if she was going to bake all the things she hoped to make today. With a twist of the dial on the timer, she wiped her hands on the towel and hurried upstairs to the shower. Today she would wash her hair and let it air dry as she worked in the warm kitchen. It would just be dry by the time it was time to leave for her shift at the market.

She pulled the pins out, letting her thick, soft hair tumble all the way to her waist. In the summer, she could wash it at night before bed and it would be mostly dry in the morning. But in the winter, the house was a bit cooler and it would still be damp when she woke.

She showered, dressed quickly, and towel-dried her hair as best she could. Then she made her way down the staircase just in time to hear the timer beeping. She pulled the muffins from the oven and placed several on a plate for her family to enjoy after chores and before they left for school and work.

The other dozen she would split into packages of four to sell at the market later that day.

Next, she started the batter for the angel food cakes. She was still busy at the stove when Caleb, Anna Shelby, and their dad came inside, shedding their coats and boots in the mudroom.

"Only twelve?" Caleb pouted as he surveyed the contents of the table.

"That will be plenty," Amy insisted as she filled his glass with milk fresh from the cooler in the barn.

"But they're tiny," he complained.

"They are normal size."

"And there are plenty of other *gut* things to fill yer stomach," Mary said as she placed the bowl of fried potatoes next to the giant bowl of scrambled eggs Amy had made just a minute ago.

"There's bacon, too," Shelby said as she carried in the plate from the kitchen.

"Oh," Caleb's eyes brightened, and he held out a hand.

Shelby's eyes went wide and instead of handing the plate to her older brother, she set it down on the far end of the table where she sat. Amy laughed aloud as Caleb frowned and Shelby shrugged.

Breakfast was always a hearty meal, but it was consumed quickly. Everyone had somewhere to go—work or school—and it was a bustling home until they all scooted out the door and loaded into one of the buggies. Caleb would take the little girls to school and then go to Silas's home to work in his large woodworking shop. Her parents would go to the market and open and run the store as they had for all the years of their marriage.

Amy heaved a sigh as the door closed behind them all. The house already smelled heavenly from the two angel food cakes she had baked during breakfast.

She started the batter for the cinnamon bread, quadrupling her recipe this time. Before Kirsten, she had never taken cinnamon bread home—it was one of her best-selling items, and she made a nice profit off it in addition to her hourly wage at the market. Now at least once a week she would set aside a loaf or two for her sister-in-law.

When at last she'd slipped the last few loaves into the oven, Amy pulled one of Silas's hand-made rocking chairs close to the woodstove. Carefully arraying her hair so it would finish drying in the warmth, she pulled her Bible onto her lap.

*"Lead me, O Lord, in your righteousness because
of my enemies—make straight your way before me."*

Enemies. Did Amy have enemies? Would she consider Lucas to be an enemy? No, but neither did she think of him as a support to herself and her family. A vision of Nathaniel's furrowed brow as he had talked with Lucas at church just days ago flitted through her mind. Clearly, Lucas had told him something that caused him to frown. Amy couldn't shake the feeling it had been about her.

> *"Not a word from their mouth can be trusted; their heart is filled with destruction. Their throat is an open grave; with their tongue they speak deceit. Declare them guilty, O God! Let their intrigues be their downfall. Banish them for their many sins, for they have rebelled against you."*

In the days after Lucas had broken things off, Amy had struggled mightily to forgive him. In her eyes, he was wrong. In her eyes, they were called to love one another. Jesus had done so even when he had encountered people who were not God-fearing. Lucas and his family had opted to believe the worst about her and her family. A belief that never proved true. He hadn't chosen love over judgment.

> *"But let all who take refuge in you be glad; let them ever sing for joy. Spread your protection over them, that those who love your name may rejoice in you. For surely, O Lord, you bless the righteous; you surround them with your favor as with a shield."*

When she thought of people who loved God's name, the faces of her family were first to appear. Her parents with their steadfast faithfulness and trust. David and Sarah and their children with their complete devotion. Michael and Deborah and their children with their kindness and gentleness. Silas and Kirsten, Grace and Benjamin, who still weathered judgment with a love and patience that bewildered Amy. Caleb, Anna, and Shelby with their almost constant joy and contentment. They had taken refuge in God, and there were so many reasons to rejoice. And yet, Amy still prayed for protection for them. She prayed against any further recrimination. She prayed their community would continue to see and understand that the heart of the Miller family was firmly in the hands of their Heavenly Father. That they desired to love and serve Him by loving and serving those in their church district…and the extended English community.

The timer in the kitchen went off, and Amy jumped up to pull the cinnamon bread out of the oven. There was just enough time to let it cool a bit while she did up her hair and changed into one of her good work dresses. Hurriedly, she finished getting ready and was sliding the warm loaves into their plastic bags when the sound of a buggy pulling up to the house signaled Caleb's arrival to take her to work.

Most likely he had a load of smaller finished wood pieces that would need to be delivered to the market. While Silas loved making big pieces of furniture, Caleb seemed more interested in crafting smaller things. Wooden toy trains. Quilt racks with turned legs. A small shelf for the wall. Some of his most popular sellers right now were thick turned candle stands. Kirsten always had good ideas for things they could make and sell, and she was usually right.

Amy quickly stuck the preprinted labels onto her wrapped cinnamon bread. She started when there was a knock at the door. Caleb would not knock.

She turned and made her way across the room, almost stopping when she saw Nathaniel through the glass pane of the door.

"Hullo," she said as she pulled the door open in confusion.

"I was over at Silas's workshop and Caleb asked if I could bring ya to the market when I went in today," Nathaniel explained as he stood on the wraparound-porch.

"You were at Silas's workshop?" Amy asked, almost in a daze.

"*Jah. Maam* is going to need more cabinets for the kitchen, so I went to see about Silas and Caleb making them."

Nathaniel's family wanted her family to make them cabinets?

"I thought yer uncle was helping ya with yer remodeling."

Nathaniel tilted his head slightly. "*Jah*, but he doesn't normally do cabinets."

"Oh." How odd. Surely Joseph Beiler would not recommend the Millers for cabinets…or anything else.

There was a long, awkward silence.

"Are ya about ready to *geh*?" Nathaniel asked finally.

"Oh! *Jah*! Just let me load up these baked goods and get *mei* coat," Amy said breathlessly.

It wasn't until she had turned around that she realized she had just shut the door in Nathaniel's face. She was too mortified to turn around and look, so she scurried back to the kitchen and quickly loaded up all her fresh baked goods into a large box.

Amy winced as the icy cold air struck her face. How humiliating that she had left poor Nathaniel out here all this time. If he didn't already dislike and distrust her, then she was good at giving him reasons to do so. But Nathaniel stood at the porch railing, calmly surveying the farmyard. He turned when she stepped onto the porch and immediately reached to take the large box from her. For a moment, Amy considered keeping hold of it. But she'd already been rude enough, so she let it go without a fight.

"I can carry it, no problem," she said as she followed him to the buggy.

"I know," Nathaniel replied. He carefully set the box inside, and she watched to make sure he didn't jostle the contents too roughly.

With ease, he turned and offered a hand to help her into the buggy. That wasn't necessary either. She had climbed in and out of buggies so many times in her life she could do it in her sleep. Besides, touching him at all seemed to scramble her brain. But there he stood, waiting. Reluctantly, Amy placed her hand in his, careful not to put any weight into her hold so he would know she didn't need him to help her.

She settled in and tried to calm her racing heart as Nathaniel rounded the buggy and landed beside her, his door snapping shut and blocking out the cold winter air.

"I'd ask what ya did this morning, but by the smell it's pretty obvious ya spent yer time baking up some *gut*-smelling treats," he said with a glance over his shoulder as he snapped the reigns.

Amy swallowed and nodded. Every time Nathaniel's leg bumped against hers, she tensed up even more. Perhaps praying for God to ease the distance between her family and some of the members of their district had been a mistake.

.⁃⁂⁃.

If Nathaniel's ears had been ringing after he brought Sally home, the opposite was true after a buggy ride with Amy. She'd been almost completely silent. Even when he'd asked her questions, her words had been few. Her reserve and her posture told him he couldn't drive fast enough to get to the market, for her sake.

It was almost worth it though. Just the smell of those baked goods was a treat. He'd eaten lunch just before he'd picked her up, but the memory of the smell made his mouth water.

Did she treat all men like they were poison…or was it just him?

— CHAPTER ELEVEN —

Amy checked her watch again. For a Friday afternoon, they had been pretty busy. Sally had even stayed an extra half hour to help with a sudden rush of customers. Nathaniel had stepped in to help them through the busy time, but now she hadn't seen him for at least forty-five minutes.

She flipped the sign to closed and locked the double glass doors. Her back ached a bit and she stretched and twisted until the muscles seemed to relax.

Her parents had done this job for so many years. Even when her mom had little babies and toddlers, she had managed to work at the market almost full-time. Of course, it was easier for Amy without a family depending on her for meals and laundry and housekeeping. When she took over the market on her own, she wouldn't have to figure out how to manage the store and a family.

Her father had never said, in so many words, that one day the market would be hers. But none of her siblings had spent the kind of time working at the market that Amy had. None of them shared her obvious love for helping the customers and running a retail business. The older *buwes* had all been mostly interested in doing their own thing—being their own boss on their own property.

In truth, Amy was grateful none of them had wanted this place. With her mom and dad working less lately, it would be only a matter of time before they were ready to retire completely.

Amy would be ready. Even today, when her dad had left early to help Michael install new overhead lighting at his dairy, Amy had stepped up to manage the customers and the other employees.

Speaking of employees, it was time to track down Nathaniel and send him home for the night.

She made her way out of the storefront, flipping off the fluorescent lights as she went, and stepped through the swinging doors to the back room.

"Watch yer step." Nathaniel's voice floated back to her.

Amy glanced down to see the wooden floor gleaming beneath her feet. As her eyes traveled its length, she saw Nathaniel in the far corner, mop in hand. Judging by the shining length of the back room, he'd mopped the whole space.

"I usually mop on Saturdays after closing time," Amy said, furrowing her brow. She'd certainly never told him to come back here and do this.

"Micah Zook dropped off some jugs of apple cider, but one got dropped and exploded. By the time I finished cleaning that up, I figured I might as well mop the whole thing." Nathaniel's back was turned to her as he pushed the mop from side to side.

For a moment, she watched as his muscles moved beneath his shirt, pushing and pulling the mop across the floorboards. Amy shook herself out of her stupor. Really, this…watching could not happen again. She had to make sure it wouldn't.

"Being careful with our suppliers' merchandise is of utmost importance," she finally managed to say, as sternly as she could.

Nathaniel paused but didn't turn to look at her. "I agree," he said simply, resuming his work.

That wasn't quite the reaction she had been hoping for. She'd wanted him to look remorseful, sorry, chastised. Instead, he seemed wholly unaffected.

But before she could think of another way to scold him, he spoke.

"Are ya ready to *geh*? I'm done here." With that he wrung out the mop and put it in the cleaning closet.

"Um, *jah*. Just let me check the temperature gauge on the cooler," she stuttered.

"I already did that."

Amy stopped midstride.

"But ya can check it again if you'd like," he offered.

Amy made her way across the freshly mopped floor to the walk-in cooler. He was right, of course.

"I saw the handle was a little broken, so I asked yer *daed* about ordering a new one," Nathaniel said as he shrugged on his coat and hat.

The door handle on the cooler had been broken for years. So long they had simply gotten in the habit of propping a small box in the doorway whenever they were in the cooler for any period of time. If not for the box, the door would swing shut as it was made to, but the faulty handle would not release from the inside. It was an annoyance, even though she was used to it.

"What did he say?" she asked, knowing she had asked her dad to order a new handle several times and he'd never done so.

"He thought it was a *gut* idea," Nathaniel answered with a shrug.

Amy pulled her own coat on and wrapped the shawl over her head, tying it beneath her chin.

"He also said it would be a *gut* idea for me to drive ya home tonight," he said as she stepped past him into the cold wind.

She could hear the reluctance in his voice without looking at his face. She sighed and made her way over to his buggy.

— Chapter Twelve —

"I put the cake in there," Ella said with a wave of her hand toward the bank of drawers in the kitchen. There was nothing fancy about it, but her kitchen was neat as a pin.

Amy pulled open the drawer and found the metal nine-by-thirteen pan precisely where it was every time she visited. She lifted it out of the drawer and stared down at the ancient thing. The bottom bore countless score lines from knives slicing through some wonderful creation. But it was the lid that always made Amy shake her head.

The cheap plastic lid no doubt came with the pan decades ago. Now the whole thing was covered with layers of masking tape. In the center of the lid, Ella had taped the blade of a butter knife, presumably for stability. It was an utter disaster.

"Ella, how about I buy ya a new pan next time I'm in town. I would love to get ya one with a nice, tight-fitting lid…metal or plastic," Amy offered, her voice louder than usual to make up for Ella's poor hearing.

"Oh, I don't know," Ella sighed. "I've gotten plenty of new pans over the years from my children and grandchildren. They keep getting me one for Christmas. I keep all of them in the entry closet." She flicked her wrist toward the large entryway. Amy's gaze swung there and back.

"Why do ya keep them there?" She smiled as she set the cake pan on the table, sat down, and pulled off the haphazard lid. "Why not just use one of them?"

"I've tried them out a few times. Trouble is none of them work as good as this one. I *like* this one. Makes better cake."

Amy stared down at the from-scratch white cake resting in the beat-up old pan, the layer of vanilla frosting as un-fancy as you could imagine. Truthfully it looked a bit boring—like it wouldn't be anything special. And yet Amy knew Ella well enough to know how deceiving that picture was. It would be the softest, most flavorful and moist cake she'd ever tasted—just as it always was.

"Now, tell me about yer week," Ella insisted.

Amy relayed stories about customers at the store, as always making sure to tell Ella some of the best questions she'd been asked that week.

"One man asked me why I didn't pay taxes. He seemed really annoyed until I assured him that I *do* pay taxes—that we *all* do," Amy sighed dramatically. "And another one asked me how old I was before I dropped out of school." Both questions were fairly typical. There were so many assumptions Englishers made about the Amish that it almost made Amy's head spin. But still, even though their lifestyle was so drastically different, there was something that drew others in. Amy had seen the curiosity mixed with gentle longing on the faces of so many outsiders over the years. Deep down they knew they would never convert—not like Kirsten. And yet something appealed to them—the simplicity, the community, the faith, the tight-knit families.

"Back in the day, we weren't quite so different, ya know," Ella said with raised brows. "Everyone drove horses and wagons and buggies of a sort. Everyone wore dresses and aprons and bonnets of a sort. Things surely have changed for the world in just my lifetime."

"*Jah*, that's true," Amy agreed.

"Speaking of change, I met the new neighbors!" Ella nodded satis-factorily. "Very nice people. Big *familye*. I don't remember all their names, but the children were very polite." Ella's land backed right up to the Shetler family farm. Where Ella's yard and small field ended, the Shetlers' property began.

"Oh," Amy said, images of Nathaniel instantly drifting through her imagination.

"And that Nathaniel seemed especially nice, *jah*? Is he a good worker?"

Unease flickered in Amy's stomach. "*Jah*, Nathaniel is nice enough, I suppose. He does work hard. Though sometimes I think he overdoes it, a bit." She shrugged as noncommittally as she could.

"Hm. Maybe someone ya could get to know better?" Ella gently suggested.

"My feelings haven't changed, Ella. I really don't want anybody," Amy murmured. Maybe too quietly—Ella's hearing aid whistled loudly as she attempted to adjust it.

"Sometimes when we're hurt, we just want to hide away forever. I know something about that myself." Amy had heard pieces of Ella's story over the years. She knew Ella's mother had died when Ella was a teenager and that her father had remarried someone very close to her age. Ella never spoke much about it, but Amy could almost feel the heartache. After a few years, Ella had moved on to be a caretaker for other families. It wasn't until she was in her thirties that she met Hank. And somehow Hank had won Ella's heart.

"*Jah*, I know ya weren't treated right a few years back. It wasn't fair, and it wasn't what ya deserved. Lucas made a mess of things for ya, but he doesn't have the power to make a mess of what God wants to do with ya. God's not finished yet." Ella spoke with such sincere gentleness that tears sprang to Amy's eyes.

"I'm content to just be with my *familye*, working at the market and visiting you," Amy said as she blinked rapidly and shook her head.

"Which is a wonderful thing."

"Speaking of wonderful things," Amy said, drawing in a deep breath and squaring her shoulders, "Ya said something once about a lesson on cinnamon rolls."

A strange expression crossed Ella's features. "Did I? *Jah*, we may have to have that lesson one day. But not yet. There are other things to learn first."

"Oh…" Amy tried to hide her disappointment.

Later, as she stood slipping into her wool coat, Ella pulled Amy into her arms and pressed her forehead against the younger woman's.

"*Jah*, we still have time yet," Ella said, her voice just above a whisper.

A lump formed in Amy's throat. And then she knew.

Ella was saving the cinnamon rolls for one of their last lessons.

Amy wiped away tears as she drove off the small yard. Hopefully, there was lots of time yet.

— Chapter Thirteen —

Nathaniel set the bag of homemade dark chocolate sea salt caramels on the counter beside his mother. She paused her stirring of an enormous batch of broccoli salad and turned her gaze to him.

"Well, what's this?"

He shrugged. "I know ya like caramels."

"*Jah*, I do! You have certainly brightened my day," she replied with a gentle smile.

Nathaniel merely nodded as he slipped a cookie out of the container that always sat on the counter. He would never say anything bad about his mother's cooking. Her food and baked goods were always very good. But after six weeks of working at the market and sampling at least one of everything Amy made, he could tell there was a difference. His mom's cookies were still good…but not quite as good as Amy's.

"*Daed* is in the shed looking at his newest toy," she said with a pert little shake of her head.

"It's here?" Nathaniel asked as he shoved the rest of the cookie in his mouth.

"*Jah*. Got here just after lunch, and I haven't seen yer *bruders* since," his mom answered, the amusement obvious in her voice.

Nathaniel quickly slipped back into his coat and made his way toward the door. He passed the barn and headed straight for the shed. Sure enough, his father and *bruders* stood in a sort of semi-circle around a large tractor. In Middlefield, they had been permitted to own some machinery. But never a tractor. The difference between this and every other tractor in the state was the presence of the steel wheels, but it would be the only way for them to actually farm the hundred acres of ground they now owned.

"What do ya think?" Nathaniel's dad asked without taking his eyes off the large piece of equipment.

"It's big."

"*Jah*. Looks like it will get the job done."

"I should think so."

"Well, we'd better *geh* back inside and get ready to go to supper," his father said with a clap of his hands.

"Go to supper?" Nathaniel asked.

"*Jah*. We've been invited to the neighbors for supper."

Neighbors? Nathaniel's stomach clenched. Things had been fine at the market lately between him and Amy. And he genuinely liked all the rest of the Millers, despite Lucas's repeated warnings. But Nathaniel knew what to do at the market to keep himself busy. Going to their home was a whole different ballgame.

⋘⋙

The Miller house stood tall and white against the already dark sky. The wraparound porch stretched along two sides of the large home, and every window on the ground floor glowed with warmth and light.

Nathaniel stopped his horse and buggy and stepped out to find Caleb ready and waiting to take care of their horses.

"*Wilkum*," Caleb greeted him with a warm smile, visible in the moonlight.

"*Denki*," Nathaniel answered, with a nod and grin of his own.

Caleb was an easy person to be around. Still, for some reason Nathaniel was reluctant to go in the house. Daniel and Mary would be there with their two little girls. And Caleb, of course. And Amy.

After settling the horses, they headed inside, where Nathaniel's brothers and sisters were already enjoying the visit. All the girls were bustling around in the kitchen, while all the boys played with the homemade wooden toys that had most likely been handcrafted by Caleb himself. A marble run. A long wooden train with six cars that hooked together and hauled cargo. A tiny semi-truck. All toys that were identical to the ones for sale at the market.

But one drew the most attention: an exquisitely crafted Noah's ark, complete with at least a dozen pairs of animals. Nathaniel doubted Caleb would be able to make those fast enough to keep up with demand.

His dad and Daniel sat in handmade rockers by the snapping fireplace. His mom and Mary were talking like old friends as they told the younger girls what to do. But there was no sign of Amy.

Caleb waved Nathaniel into a chair along the enormous trestle table that stretched between the kitchen and living room. The older men came and joined them, still deep in conversation. Nathaniel tried to dial in to what they were saying. Something about fertilizers and crop yields.

There was so much chatter and noise in the bustling space that he never heard her footsteps on the stairs. But then all of a sudden, there she was, breezing into the room. She'd changed. At work today, she had worn a light blue dress, but this one was almost emerald green. Nathaniel mentally kicked himself for even noticing.

Thankfully, Amy sat at the other end of the long table.

Mary was a wonderful cook. Nathaniel ran out of room on his plate for all the delicious food he wanted to eat. Caleb apparently intended to eat until there was nothing left and refilled his plate more times than Nathaniel thought possible.

"For dessert we have apple crisp and cappuccino fudge cheesecake," Mary announced with a glance over her shoulder into the kitchen where Amy stood slicing the treats.

"How's a guy supposed to choose?" Caleb cried in exasperation.

"A guy could show some restraint." Mary leveled a firm look at her son.

"Or maybe a guy could have one of each?"

"Not likely," Mary said with finality, then proceeded to take orders from everyone else before asking Caleb which he had finally settled on.

Nathaniel chose the cheesecake and wasn't disappointed. He'd seen some fancy-looking cheesecakes in advertisements and even at grocery stores on the rare occasions he went to one. But this one put them all to shame. Every piece boasted a fine latticework of glistening ribbons of chocolate icing. Before he had even taken a bite, Nathaniel wished for a bigger slice. But once the decadent dessert hit his tongue, he was glad for the narrow piece sitting before him. It was so rich he knew he'd have a job just finishing his portion.

"If I finish this piece of cheesecake, can I have the other?" Caleb winked at his mother.

"Yer *bruders* were the same way or I would worry about ya," Mary sighed, shaking her head.

It was fascinating to be in another home, watching another family interact. It wasn't that Nathaniel's family meals were boring. They were spirited and entertaining in their own right. But the way the Millers laughed and had such rich senses of humor was a delight to him.

Long before all the coffee was finished, the children were excused to explore the farm.

"You go on too, Amy," Mary encouraged. "Ya worked hard enough all day long. Ya needn't help with all the cleanup."

Nathaniel watched as Amy merely dipped her head and nodded. With slow, graceful steps she made her way to the porch. Amy was the only person over the age of ten outside. The rest all sat indoors, reading the newspaper or playing Mexican train dominoes.

"We best be going soon," Nathaniel's father murmured to him after a long while.

Nathaniel merely nodded, stood, and made his way outside to find his younger siblings. It was beginning to feel more like spring, but there was still a chill in the air. Hopefully his little *bruders* had found a warm place to play.

The horse barn was quiet, and the other small outbuildings were, too. He stood in the yard, listening for some kind of clue as to the children might be. Then he heard it.

Singing…coming from the main barn. He made his way over and slipped in through the unlatched door.

"Okay, Matthew, yer turn. What is yer favorite song?" Nathaniel heard Amy's voice up in the hayloft.

"*Das Loblied*," answered his youngest brother.

"Oh, that's a *gut* one!"

Then, with perfect pitch, Amy began singing the words. Her voice lilted in the slow, even way all Amish people sang. But it was so gloriously beautiful goosebumps prickled his arms. Matthew's young voice joined timidly with Amy's, and soon all the children were singing right along with her.

Nathaniel stood quietly on the ground floor, closed his eyes, and let the music wash over him. He'd heard his mother and sisters sing as they worked in the kitchen or on some sewing or quilting. But Amy's singing was unlike anything he had ever heard. Her tone was so perfectly pure and strong. It was almost too good for mere sons of earth.

Too soon she was done, and the world around Nathaniel became perfectly still and silent, as though she had just finished conducting a choir of heavenly hosts.

๑๑ ๑๑

Amy was startled to see Nathaniel standing at the bottom of the ladder. Had he heard her singing? Well, that would be embarrassing. But his face gave nothing away. He merely watched and waited until his brothers were safely down the ladder.

The children bounded back toward the house without care for the light of the lantern Amy was carrying.

"It's a nice night," Nathaniel said as he stared up at the glittering sky above them. "Maybe we're done with *schnee* for a while."

"That's a dangerous hope in Iowa," Amy laughed lightly.

"*Jah*, that may be true," he admitted, grinning.

"Did ya make that cheesecake?" he asked as they neared the horse barn.

"Oh, uh, *jah*. I did."

No one would ever know just how much she'd put into making that dessert. The ingredients alone had been costly. The time had been the second price. She'd spent all of four hours last night preparing it. It was too fancy. She knew that. And the thought of serving it to their new neighbors made her terribly nervous. But she had longed to try the recipe since she had found it in the magazine from the library. And it was fun to make something new and spread her own wings every once in a while.

"It was *appleditlich*," Nathaniel said, his voice suddenly warm and appreciative.

"*Denki*," Amy mumbled as she hung the lantern on the hook near the door. "I'll let Caleb know you're getting ready to *geh*." She turned and hurried back to the house. No need to reveal any more about herself to Nathaniel. She was perfectly happy keeping to herself, free from the opinions of a *mann*.

— Chapter Fourteen —

"Excuse me, young man," said the elderly English woman. "My but you are tall!" She craned her neck to look up into his face.

Nathaniel smiled, enjoying her look of surprise.

"Would you happen to have any more jars of this locally harvested honey in the back room?" she asked as she held up a small jar for his inspection.

"I will surely go look and see." Nathaniel turned and made his way to check the stock.

Just as he had found the box of jars, he heard Daniel's voice behind him.

"I saw them pouring concrete at yer place this morning."

"*Jah.* Feels like spring has arrived, and I know Uncle Joseph is eager to get started on the addition," Nathaniel answered as he hefted the box into his arms.

"He'll have it finished in no time," Daniel said cheerfully.

Interesting how Nathaniel had heard more than a few negative comments about his employer from his uncle, but Daniel never spoke ill of anyone.

Nevertheless, the sooner that addition was done the better. Nathaniel loved his *bruders*, but sleeping five in such a small room was taxing. Matthew moved almost as much in his sleep as he did when he was awake, and more than once Nathaniel had woken to a pair of three-year-old feet kicking him in the back. The new addition would have a large bedroom for the three girls to share, a smaller bedroom for some of the boys, and an additional bathroom all upstairs. Downstairs would be an enormous living room—big enough for his mother's quilting frame and plenty of chairs and couches for the whole family. His mom would soon have a much larger kitchen full of brand-new, handcrafted, custom kitchen cabinets. Silas had already begun working on them.

"Here ya go," Nathaniel said as he returned to the woman who had asked for the honey. He placed the jar in her wrinkled hand and slid the rest onto the shelf.

"Oh, wonderful! Thank you so much! I put this in my tea every day," she explained.

"My *maam* likes tea with honey, too," Nathaniel said with a broad smile.

"And so nice to have this instead of some mass-produced, preservative-laden stuff," the woman added as she put two jars in her shopping basket.

"Fresh from the bees is the way it should be," he laughed.

The customers were fast becoming Nathaniel's favorite part of the job. Sure, there were a few bad apples in the bunch. Even in just his first months at the market he'd been asked a few point-blank, personal questions or caught someone staring. But he'd learned a lot from simply observing the way the Millers interacted in those challenging situations. A gentle smile and a nod warded off staring most of the time. A humorous answer or a quick, honest response took care of the interrogators. Gone were the days of running and doing work as fast as humanly possible. This place was about connection.

Who would have thought running a store would be about making and maintaining relationships? Just the way God had intended, just the way the Amish built their communities.

The market was wonderful for Nathaniel.

⊷ oe ၅๑ ⊷

Amy watched as Nathaniel smiled at the old woman, his eyes crinkling at the corners and his teeth white against his skin. White like his shirt. A total contrast to the dark hair on his head. It worked in his favor. There was kindness and gentleness in his way with the customers that set her heart at ease. She hadn't been sure at first—not after his meddlesome rearranging in that first week. But she had been watching him, and he always seemed ready and willing to help anyone, no matter what they needed. Sometimes he even tried to jump in and help her. *That* she appreciated a little less. There wasn't much of anything here she couldn't do herself. Though maybe lifting some of those boxes was beyond her ability. He carried them like they were nothing, but she knew better. Still, there were two-wheeled dollies and pallet jacks for those heavy things.

These thoughts followed Amy all the way home and still filled her mind as she sat at the kitchen table that evening.

"I was thinking of taking some more time away from the market this spring," Daniel said, drawing in a deep breath and letting it out slowly. There was a peaceful, hopeful look on his face. Evidently the idea did not worry him at all.

"Uh oh," Caleb muttered under his breath.

"Not to worry," Daniel said, easing the tension. "Nathaniel has things well in hand."

For a moment Amy bristled with quiet indignation. *Nathaniel* had things well in hand? She was quite sure *she* was the one who had things well in hand.

"But isn't he going to be busy with field work soon?" Caleb asked.

"*Jah*, I know he is going to be needed more at home, so we will adjust his hours and mine a bit."

Amy fought another wave of irritation. Was there a reason she hadn't been consulted in this rather significant discussion?

"Amy still takes Tuesdays off. It is our slowest day, and we are happy to handle things for her while she is not there," Daniel continued. "Nathaniel will also take Tuesdays off, so yer *maam* and I will work then. That will allow him to farm in the mornings, work at the market in the afternoons, and be home in time for supper."

Caleb nodded. Amy sat still and silent.

"I realize ya would rather be doing woodworking with yer *bruder*. Yer *maam* and I want to encourage that, so we've agreed to free ya from yer responsibilities here at home to a certain extent," Daniel said to Caleb.

"Meaning?"

"Meaning I will be home most afternoons when Nathaniel is at the market. No need to have both of us there doing the same thing. I can help *Maam* with the garden and the orchard. You can focus on being a help to yer *bruder*."

"Amy has the market under control all on her own." Mary turned to her daughter with a warm smile.

Amy's smile in return was subdued but grateful.

"*Jah*. Amy does *gut* work," Daniel said.

Somehow, his words didn't feel like enough.

— Chapter Fifteen —

Spring came surprisingly fast. Gone was every trace of snow, and warm sunshine dried up the mud puddles that had dotted the gravel parking lot at the market. At least that would make for a lot less sweeping and mopping, Nathaniel noted as he adjusted the brim of his straw hat. He carefully tied Susie, his horse, behind the store, making sure she had plenty of food and water for the afternoon. A shiny blue and chrome bicycle sat in the corner of the lean-to shelter that hung off the back of the market.

Bicycles were against the *Ordnung* in his old district. They were allowed—even welcomed—here, but it still felt strange to see people pedaling away down the gravel roads. Most likely even his uncle and aunt had a stash of bicycles on their farm. It intrigued him. He'd never learned how to ride, of course. But it sure would be handy to just hop on and bike down the road instead of hooking up the buggy and managing a horse all day long. The basket on the back told him it most likely belonged to Amy or Sally. Given how far he had driven to take Sally home, he doubted it was hers.

So Amy then. The mental image of her pedaling away made him smile for some reason.

Nathaniel trod lightly up the steps and tugged open the solid metal back door. Judging by the full parking lot, there would be plenty for him to do today. He stepped through the swinging doors to the storefront. Shoppers, Amish and English, were ambling down various aisles. Sally was talking a mile a minute as she helped a bonneted woman with some fabric bolts. Amy was stationed behind the checkout counter, smiling brightly as she chatted with an English family. For a few seconds, he just watched her.

She had such an ease and grace with everyone who entered the building. She was sweet and unassuming, yet so capable and sure of herself. He knew there were no questions she didn't know how to answer. Even when people asked something about Silas's furniture pieces, she didn't flinch. She knew how he had constructed them, what tools and processes he used, what the different types of wood were, and what finishes he had applied. Her words were always delivered with a perfect balance of warmth and self-assuredness. And they always came with a gentle smile.

At least the customers got the gentle smile. Come to think of it, Nathaniel was the only one who seemed to get a more strained version of her. There was a flicker of wariness in her eyes nearly every time he caught her looking at him. And though that happened very rarely, he was certain her eyes were on him more than he realized. She seemed to distrust him. Whether that was because of her past or his family connections, he couldn't guess. Maybe both.

Yes, real smiles from Amy were rare in Nathaniel's personal experience. Perhaps that was why he was so distracted by watching her interact with customers.

Suddenly Amy's eyes snapped and landed precisely on him. He felt her gaze sharpen and almost pierce him where he stood. Weakly, he lifted a sweaty palm and waved a greeting. She nodded once with a tight smile and turned her attention to the next customer in line.

Normally Amy had a list of instructions for him—all of which were somewhat unnecessary. After months of working here, he knew what needed to be done. But he always listened patiently, just in case she mentioned a special project for the day. Surprisingly, today she didn't seem to feel the need to give him a to-do list, so he wandered back to the back room to start on his routine.

A chime sounded by the glass-windowed delivery door. Nathaniel spied the brown-clad delivery man standing on the wooden deck that surrounded the storefront.

With a quick scrawling signature, Nathaniel swiped the pen across an electronic gadget and handed it back to man, who was already walking away. He watched as the man hopped, turned, and scurried down the steps and across the lot to his big brown truck. Evidently, he was in a hurry. Nathaniel could identify with that kind of work, but it was definitely not the pace of the market.

He lifted the medium-sized box, making sure to not be rough with it, just in case the contents were breakable. It felt solidly full. Not heavy, but not light. He set it on the worktable and tugged the box cutters out of his pants pocket, then slid the blade carefully across the tape and pulled the flaps open. A single white piece of paper covered in block-style writing met his gaze. Immediately he knew this was one thing he had to get the boss's approval on.

And he didn't mean Daniel.

৯৫৯৯৯

"Did ya get the back room mopped yet?" Amy asked over her shoulder as she heard Nathaniel's steady footsteps approach from behind. The day had been busy—more tourists were out and about in the spring in Amish country. The family-owned greenhouses would do wonderful business over the next several months.

"*Jah*, I did that," Nathaniel answered, his low voice giving Amy strange goosebumps. Her words sounded almost shrill and unsteady compared to his calm, even tone.

"And how about checking on the cooler?" she continued, her voice even higher than before, much to her annoyance.

"Did that too." This time it sounded like he almost sighed.

"Maybe ya could—"

"I have something I need to show ya," Nathaniel interrupted as Amy turned to face him. The hands on his hips and the serious look on his face worried her.

"What happened?" she asked, her eyes widening.

Nathaniel's face crinkled, and he shook his head. "Nothing *happened* exactly. We got a delivery," he said as he tilted his head toward the back room.

"Okay, so what we need to do is catalog the items…" she began as she stepped past him. How many times would she have to give him this same speech? Amy breezed through the swinging doors and stepped up to the table.

It was empty.

"Where's the delivery?" she asked turning to Nathaniel, hoping he hadn't already unpacked it or put it on the shelves.

With slow strides he moved past her and reached up high above his head. She tried, *really tried*, not to stare as his long arms pulled the box off the shelf. His short-sleeved shirt was of course made to fit him perfectly. Amish homemade shirts were not baggy. She could clearly see how broad his shoulders were compared to his trim waist.

Nathaniel set the box down on the table in front of Amy and slid it toward her. She pulled the flap open and stopped.

A note. That same block-lettered handwriting. And beneath it…her breath caught. Surely not.

"Please donate the money from the sale of this quilt to the community fund," she whispered.

"The mystery continues." Nathaniel's voice interrupted her whirling thoughts.

"Have ya touched it yet?" she asked sharply, her eyes shooting up to his.

Nathaniel raised just one eyebrow and then slowly shook his head. "I thought you should be the one to unpack it."

Amy released a breath and reached in to pull the plastic-wrapped bundle from the box.

"I washed the table off for you already," Nathaniel said as she cradled the layers of folded fabric in her arms.

Well, that was thoughtful. Amy let out a breath as she laid the bundle down on the work-worn surface.

With slightly shaking fingers, she opened the plastic and slid the bundle out. She couldn't stop the gasp that escaped her lips. Even folded, the quilt was stunning. This one was so different from the last—almost an opposite. Brilliant colors stitched together to form squares that made parts of larger squares, all edged in a solid black border and all quilted to such perfection it was almost impossible to believe.

Carefully between the two of them, Nathaniel and Amy unfolded the quilt onto the table, letting it drape gently over the edges like the most beautiful tablecloth that had ever existed. For a long while, Amy just stared at it.

"It came by delivery." Nathaniel's quiet voice interrupted her thoughts yet again.

"Last time it was just set down on the doorstep for us to find in the morning."

"Seems smarter to have it delivered than risk having it sit outside." He was right, of course. Again.

"No return address?" she asked, suddenly hopeful.

Nathaniel shook his head, quickly dashing that thought. "No. Still very anonymous."

Amy traced the quilted lines, her fingers barely grazing the fabric.

"It has to be a single Amish woman," Nathaniel said, his brow furrowed as he stared down at it.

"Why would ya say that?" Amy asked curiously.

"No married woman would have the time to make such a piece. She'd be busy with *kinner* or other household chores. And I think she's younger because these colors are not ones *mei mudder* would choose."

"Don't ya like it?" she asked in surprise.

"I don't know how ya could *not* like it." He shrugged. "It's stunning. Anyone would think so. I just think it looks like it's done by someone with more...youthful...tastes."

"That's not something we could see in the white one." Amy frowned as she gazed back down at the quilt.

"Is this a pattern you've ever seen before?"

"*Nee.* She must have made the pattern up herself."

Nathaniel laughed. "But who could do that? How are there still new patterns to be quilted?"

"An artist could do that," Amy breathed, still captivated by the quilt's beauty.

"Don't ya have any idea who it is? I mean, you have quilting bees and things, *jah*? Surely, you've seen someone there who sews like this." Nathaniel shook his head in wonder.

"*Nee*, I don't know anyone who can sew quite like this," Amy answered quietly.

"But surely ya have *some* idea."

"I don't. And I don't want to think about it anymore."

"Why not?"

"They want to be anonymous, and I don't want to take that away from them."

Nathaniel tipped his head to the side, acknowledging her words. "Okay. We'll let the mystery continue."

"There's no mystery," Amy said calmly. "It's just a quilt that we need to catalog, price, and hang up."

"Whatever ya say, boss." Nathaniel grinned.

— Chapter Sixteen —

"Well, we have to learn some time," Nathaniel muttered as he surveyed the two-wheeled bicycle sitting in front of him.

Gideon warily eyed the second black bicycle they had just pulled out of Ella's shed.

She'd asked if they had any bicycles, and for some reason they had said no. And then Ella had offered up the two she had in storage. "I won't be needing those anymore," she'd laughed. There was just no way to turn down their sweet old neighbor, so Nathaniel had agreed. But now they had to get the bikes home. Cutting through the field would make for a much shorter trip, but the spring thaw and recent rain made that route a muddy and almost impossible option. Going around the farmland block on the gravel roads was a better choice. But it sure would go faster if they were riding the bikes rather than walking them.

"How hard can it be?" Nathaniel mumbled as he grabbed the handle-bars and swung a leg over.

"You first," Gideon said with a crooked smile.

"Right."

Nathaniel lifted his supporting leg, placed it on the pedal, and gave it a push down. The bike wobbled precariously as it shifted forward slightly. Nathaniel fought for balance, but there was none to be found on such skinny tires. With a sway to one side and then the other, he felt himself going down. He managed to half catch himself, but the gravel still bit into his hip as he landed.

He shot up and dusted off his trousers, thankful he hadn't ripped them. He turned to see Gideon doubled-over, hands braced on his knees, wheezing and laughing so hard the sound carried over the clattering approaching of the buggy.

Wonderful. An audience.

The buggy slowed and then stopped. Amy slid out, Caleb exiting the side opposite her. This really couldn't get any worse.

"Are ya okay?" Amy asked. At least she had the good grace to have a worried frown. Caleb was fighting a smile and losing the battle.

"*Jah*. I'm fine," Nathaniel insisted, his words short and too defensive. He dusted his hands again and picked up the bike.

"Can we help?" Caleb asked, his smile broad and no longer hidden.

"I think I can manage," Nathaniel replied, rolling his eyes.

"I think what Caleb means is that we would be happy to help ya learn how to ride," Amy said, sending a castigating look at her younger brother. "It won't take long for ya to get the hang of it."

Nathaniel considered her and then considered the bike. Was there some trick to this he didn't know? Maybe they *could* help. And maybe that would save him any more injuries.

Still, a casual shrug was all he could manage.

"Riding is about momentum and balance," Amy explained. "Pedaling and moving forward actually helps ya balance better."

Nathaniel swallowed and considered the bicycle.

"When you are on the bike, use yer body weight to make tiny adjustments for balance. Don't pull on the handlebars or stop pedaling," she instructed.

Nathaniel glanced at her face and was relieved to see her serious, almost furrowed brow. At least she wasn't laughing at him. Like Gideon. And Caleb.

"Okay," he huffed as he threw his leg back over the bicycle.

"And remember—when ya want to stop ya gently squeeze the brakes here and put out yer leg to catch yerself," she said as she tapped brake on the handlebars.

"Right. Which leg?" he asked, grimacing at his own ignorance.

"Well, whichever one you're about to fall on, I suppose," she answered with a shrug. He didn't dare look at her face this time because he could hear the slightest hint of amusement in her reply.

Caleb began laughing in earnest behind him.

"Try again," Amy encouraged, all traces of humor gone in her face and quiet voice.

Nathaniel drew in a deep breath and pushed awkwardly off his supporting leg. The bike wobbled precariously again.

"Pedal!" Amy encouraged him.

Nathaniel shoved one pedal down and then the other. The bike wobbled but moved forward.

"*Gut*! Keep pedaling!" Amy called as he put distance between them.

Nathaniel's slow pace and the gravel beneath him made for a bumpy ride. But as he urged the bike forward, he began to find a rhythm. Soon he knew what she meant by making small adjustments with his body weight.

"You're getting it!" Amy cheered.

Nathaniel was several yards down the road and decided it was time to turn and make his way back to where Gideon, Caleb, and Amy were still standing. He turned the handlebars but too sharply. The bike jolted and lurched, and he could feel it leaning too far. Quickly he squeezed the brakes and threw out both legs. With a couple bouncing hops his leg caught him, and he was relieved to see he'd stopped without falling.

With another wobbly start, he was on his way back to the small group.

"That was gut!" Amy praised with wide, sincere eyes. "Ya caught on quickly!"

Nathaniel ducked his head, embarrassed while also drinking in the praise.

"I think ya better give it a go, too, Gid."

Gideon's smile faded, but his face took on a determined set. Following Nathaniel's lead, Gideon made his own shaky start. He traveled about seven feet and abruptly braked and stood, gathering his wits and courage. Another few false starts, then Gideon suddenly took off, his feet pushing the pedals down rapidly. Unlike Nathaniel's horrible example, Gideon managed to turn the bike around, using the entire width of the road.

Caleb struggled to control his amusement, but Nathaniel and Amy called out encouragement.

"Good job, Gid!" Nathaniel cried as Gideon turned and started back toward them.

"He caught on fast, too," Amy said.

"It will be nice to just hop on one of these and go," Nathaniel mused, immediately feeling a strange feeling of guilt. So much of Amish life was about taking things slow, not doing things the easy or fast way. Maybe that's what he had hated so much about the work at the factory. He'd never been taught to rush through anything in life. In his old district, they'd only been permitted to use scooters. Anything else would presumably allow them to go too fast or too far. The rule had never felt burdensome or irritating to him. But the idea of just climbing on this bike and getting to work in mere minutes, without the hassle of hooking up a horse and buggy, seemed awfully appealing.

"*Jah*, it is handy."

"*Denki*. For teaching us," Nathaniel said quietly.

"Ach!" Amy waved a hand casually. "You didn't need much help. After some more practice, you'll fit right in."

He didn't know why but her generous praise surprised him. He'd half expected her to laugh, like Caleb, and make him feel stupid. Instead she'd offered just the right amount of instruction. Not too little. Not too much. And never once had she seemed condescending. She was different at the market. That was obviously her territory. It meant something to her—something more than just a place where she worked. He tucked that away in his memory.

Still, he wondered. Did Daniel realize how Amy felt about the market? He wasn't so sure.

— CHAPTER SEVENTEEN —

The sky had grown steadily darker over the past hour. Ominous clouds seemed to chase away all their customers, until Amy, Sally, and Nathaniel were left alone, standing at the glass front doors and watching the weather roll in. The wind suddenly kicked up and some of the hand-crafted wooden swings outside blew wildly.

"I'm sure glad those are as heavy as they are," Nathaniel observed. Just last week Ira Bontrager had stopped by to drop off outdoor furniture pieces he had made over the long winter months. The trailer had been full of Adirondack chairs, swings, and even a picnic table. After unloading all of that, Nathaniel knew it would take a terribly strong wind to blow them over or do them any damage. A good thing since none of them would want to be out in the storm anyway.

The sky abruptly opened and the rain came down in sheets, blurring their view of everything past the wooden porch just outside the doors.

"This calls for coffee, I think," Sally said, snapping her fingers and spinning so her skirts swirled about her legs. Mere seconds later she was back with a package of three whoopie pies from the baked goods table.

"My treat," she said, sliding a five-dollar bill out of her apron pocket and getting her own change out of the cash register.

"I'll get the coffee," Nathaniel offered. He turned and headed toward the back where they kept a coffee maker before Amy could argue. Judging by her sudden jerky movements, she wanted to protest. But there wouldn't be any customers in a downpour like this. And it was as good a time as any for them to take a little break.

Nathaniel returned shortly, three coffee mugs looped through his long fingers. Sally had made short work of opening the package of whoopie pies and setting up chairs near the door where they could watch the storm.

Nathaniel waited until the two girls sat down, Sally just as comfortable as could be and Amy looking oddly resigned and stiff. He sank his teeth into the whoopie pie and closed his eyes as the mixture of soft chocolate cake melted with the light and fluffy white whipped filling.

"Oh, Amy…I've had hundreds of whoopies pies but never one this *gut*!" Sally breathed, a look of deep satisfaction on her face.

Nathaniel hid a smile. He knew what she meant. It was such a common treat for their people, but Amy's were so much better than anything he'd ever had before.

"*Denki*," Amy murmured.

"I don't know when I've ever seen it rain quite this hard, do you?" Sally asked, casting a look out the glass doors.

Nathaniel shook his head. "Doesn't rain like this in Middlefield too often."

"I remember a time," Amy said quietly.

Both Sally and Nathaniel turned their gazes to Amy in curiosity.

"Oh? When was that?" Sally pressed.

Nathaniel watched as Amy stared out at the rain. She seemed mesmerized. Almost lost in a memory.

"It was the day of Rebecca Lapp's quilting bee. Kirsten and I and my two little *schwesders* were on our way home and an awful storm snuck up on us." Amy's eyes fell to the coffee mug in her hands.

"Oh, I think I remember that!" Sally gushed.

"We were still miles from home, but somehow Silas knew and came and rescued us," Amy almost whispered, her voice and demeanor the opposite of Sally's.

"Oh, that Silas," Sally sighed loudly. "He surely is Kirsten's champion."

Amy grinned then and nodded. "*Jah*. He always has been."

"It's a blessing he was able to find ya and get ya home safe!"

"It is. It was my fault, really. I should have been minding my surroundings more carefully." Nathaniel watched as Amy's shoulders slumped. This posture was so different from the way she normally carried herself that it bothered him.

"Everyone makes mistakes, Amy," Sally gently reassured her.

"*Jah*. I made a bunch of them back then," Amy agreed, her eyes still downcast.

Lucas. She hadn't said his name, but Nathaniel knew he was one of the mistakes she was referring to. He braced himself for Sally to blurt out the obvious. Even he, the newcomer, knew Lucas had broken Amy's heart, and Sally wasn't one to consider words and not say them. But for several long moments there was quiet.

A sudden lightning strike nearby jolted them out of their quiet.

"Oh my goodness!" Sally cried, hand pressed against her throat. "That was too close for comfort!"

"Will Susie be okay?" Amy asked, turning suddenly to Nathaniel.

She knew the name of his horse? How did she know the name of his horse? And how did she know he hadn't ridden his bicycle that day? He'd been riding it to work for the better part of two weeks now.

"Oh. *Jah*. I'm sure she's fine." Just to be safe, he'd check on her soon. The shed at the back of the building was a dry, secure place. After his father had predicted this storm this afternoon, he'd decided against the bicycle.

"Well, Amy, *denki* for the wonderful treat!" Sally said, rising quickly and tidying up the napkins and coffee mugs.

"I think we should thank you for buying them and sharing them with us." Amy smiled gently.

"I'm the one thanking both of you ladies. I did nothing," Nathaniel quipped.

"Don't be silly. You always make us feel quite safe and looked after." Sally waved her hand wildly in the air as she turned to go to the back room. "It's nice to have a *mann* here to watch over all those things we can't do ourselves."

The door swung shut behind her. Nathaniel turned to Amy and saw her smirk.

"Is there anything ya can't do yerself?" he asked, his smile crooked.

She glanced at his face and returned his smile. "Well…no. Probably not."
He nodded. "That's what I thought."

✾❧✾

Amy sat on the edge of her bed, the light from the gas lamp shining steadily and filling the room. It was always a strange relief to come home and be free from the glare of fluorescent lights. The room seemed so cozy and warm bathed in a soft yellow glow.

The rain continued to fall gently against her windowpane. Nathaniel had insisted on driving her home even though there had been a break in the weather for a few hours.

"The roads are too muddy for a bike ride," he had said as he shook his head.

As much as it had annoyed her to admit it, he was probably right.

Always looking after them. That's what Sally had said. Ridiculous. At least, that's what Amy thought at first. She didn't need a *mann* looking after her. She didn't *want* a *mann* looking after her. She could handle everything at the market, just like Nathaniel had said. And yet, it was nice to have someone tell her she didn't need to brave the muddy roads on a bicycle.

But there was no need to get used to any of this. As soon as field work began, Amy had a suspicion Nathaniel's time at the market would become far more limited. In fact, she didn't see how he could keep up with helping his *familye* and working even part-time. Yes, he would probably quit. If not now, then surely when harvest came around. And if not then, well, someday he would marry and farm his own piece of ground.

No matter. By then maybe the market would be hers and she would be free to make all her own hiring decisions. Sally, for example, had been an excellent choice on her part, even if she did talk a bit too much. As charming as she was, Sally had never dated anyone. Which was a shame. If someone could put up with her near-constant stream of conversation, she would be a wonderfully sweet partner in life.

Amy knew what a *gut* marriage looked like. She was surrounded by them. First her parents. Then one by one her older *bruders*. Watching

Silas and Kirsten find each other and fall in love had shown her just how amazing and redemptive love could be.

There was a time when she had wanted that for herself. When she and Lucas had started dating, everything had felt just exactly right. Perfect. Like it was meant to be. And she had fallen head over heels for that boy. Crazy silly girl that she was, she'd believed she had found her forever. At the time, it'd seemed like Silas was making all the wrong choices and she was making only the right ones. She had been so sure her life was on the perfect path and that her *bruder* was out of his mind.

How wrong she'd been…and in so many ways. She'd been wrong about Silas. She'd been wrong about Kirsten. She'd been wrong to judge their relationship and make Kirsten's transition to Amish life so difficult at times. She'd been wrong about Lucas.

All it took was one look at baby Grace to realize how wrong she had been. Grace's arrival had changed all of them, but especially Amy.

Gone was all the judgment and anger she had felt toward Kirsten and Silas. Gone was all the bitterness she had felt toward Grace. If such a beautiful, sweet little baby had pushed Lucas away…well…then good riddance. She certainly didn't need him.

She could do just fine all on her own.

— CHAPTER EIGHTEEN —

The roar of the giant machine beneath him didn't feel normal. He'd learned to drive a forklift at the factory, but that was definitely not the same as driving a tractor. They were so very loud! And almost frighteningly powerful.

Nathaniel pressed the clutch down and slipped the tractor into gear, feeling it respond almost immediately. He tried to ease off the clutch, but the tractor jerked forcefully. He tried again, this time slower, and felt it move a bit more smoothly.

Once the disc was lowered into the ground, he began turning over the soil, one long row at a time. In just a few hours, he had more done than he would have accomplished in two days using the draft horses.

On the edge of the field, he spotted Becca and Matthew, awaiting his approach. He slowed as he neared the end of the row and turned carefully to the starting point of the next pass. He slipped the tractor out of gear and waved Matthew over. Matthew ran, tumbling and stumbling over the deep furrows of freshly turned earth. Becca followed and helped the small boy up the steps to Nathaniel's waiting arms.

"You want to try it out, *jah*?" Nathaniel smiled at Matthew's wide, bright eyes. His small straw hat bobbed furiously as he nodded.

Putting Matthew on his knee, Nathaniel wrapped one arm around his *bruder's* waist and with the other put the tractor into motion. Placing a gentle hand on the steering wheel to keep Matthew from over-steering, he let the small boy guide the tractor down the long row. Occasionally Matthew would giggle, and sometimes he would stick his tongue out between his teeth.

Nathaniel's youngest *bruder* would grow up with such a different life. He would soon know how to ride a bicycle of his own. He would help their dad farm all these acres with this tractor. He'd live in a house with gas-powered appliances. Nathaniel was sad and happy for him at the same time. Life with more conveniences often had more challenges. That was something he was beginning to learn. Just yesterday, his mother's gas-powered washing machine had gone out. His dad had spent the entire day trying to repair it, only to give in and call a repair man. Of course, his mom knew how to do the wash without the machine. She'd been doing it by hand her entire life. But in just the few months they had lived here, she'd grown to love some of those new comforts.

"Look! You can see the market!" Matthew squealed as they crested the top of a small ridge.

Sure enough, there was the market, cars lining the parking lot. Looked like a busy day. Nathaniel hoped Daniel and Amy were managing okay without him. His shift started in a few hours, but taking in the bustling scene made him long to go in early.

"That was fun!" Matthew said exuberantly as Nathaniel carried him down the tractor steps nearly an hour later.

"Thanks for working so hard." Nathaniel smiled, setting the small *buwe* on the ground.

"*Yer wilkum*," Matthew called over his shoulder as he ran to the house.

Nathaniel hurried after him. After a quick shower and lunch, he'd set off for the market...even if he would be a little early.

⁓ೋ❀ೋ⁓

On Tuesday, Amy slid the mop over the last bit of hardwood floor. The surface gleamed like a mirror. At least Ella wouldn't have to worry about doing her floors for a while.

"It doesn't get too dirty with just little old me puttering around here, but I surely do appreciate ya doing up my floors for me," the small, white-haired woman said as Amy came back in the house after dumping out the mop water.

"It's no problem, Ella," Amy assured her.

"Ach, you young people in our community are so helpful to me. I'd be lost without ya."

The timer on the oven sounded, and Amy quickly stepped into the kitchen to pull out one last pan of chocolate chip cookies.

"You really can't go wrong with a classic," Ella said, drawing in a deep breath.

Amy's mouth watered as she slid the oven mitts off. According to Ella's instructions, the cookies had to cool on the pan for a few minutes.

"Oh, look!" Ella exclaimed, squinting through her glasses. "I think I see the Shetlers out in the field today."

Amy's eyes snapped up to peer out the kitchen window at the field just across Ella's yard. Nathaniel and Gideon stood on a planter, driving a team of four giant draft horses.

"I thought they had a tractor," Amy murmured under her breath.

"*Jah*, they do." Amy turned a bewildered gaze on her old friend. She spent most of her time shouting her side of the conversation so Ella could hear. How she had just heard Amy, she didn't know.

"Here, take them some cookies from me, will ya?" Ella said, sliding a half dozen fresh, gooey chocolate chip cookies onto a plate.

A thousand arguments raced through Amy's mind. Nathaniel wouldn't want to stop for cookies. He had too much work to do. Amy didn't want to walk through the field after she'd just washed Ella's floors.

"Off ya *geh*," Ella commanded with a surprisingly firm shove.

Amy walked with wooden legs across the yard and stood for a moment, considering the best way to get the *buwes'* attention. This was the part she was bad at—drawing attention to herself. She was much better at baking and being an unassuming store clerk. A glance over her shoulder revealed Ella standing in her doorway, shooing Amy into action.

With a sigh, Amy stepped into the warm earth. Parts of it were soft, but clods of dirt made her progress slow. She knew almost instinctively when Nathaniel and Gideon had spotted her. The creak and rattle of the harnessed horses quieted as they slowed and came to a stop.

"Ella asked me to deliver these to ya," Amy said, feeling flushed even though the weather had not yet turned very warm.

"*Denki* to Ella and to you for bringing them out," Nathaniel replied as he took the plate from her hands. Amy figured she'd have to just sit here and wait for them to eat so she could bring the plate back. Nathaniel offered it to Gideon first, who quickly slipped two cookies and took a large bite. Without pause Nathaniel offered the plate to Amy, and as much as she wanted to refuse she simply couldn't. Amy slid one off the plate and watched as Nathaniel took two for himself. He took a massive bite, and the chocolate from the cookie left a smear on his bottom lip. Amy stood transfixed as he swiped it away with his thumb and licked his lips clean.

"I thought ya bought a tractor," she said, her voice sounding hoarse and strange.

Nathaniel's mouth twisted as he chewed and then swallowed. "*Jah.* We did. Couldn't quite get it to work the way we wanted it to this morning with the planter, so I figured I'd just do this the old-fashioned way."

"Oh."

"Thanks again," he said, handing a suddenly empty plate back to her.

"*Yer wilkum,*" she replied as she turned to make her way back to where Ella was still standing in her doorway, a satisfied smile on her face.

"Such nice young men." Ella's grin crinkling into every wrinkled groove of her face.

Amy met the eyes of her old friend and stifled a sigh.

— CHAPTER NINETEEN —

The car pulled into the parking lot just after closing time. Nathaniel peered out a window in the storeroom. It wasn't all that unusual for a customer to stop after normal business hours. And normally he wouldn't mind letting them in just the way Daniel always did. But something seemed off. They hadn't pulled into one of the parking spaces along the building. They'd merely stopped in the middle of the lot and gotten out.

Three young men dressed all in black.

There was something deeply menacing about them. Their clothing. Their walk. Their loud laughter.

Behind him, he could hear Amy doing a quick inventory in the walk-in cooler. There was no time to lock the front doors, which the young men were headed toward. Even if he did, they didn't strike him as the kind of people who would be deterred by a lock.

With quick, determined steps he hurried to the cooler.

"Stay quiet," he commanded, then shut the door. He'd been meaning to replace the handle and locking mechanism on the door. The new one came last week, but he just hadn't gotten around to it yet.

So now, Amy was effectively locked in the cooler.

Nathaniel spun on his heels and headed back to the front. The unwanted guests would expect to find someone here if the doors were open. Nathaniel made it halfway to the front when they sauntered into the building.

All three had smooth-shaven heads. They were at least as tall as he was, wearing black t-shirts or sweatshirts, black jeans, and random chains hanging from pockets or around their necks. None of them looked like the kind of customers they normally had. The one in the middle tugged the hood back from his head. What Nathaniel saw made his hair stand on end. He hadn't been able to see before all the black ink swirling on the guy's arms and neck. More alarming were the black marks on the guy's face. And there were so many piercings.

Instantly, all three settled their gaze on Nathaniel.

It was then he felt it—a sudden heavy presence filling the room. Part of him wanted to run. He was fast. He could probably outrun them. But he couldn't leave Amy in the building alone. Not in the face of this… evil. Yes, that was what it was. It was evil. Nathaniel stood his ground, knowing things were not going to end well.

"Oh ho! Lookee here! We have one of them A-mish boys!" cackled the grotesquely painted leader. He loped slowly and menacingly toward Nathaniel.

"We're closed," Nathaniel said as firmly and calmly as he could.

This was met with a chorus of laughter.

"Shit. I think he's scared," the leader scoffed. "You scared of me, baby boy?"

The liquid in the bottle clutched in the leader's fist sloshed noisily as he slinked to a stop, inches away from Nathaniel's face.

He was skinny and so pale Nathaniel wasn't sure he'd ever been out in the light of day. Dark black coal lined the guy's eyes.

Nathaniel could take him. He was no stranger to hard work, and that made for a lot of muscle. More muscle than these lowlifes had, that was for sure. But was he stronger than all three? Well, that he doubted. Alcohol and drugs did strange things to people, and there was no doubt both were at play here. Were they armed? Easily possible. And he was, as the leader had accused, very much Amish. And Amish were steadfastly against any violence of any kind.

Nathaniel refused to be intimidated by the sneer accentuated by the layers of black swirls. He stood resolutely still and calm. For the briefest moment, he let himself listen for Amy. There was no sound coming from the cooler. No thumps or whacks or shouts or screams. No hint there was someone else in the building.

Please stay quiet, Nathaniel silently pleaded with her. *God, whatever happens to me, please keep her safe.*

When Amy didn't return home on time, someone would come looking for her. Surely they would come and find her in the cooler.

"Sure don't have much to say do ya, A-mish?" the leader snickered. The smell of his breath almost made Nathaniel wince.

"I think ya should go," Nathaniel said evenly, after their hoots died down. "Do you?"

All traces of humor or amusement left the leader's eyes. And the evil presence that surrounded the three seemed to fill him. Pure hatred filled his eyes.

Keep her safe and still and hidden, Lord.

"How about you make me?" threatened the leader, still inches from Nathaniel's face. The two men behind him stilled and waited.

With as much intensity as Nathaniel could muster, he simply stared back at the young man. He would not throw a punch. He would not use physical force. But neither would he be a doormat. Not if he could help it.

The leader shoved him, but Nathaniel had braced for it. With hardly a step, he stood his ground. This evidently angered the painted man. The second shove was harder, more filled with rage. Still, Nathaniel stood. Seconds later, a fist met Nathaniel's jaw. It took three punches before he went down. The world was growing darker as he climbed to his knees. The kick to his ribs felt like a sledgehammer. The kick to his stomach knocked all the breath out of his body, and he let the rest of the darkness overtake him.

The last thing he heard was their laughter.

⚜

Nathaniel came to with a choking gasp. The storefront was empty and dark. The glass doors were shut tight. He lay on his side, trying to blink the room into focus.

Were they gone or just hiding? How long had he been out? What else had they done?

Amy.

The thought of her spurred him into movement. With a growl, he rolled to his side. It felt like someone was stabbing his chest and back. He coughed hard a few more times on his elbows and knees, with his forehead pressed against the floor. Nathaniel desperately prayed for the room to stop spinning. He turned his head and stared at the clock on the wall by the cash register, willing it into focus.

6:35.

His hands gripped his head, as though that would make everything stop moving. He drew a deep breath in, feeling another piercing pain in his side. Slow, shallow breaths, then. His jaw ached. His eye was rapidly swelling shut. But nothing hurt quite as much as his ribs. With every ounce of effort he could muster, he pulled himself unsteadily to his feet and mashed his broken hat onto his head. With stumbling feet, he propelled his body to the front glass doors, switching the latch to lock.

Through the glass he saw the parking lot was dark and empty.

Drawing rapid, shallow breaths, Nathaniel turned and awkwardly limped toward the cooler.

Please be there. Please be safe inside.

He yanked on the door and felt the rush of cold air blow over him in welcome relief. His eyes slowly adjusted to see Amy sitting on the floor right in front of the door.

"Amy," he rasped. It hurt so much to just say her name.

"W-w-w-w-w-what k-k-k-k-k-kind of a j-j-j-j-j-joke was th-th-that?" she accused through her violently chattering teeth.

Nathaniel wanted to bend and pick her up. He wanted to carry her out of the store and never look back. But there was just no way. The cracked ribs he suspected he had would never allow him to expend that kind of effort.

"I'm sorry," he lied. She stared at him blankly. He was the furthest thing from repentant.

"Let's *geh*," he said, his pulse slowing now that he could see she was safe. He offered her his hand and grimaced as she pulled on his arm to haul herself up.

"S-s-s-s-s-s-so c-c-c-c-cold," she stammered, her arms wrapped around herself.

Nathaniel turned and grabbed a quilt off the shelf nearby and wrapped it around her shoulders. She stumbled stiffly ahead of him to the back door. The air outside was warmer than the cooler, but it would take a hot summer night to make her more comfortable. And hot summer nights were still many weeks away.

Nathaniel worked as quickly as he could. Throwing the harness over Susie's back was excruciating. He slid the bit into her mouth and a small cry escaped him as he stretched up to put the bridle on over her head. He hooked up the traces to the buggy and stood, leaning against Susie for a few seconds, trying to catch his breath.

"In ya *geh*," Nathaniel gestured to Amy.

Woodenly she climbed in and sat with a heavy thump. Nathaniel limped around the front and untied the reins from the rail. He pressed his forehead against Susie's long nose.

"Get us to Amy's house, Susie," he begged in Pennsylvania Dutch.

⋅ೂ❦ ❦ೲ⋅

Over the years, her brothers had played plenty of pranks on her. Amy had been locked in horse stalls, left high up in apples trees, and even found a frog in her bed once. But never once had anyone ever pulled a stunt like this.

The shivering was almost painful, unbearable. Had she been in the cooler for hours? It had certainly seemed that way. One minute she was taking inventory and the next minute Nathaniel's voice was ordering her to be quiet, just seconds before the door thumped solidly closed. All light, every speck of it, was extinguished. There was only pitch blackness all around her. At first, she had waited. Waited for Nathaniel to open the door and explain himself. But as the minutes began to pass, a chilling realization crept over her. He wasn't hurrying to open the door and let her out. He had deliberately locked her inside the cooler, knowing the handle was broken, and left her there.

Why? Why would he *do* such a thing?

Did time pass more slowly in the black, frigid interior of the cooler? It certainly seemed to. The cold became more and more painful, and Amy willed herself not to cry. This prank went beyond teasing. Teasing she could handle. Whispers she could handle. Even outright doubt of her commitment to the community she could handle. But this—this was just mean.

When the door finally opened, the air of the back room felt tropically warm. Even so, she couldn't stop her shivering. Her hands were numb; she couldn't bend her fingers. Her toes would not cooperate, and keeping her balance was hard.

Sitting on the back steps, wrapped in a quilt while Nathaniel hooked up the buggy, felt like an eternity in and of itself. But she had no choice. She could not ride a bike or walk home in this condition. She had to accept the ride.

He was quiet, so he must know how bad the joke had been. He must be filled with some regret. But that wasn't going to stop her.

"W-w-what kind of a p-person are ya?" she spat, her eyes fixed on the road in front of her as they slipped across the highway onto the gravel.

"Who d-d-does something like that?"

He sat silent, saying nothing.

Her body still shook. In absolute silence, he reached an arm around her shoulders and pulled her close to his side.

"Don't touch m-m-me," she demanded. But even her own ears could hear the weakness in her command.

The warmth of his body against hers felt too good to pull away. She leaned into him. If he was going to play a prank like this, then he was going to have to pay. She pressed against him, letting her shivers come in violent bursts. But Nathaniel was silent. Absolutely silent.

Amy stared out the windshield, practically willing that horse to go faster—to get her home faster. When the buggy creaked to a stop beside her house, she jerked her body away from Nathaniel and propelled her frozen limbs out the small buggy door.

Her father pulled the door to the house open, light spilling out, before she even rounded the buggy.

"There you are," he said warmly, but his smile faded as he caught sight of her face. Amy couldn't have stopped her frozen limbs from stomping up the wooden stairs of the wraparound porch if she had tried, but it seemed appropriate given her emotions.

"What happened?" Daniel asked, reaching out to steady her and pull her toward the house.

"Ask him," Amy hissed with as much venom as she could muster.

Daniel turned to Nathaniel, who was leaning out of the door of his buggy. Amy wrapped the quilt tighter around herself and left Nathaniel to beg for forgiveness from her father. Maybe for once Daniel Miller wouldn't be so kind and generous.

— Chapter Twenty —

Nothing in the world had ever felt quite so good as the warm bath her mother drew for her. Amy lingered in the sweet-smelling bubbles until the water began to cool. Even so, when she climbed out she could still feel a chill. The cold was no longer surrounding her, but it lingered in her. She wrapped herself in her winter pajamas and her bathrobe.

There was a knock on her door as she sat on the edge of her bed, combing out her wet hair.

"*Jah*," she called quietly.

Her dad walked in then. Had he ever been in her room before? Maybe when she was sick once as a child. The look on his face confused her.

"We need to talk about what happened tonight," he said as he sat next to her, making her bed slant.

"Did he apologize?" she asked. How Nathaniel could have done this to her—why he'd done this to her—she wanted answers. But she also dreaded them.

"Sometimes things are not as they seem," Daniel murmured gently. With careful, quiet words he told the story of what Nathaniel had gone through that evening.

"He sacrificed himself to protect me?" Amy asked, the tears clogging her throat.

"*Jah*. It would seem so."

"Is he okay?" she squeaked, a few tears trailing down her cheek.

Daniel paused a long time.

Amy's gaze shot to her father's face, and in the low lamplight she could see the worried pinch of his brow.

"*Daed*?"

"I think he will be okay. I helped him home and talked a while with his parents. After he gets home from the emergency room and has some time to heal, I think he will be okay."

"Emergency room?" she breathed.

"He took quite a beating."

"I didn't know," she choked.

"*Jah*. He knows," Daniel said with a quieting pat on her knee. "You should get some sleep, *dochder*. Tomorrow we'll *geh* to the store and see if they did any other damage."

Amy sat like a statue as her father left the room.

⟡

Amy sat nestled in the back of the buggy, her mother close at her side. Daniel and Caleb sat in the front. The silence was deafening and welcome. Sleep had come so fitfully last night. Her imagination running constantly. Even Caleb, normally so lighthearted and joyful, was subdued and quiet today.

The parking lot of the market looked like it always did. None of the outside furniture pieces or flowerpots had been disturbed. Everything looked perfectly untouched. But they were all braced for the worst. Nathaniel had been too injured to take time to examine the storefront. He had only known the glass doors were intact and locked.

Daniel pulled the buggy to the back and quickly unharnessed Ginger with Caleb's help. Another buggy pulled into the lot and around to the back of the building. Silas's tall form unfolded through the small door.

"Here to check on yer furniture?" Caleb called.

Silas dipped his hat-covered head, but Amy could see him shaking it. "*Nee*. Here for something more important."

He didn't have to say the rest. They'd all become pretty good at filling in the blanks when it came to Silas. Amy tried to swallow the lump in her throat brought on by his few words. They were all here together because they were family. And this mattered to the family.

Daniel opened the door and Caleb ushered Amy up the stairs right behind him. The back room looked as it should—exactly as it had last night. Neat and tidy. Floor freshly mopped. That was the last thing Nathaniel had done before the incident. Amy tried and failed yet again to swallow the lump in her throat.

"This safe is untouched," Daniel said as he examined the large metal box in the back corner behind his desk.

"Praise the Lord," Mary whispered.

Silas and Caleb were moving toward the storefront. Amy followed numbly in their wake. All their suppliers trusted them to sell their precious homemade products. If those criminals had so much as smashed one jar of jam, she was going to lose it.

Silas's long legs carried him through the room the quickest. He stepped behind the counter, no doubt checking the small safe they kept there.

Caleb had fallen off Silas's pace and stopped. Amy's eyes caught on the spot where he stood transfixed. A dark, reddish-brown patch stained the wood floor.

Blood.

Nathaniel's blood.

A pool of it.

"He's okay?" Caleb asked his dad, an uncharacteristic note of sadness in his voice.

"*Jah*. They called late last night when he was released from the hospital. I checked with his *familye* this morning, and he is resting," Daniel reassured them, though his eyes were also fixed on the spot.

Amy fought a wave of nausea. If he had been hurt badly enough to bleed this much, how had she not noticed? What injuries did he have? She didn't know. She hadn't realized. She never saw...

Mary rolled in the mop and bucket, and Amy quickly took both from her hands.

"Amy, ya don't have to do this," Mary soothed.

Amy just shook her head and wordlessly wrung out the water. The small mess cleaned up quickly—much more quickly than the lingering effects of the beating would.

After Silas, Daniel, Caleb, and Mary inspected the rest of the building, it was determined only a few small candy items had been taken—nothing of substance. Nothing that would warrant beating Nathaniel. Had they simply demanded an item he would have given them whatever they wanted. Amy knew that in her bones.

She stood staring at the shiny floor, all traces of blood washed away. Her water was a sickening reddish color.

Daniel stopped and stood next to her, his hand so gentle on her shoulder.

"I want to see him," she mumbled thickly. She needed to see if he was okay. She needed to thank him for his selflessness. She needed to undo the angry words she had thrown at him in the aftermath. She needed to make it right.

CHAPTER TWENTY-ONE

So many ice packs. Nathaniel pulled away yet another that had gone limp and liquid. He'd never been much of a back-sleeper, but there was simply no way for him to rest on his side with his three cracked ribs. The four stitches in his brow had been less daunting than he thought they would be. If he laid very still and took shallow breaths, he at least felt like he wasn't dying. But even the smallest movements brought sharp, shooting pains that only ebbed into dull aches.

The trip to the emergency room had lasted plenty long enough for his taste. Still, it paled in comparison to his ride home with Amy. Never had two miles crept by so slowly. The violent shivers that wracked her body as she sat pressed against him had been a torture in more ways than one.

At least she had been spared.

His prayers had been answered.

Soft footsteps sounded on the stairs, and Nathaniel rolled to his uninjured side, facing the room instead of the wall. Likely his mom was on her way with another ice pack. One that would go straight to his ribs. He closed his eyes, wishing for sleep. If he could just sleep for the next several days, maybe he would wake up feeling a bit better.

A long pause told him the footsteps had stopped at his doorway. He cracked open an eye—the one not swollen shut—to see Amy standing in the doorway of his room. She was nervously wringing her hands and nearly biting her lip off.

"Hullo."

Nathaniel said nothing. He was desperately torn, wanting so badly to see her healthy and whole and also wishing she wasn't standing there looking at him when he was like this.

"May I come in?" she asked, her voice trembling slightly.

"*Jah*," Nathaniel croaked. At least he could say that without moving his jaw.

She entered and sat in the small chair his mother had pulled up to his bed earlier that afternoon.

He watched as her eyes scanned his face. The wounds on his head were painful, no doubt. But he could live with those easier than the cracked ribs. Those she couldn't see. And he was grateful.

"How are ya feeling?" she asked, her voice barely above a whisper.

"Great," he mumbled, pressing the side of his face deeper into his pillow. If he buried his head deep enough, she wouldn't get a good look at the black eye and the stitches.

"I doubt that," she said gently.

"How was work?" he asked. Those three small words cost him plenty of pain. The protest in his jaw was intense, but he hid his grimace.

"Okay," she said timidly. "*Daed*, *Maam*, Caleb, and Silas were there with me today."

"That's *gut*," he said, letting his eyes close. It had been his one stipulation when he'd brought her home. He'd outright demanded that Daniel find someone to stay with her, lest those crazy guys came back.

"I wanted to apologize for the things I said to ya last night. I didn't know—" Amy's voice broke off, and he watched as she fought a wave of emotion.

"It's fine," he soothed.

"*Nee*. It's *not*. I had no idea you had been hurt. I should have been thanking you and helping you."

"I just wanted to get ya home and safe," he murmured.

"Thank you isn't enough," she said, and now he could see the tears welling in her eyes.

"You sitting here unharmed is all I need."

Amy stayed for several more minutes, telling him about the customers they'd had that day, the funny questions some of them had asked her, and the items they'd restocked. It was the most she had ever willingly spoken to him. He didn't say a word, just listened, watching her try to look anywhere but at his face and then wincing when she unavoidably did.

"Is there anything I can bring for ya? I know yer *maam* and *schwesders* are taking *gut* care of ya, but if there is something I can bake..."

"I wouldn't turn down anything you baked," he said, grinning as much as he could manage.

Her face brightened then.

"Okay," she said with a bit of eagerness. "I'll see ya...later." She stood and smoothed her hands down her dress. The slight movement caught his gaze, and he followed her hands on their path with his eyes.

"*Jah*," he breathed. "I'll see ya later."

ༀ

The room-temperature butter landed with a smack in the bottom of the mixing bowl. All the best recipes started this way. Cream the butter with the sugar. Amy dumped in the measured amounts. Maybe Ella could just scoop it out with a regular old spoon, but Amy would always need measuring cups.

She churned the soft dough, switching arms when one got tired. By the looks of Nathaniel's jaw, he wouldn't want anything that required a lot of chewing. Something smaller and easier to handle would be best. So far, she had two loaves of cinnamon bread, a peanut butter pie, and a batch of sugar cookies. It was probably too much. She was overdoing it. She knew she was. But it was just the smallest thing she could do after what he had done for her.

Never did she think she would be grateful for being locked inside a cooler for over half an hour. But because he'd had the foresight to do it, she'd been spared what could have been an even uglier encounter.

Satanists. She'd heard her father say the word today and it gave her the shivers. Several other smaller businesses had had run-ins with this same group of troublemakers. They came in, threatened people, sometimes roughed the place up, and usually stole something. To date, Nathaniel was the only one who'd been beaten.

It could so easily have been her. And it could so easily have been so much worse.

Surprisingly, she hadn't heard any chatter about it at church today. Nathaniel's whole family had been there without him. It was surprising how much she'd missed his presence. She had never really thought of him as a friend, but often he would nod hello and perhaps exchange a few words with her after the service. Today there'd been none of that, and she'd felt oddly lonely.

No one seemed to know or care where Nathaniel was or what had happened to him. The Shetlers didn't appear eager to explain his absence.

No matter. She was content to simply give him the time to heal and to bake enough good things to distract him from the memory of the incident.

⋅෧෬ ඉ෨⋅

"I just don't understand it." Ella shook her head, her brow furrowed in deep worry lines. "Why would someone do something like that to such a nice young man?"

"*Daed* says Nathaniel felt the presence of evil when they were goading him," Amy answered gently.

Ella simply shook her head.

"He's taking some time off. To heal. He looks pretty rough."

"Do ya think he'll come back?"

Amy's head snapped up. "What do ya mean?"

Ella shrugged. "Might be something like that would put a person off of a job."

That was certainly possible. Would Amy be able to keep working at the market if it had been her? She didn't know right off. Maybe. But maybe not.

"I hope that isn't the case," she murmured, staring down at her fingers in her lap.

"Me too," Ella said, leaning forward to hold Amy's hands in her own gnarled ones. Ella's skin was so thin you could almost see through it.

"He's so strong. I can't believe they even dared to try hurting him," Amy wondered aloud. Nathaniel could lift anything. Amy had seen him do it. And her dad had said Nathaniel's hands were completely uninjured, meaning Nathaniel hadn't thrown a single punch.

"Ach, he overpowered them." Ella waved her wrinkled hand.

"What do ya mean?" Amy asked, confused.

"Seems to me the *mann* with the most strength is the one who doesn't lose himself in violence," Ella said firmly. "Now, how about we get started on a lemon friendship bread."

— CHAPTER TWENTY-TWO —

Nathaniel slowly made his way across the yard to the horse barn. Simple walks were good and a welcome part of his healing. Sleeping still presented some challenges. So many times, he'd tried to roll over in his sleep and woken up in extreme pain. Bending or twisting were absolutely out of the question. Which pretty much eliminated most of the things he did at the market. He hadn't been back since the attack. But even though he wouldn't be able to stock the shelves, accept deliveries, or even sweep the floor…he wanted to be there.

With careful movements, he reached out and opened the door to the barn, stepping inside the dimly lit space. It was early, and the horses were still enjoying the warmth of their stalls, munching on their breakfast.

He made his way over to Susie's stall and stepped inside next to her. She turned her head to peer at him before she went back to her breakfast. Nathaniel picked up the brush and began combing the shavings and dust out of her mane. Even this simple task was proving more challenging than he had anticipated.

Amy, Daniel, and Caleb would be making their way to the market soon. He didn't really want to be outside to wave as they drove by. His face was healing well. The puffiness and swelling around his eye and jaw had almost disappeared. But not the bruising. The bruising was worse than ever. He'd been busy avoiding everyone who stopped on the yard.

And that had been no small trick. Uncle Joseph and his building crew had been buzzing around all week to prepare for the construction work planned for next week. He never meant to keep the attack a secret from anyone. But it sure was easier if no one knew. Otherwise, they would all want to pay him a visit. The only visitors he had accepted were Daniel and Amy. Daniel stopped by most days after closing time. Nathaniel had been able to give him a more complete accounting of what happened. He remembered all the parts where he'd been conscious. And he'd given more than a few pointed instructions on not leaving Amy and Sally at the store without someone there to protect them.

"Caleb and I will both be there every day until we are certain it is safe," Daniel had reassured him.

That should be satisfactory. That should be sufficient. But it just didn't feel like enough. A whole army of Amish men probably wouldn't feel like enough.

"I know it doesn't feel like it now, but it's lucky you were there," the police officer's words came back to Nathaniel. "There's no telling what kind of assault could have happened if they had found the girl."

A wave of nausea rolled over him. That thought had occurred to him as he'd prayed God would keep her hidden. But to hear it confirmed by the officer who took his statement—well, that made it more real.

That couldn't happen to Amy. They could break every one of his ribs and beat him to death before he would let that happen. She was feisty and strong and tough in her own way. But no, there could be no chance of someone ever hurting her that way.

Amy. She'd been by several times to see him. Which was embarrassing. The sympathy in her eyes was almost more than he could stand. *Jah*, he looked bad. He knew it. At least she couldn't see the dinner-plate-sized bruise on his ribcage. She'd brought so many treats he was reasonably sure he would need a new set of trousers by the end of the week.

As humiliating as it was to have her eyes search his face, lingering on his cut lip, peering up into his black eye, it was worth it. She told him interesting stories from the market, though never funny ones. It was excruciating for him to laugh. She asked for his opinion on where to put a recent shipment of handmade baskets in the back room. They'd talked about ways to make the store safer for the employees. It had quieted his heart to hear her talk about the market with passion and interest. He had worried she would be too frightened to go back. What if the beating had scared her away from the market for good? But no. Her love for the store was still there, and it comforted him to know she had been spared from fear or scarring memories.

Nathaniel stopped brushing Susie and stood staring at her for a long moment. This was the cycle of his thoughts. All day. Every day. They hadn't changed. They hadn't lessened. His entire focus had become Amy and the market.

He'd tried to force himself to think of Miriam last night. But he was having trouble remembering exactly what her face looked like. He'd recognize her, of course, if he saw her. But just right off he couldn't recall the exact shape of her face. And yet he knew all of Amy's expressions. He knew the precise line of her jaw, the hue of her skin, the color of her eyes. And he could still remember the feel of her in his arms that day when she'd slipped on the front porch. The sound of her singing in the barn loft would haunt him for the rest of his life. No one else could sing like that.

There was only one thing he could do. He let the truth sink in deep.

He had to go back to Middlefield. As soon as possible.

⚬❧ ❦⚬

Amy placed a warm loaf of lemon friendship bread on the sheet of foil and drizzled icing over the top. Leave it to Ella to take a standard recipe and add a new flavor, creating something new and wonderful out of something so commonplace.

With careful folds, she brought the edges of the foil together and pinched them shut. There were six small loaves to sell at the market today, one large loaf for the *familye*, and one large loaf for Nathaniel. He seemed genuinely pleased to get her daily delivery of treats. Truth be told, it calmed her heart to see him getting just a little better each day. The swelling was gone, leaving just the grotesque purple bruises in their wake. But she thought even those had looked a little more faded yesterday.

"There are strange healing powers in homemade gifts," Ella had said yesterday. "When the heart is healed, the body will follow."

Amy certainly hoped that was true. She felt partly responsible for Nathaniel's injuries—something Ella had chastised her for. If she could be a small part of his healing, it would ease her mind.

"Off to the market," Caleb called in a singsong voice. "Again." He sighed.

"There are worse places."

"*Jah*. Sitting in this house while ya bake and refuse to share is one of them."

Amy rolled her eyes. "I share with ya more than I don't."

"But the fact is sometimes ya still don't share. So there's that."

"Get in the buggy," Amy said in exasperation. Caleb had not exactly loved his time at the market this past week. But he'd endured it in good humor. Hopefully, it wouldn't be too long before Nathaniel was back to work.

"Stop here for a moment," Amy said as they neared the Shetlers' farm.

"You know, I've heard it said that the way to a *mann's* heart is through his stomach," Caleb quipped.

Amy's face flamed despite her utter annoyance with her younger brother.

"If that was true, half the county would be in love with me," she retorted.

He nodded in mock seriousness. "I'm glad to see humility is still one of yer greatest qualities."

"Just pull over," Amy sighed impatiently.

Caleb guided the buggy into the Shetlers' driveway and pulled it to a stop. The yard was quiet and still. Strange. Usually when she drove up, Nathaniel was quick to meet her outside—almost like he sat by a window watching for her. But no one came out today.

"I'll just *geh* knock on the door." Amy slid off the bench seat.

"Make it snappy," Caleb ordered, though she knew he was joking.

After a few timid knocks, and Becca pulled open the door. A frisson of worry wound through Amy. Was Nathaniel not well enough to answer the door? Where was he?

"Oh, *guder mariye*, Amy! *Wie geht's?*" Becca greeted her with a warm smile.

"I'm well, Becca. *Denki.* Is Nathaniel home?" Amy asked, her face flushing. This was not something she normally did—call on a *buwe*. It was so much easier when he just came out of the house and met her in the yard.

"Oh, *nee*. He's not home," Becca said, frowning slightly. "I thought maybe he mentioned it to ya."

"Mentioned what?" Amy asked, dread pooling in her stomach. Why did this feel so bad?

"Well, he decided to go back to Middlefield for a while. Left this morning. He wanted to visit some old friends, I think. That and his face looks so bad, *jah*? I think he just wanted some time to heal up."

"Oh," Amy breathed woodenly. He'd left. He'd gone back to Middlefield. Middlefield where there were no violent, unprovoked attacks. Middlefield where there was no market to work in each and every day. Middlefield where he wouldn't be bothered by her visits.

"I'll tell him ya stopped by if he calls," Becca offered. The look on the girl's face said she knew she had just delivered disappointing news.

"*Nee*, that's not necessary. I'll see him when he gets back," Amy reassured Becca as she backed away from the door.

"Not home?" Caleb asked as she climbed back in beside him.

"*Nee*. He went back to Middlefield," she said, annoyance coloring her voice.

"Oh. So more time at the market for me then."

"I'm as thrilled about that as you are."

৩৫ ৯৯৹

It was well after midnight when Nathaniel stepped off the train. Splurging on a sleeper for his trip wasn't something he would normally do. But being able to lie down had made his trip far more bearable than riding in a regular seat for the entire fifteen hours. With a careful swing, he tossed his bag over his shoulder and made his way across the covered outdoor portion of the station.

He tugged the brim of his hat lower, trying to hide his bruised and battered face from the glare of the fluorescents. Not only was he well-rested, but he'd enjoyed the privacy of his cabin. Truth be told, he was growing more accustomed to stares and curious looks from Englishers after all his time at the market. But most of the looks he got lately included shock at his bruises.

A familiar form stood waiting near the parking lot.

Elam. His best friend for most of his life. Except for the past several months in Bradford, Nathaniel couldn't remember a day when he hadn't seen Elam. They'd grown up only a half mile apart. They were the same age. They'd even worked together at the RV factory. Just seeing his goofy grin made Nathaniel realize how much he had missed his friend.

Elam stuck out his hand and shook Nathaniel's firmly.

"*Du gucksht gut,*" Elam drawled with a crooked grin.

Nathaniel snorted a laugh. He knew he didn't look good at all.

"The reports of yer injuries were woefully inadequate," Elam continued, his grin still firmly in place.

"Still better-looking than you," Nathaniel quipped. At that Elam threw back his head and laughed loudly.

"That you are," Elam finally agreed. He waved his arm. "The car and driver are over here."

"*Denki* for picking me up," Nathaniel said, struggling to make his legs keep up with Elam's strides—something that was normally easy for him to do.

"Sleep is for the weak." Elam grinned again. "We'll be home in a few hours and we can both get some more rest."

"Sounds *gut* to me," Nathaniel agreed easily.

"Miriam is already planning the breakfast of a lifetime." Elam laughed as he rubbed his stomach.

At the mention of her name, Nathaniel's stomach flipped. That Miriam was Elam's younger sister by a few years was not going to help matters.

— Chapter Twenty-Three —

Amy sighed in disgust. There in the corner of the back room was her younger brother, sprawled on his back with his hands behind his head, sound asleep. She'd sent him back here to clean up—not to nap.

"Caleb!" she said sharply.

He jolted awake, spied her angry face, and resumed his reclined position.

"Can't a guy get a little rest every once in a while?" he asked, closing his eyes and drawing in a deep breath.

"*Nee*! You are here to work! Not take naps!"

"You are a slave driver. I don't know how Nathaniel puts up with ya," he mumbled as he pulled himself up to a sitting position.

"Nathaniel never naps!" she snapped.

"Not that ya know of any way," Caleb said with a smart tilt of his head.

"Nathaniel works hard every day. Which is more than I can say for you. The wonder is Silas puts up with ya!"

"Ah, but I like working with Silas. You…less so," he replied, finger pointing up at the ceiling.

Amy jabbed her finger at the messy pile of boxes near the loading doors. "Get to work breaking those down for the recycling truck or I'll make ya work through yer lunch hour."

Caleb's eyes shot from her to the piles of boxes and back to her again. That threat seemed to get his attention.

She watched as he unfolded his long limbs and stood, towering well over her. She tilted her chin up to meet his annoyed look and watched as he turned to the pile of boxes.

Oh, it would be good to have Nathaniel back again. At least he'd told her father about his trip, but for some reason it smarted that he hadn't mentioned it to her. But something more than that bothered Amy. Why go now and not wait until his injuries had healed? What couldn't wait until later?

⋅☙ ❧⋅

Breakfast casserole, bacon, blueberry pancakes, and cinnamon rolls. Nathaniel's mouth watered as he sat surveying the enormous spread.

"I sure do like it when ya visit," Elam joked as he sat across the table.

Miriam appeared from the kitchen for the first time.

"Hullo, Nathaniel. Welcome home," she said with a warm smile.

"*Denki*, Miriam." He swallowed. Home. Was this home? His old house was just down the road. The countryside was as familiar to him as the sound of Susie's trotting footsteps. He knew more faces here than he did in Bradford. He recognized voices. He knew every single person's name. The smells, sounds, and sights were all so well-known. But home?

Home was where Matt snuggled up to Nathaniel at three in the morning because the thunder outside frightened him. Home was where Becca and Rachel sat in the living room most days working on quilt blocks. Home was where he could stand on top of the low ridge on the southern side of their property and see the market. Home was Amy's smiling face behind the counter as an Englisher asked her if she knew how to drive a horse and buggy by herself.

As much as he loved Middlefield, it stunned him to find that his heart wasn't really here anymore.

"I need some help, if you're feeling up to it," Elam said, interrupting his thoughts.

"Mm," Nathaniel murmured. There really wasn't much he could do these days without aggravating his cracked ribs.

"I bought a horse. A two-year-old colt. He's been broke, but I cannot get a collar and harness on him to save my life." Elam shook his head. "Thought ya could maybe help me out a bit."

The last time Nathaniel had harnessed a horse had been the night of the attack. Throwing the harness over Susie's shoulders and getting her in the traces had been all he could do. But he might be able to coach Elam. The alternative was sitting here inside the house with Miriam fussing all over him. Which would have been appealing a few months ago.

"I'll see what I can do," Nathaniel agreed.

⊷ঞৎ৯৹

Amy sat down wearily on the front porch swing and gently pushed it into motion. There were two additional buggies in the side yard and a house full of voices. Another buggy rattled up the lane. A Saturday night family dinner. Michael and Deborah and their three children were here, along with David and Sarah and their five children. And now Silas and Kirsten and their two *kinner*. It would be more than a full house tonight. Even the enormous farmhouse extension table Silas had built all those years ago for their mother would not be big enough. Amy had escaped to the porch just as Daniel and Caleb were setting up a folding table and chairs in the spacious main floor.

"There you are."

Kirsten's voice startled Amy.

"*Maam* and Sarah and Deborah insisted they had things handled, so I stepped out here for some fresh air," Amy said with a smile.

Kirsten lowered herself onto the swing and took a deep breath.

"It's a lovely evening," she said quietly. "How was work?"

"Oh…fine." Amy shrugged. Truth was her days were both far more exciting than they needed to be and dreadfully boring at the same time.

"How's it going with Caleb?" Kirsten asked, a knowing grin on her face.

Amy rolled her eyes. Caleb was the reason the past two weeks had been more stressful than usual.

"Not so good then," Kirsten observed.

"He does fine when he works. Trouble is he just doesn't work quite enough." Amy twisted her mouth to the side.

"Hm," Kirsten mused. "He's never like that with Silas. I wonder if it's because he doesn't dare contradict Silas or because he likes the work that much more."

"Both."

"*Jah*, you're probably right."

"So, when are ya going to tell us all yer news?" Amy asked quietly with a gentle smile.

From the corner of her eye, she saw Kirsten's eyes snap to her face. "How'd you know? Did Silas tell you?"

Amy shook her head and laughed. "No. But when he comes around asking for cinnamon bread, that tells me something."

"Oh, good grief," Kirsten groaned, rubbing a hand across her forehead. "I'm nearly fifteen weeks along already. I think he's going to say something tonight. Maybe. You never know with Silas."

"Did it help? The bread?" Amy asked with a warm smile.

"Oh, yes! It's just about the only thing I can nibble on throughout the day that keeps the morning sickness at bay."

Amy laughed. "I remember that with Ben, too."

"One day, it will be your turn. You'll have to give me your recipe so I can make it for you," Kirsten said, her voice gentle and kind.

A dull ache pulsed in her chest. Amy loved children—babies most especially. Giving up the dream of having a family of her own was the only hard part about deciding never to marry. She tried to fill that void with her nephews and nieces, but it wasn't quite the same. She knew that. As much as they loved her and she them, it wasn't like having children of your very own. But for Amy to have a baby would mean she needed to have a husband. And that was something she had absolutely no intention of doing.

Amy rose and stood at the railing for a moment, staring ahead, not knowing how to respond to her sister-in-law. She heard the creak of the swing and felt Kirsten's arm gently circle her waist.

"You may have given up, *schwesder*, but I haven't. God has a funny way of making his own plans for our lives."

With a gentle tug, Amy let Kirsten tow her into the bustling house.

⋅⊙⊙⋅

"Care to go for a walk with me?" Nathaniel asked as Miriam placed the last dried dish in the cupboard. He'd been with his friends for the better part of two weeks now. The rest of the family was gathered in the living room—all twelve of them.

"*Jah*, that would be lovely," Miriam answered with a bright smile.

The air was crisp but fitting for the first week of May. Back home the planting would all be done by now and the addition on the house would be well under way.

Home.

It was not here anymore. He'd been so sure when he left that he would one day be back for Miriam. And truthfully, he was back because of her. But not in the way he'd planned.

They sat in silence on the bench of a picnic table outside, facing away from the tabletop.

"You like it in Iowa, *jah*?" Miriam asked quietly.

"Iowa is home now," Nathaniel agreed with a slow nod of his head.

"Tell me about it?"

Nathaniel wrestled with the words to say. "We farm a hundred acres. Just a mile away is the Amish Country Market, where I work. We have *gut* neighbors, and I've made some *gut* friends."

"Why all this work at the market? I thought ya moved away for farmland?"

"Farming is *Daed's* love. I like it…but maybe not quite as much as *Daed*." Nathaniel shrugged. "The job at the market came up this winter when there wasn't much to do. It was close by, convenient, and the right number of hours. It wasn't until I started working there that I realized how much I enjoyed it. It's busy but not rushed. There are always people to talk with, people to help. It's easy to make someone's day with a friendly word or a smile."

Snippets of conversations he'd had with English customers drifted through Nathaniel's mind. The more he had to explain his way of life, the more he came to appreciate the reasons why his people lived the way they did.

"But not all the English have been so nice to ya," Miriam murmured.

Nathaniel shook his head. "*Maam* says I was in the wrong place at the wrong time…but I actually think God put me there at that exact moment for a reason."

"To get hurt?" Miriam frowned.

"*Nee*. To protect *mei* friend, Amy," he answered.

"I've heard her name a few times now."

Nathaniel swallowed.

"You and I have been friends for a long while, Miriam. I know we even talked about maybe having a future together after I got settled in Iowa. But I care about ya, and you deserve my honesty…"

"Does she love you?" Miriam asked, a hint of pain in her voice.

Nathaniel could not help but snort. "*Nee*. Not even close."

Miriam drew in a deep breath and stared ahead. Several horses stood grazing in the pasture.

"I'm glad ya told me," she said eventually. "It's *gut* to know what you are thinking."

"I'm sorry, Miriam," Nathaniel said, forcing the words out.

"I think you'll be just fine," she answered, her eyes focused on Elam's new colt grazing contentedly on the other side of the fence. Nathaniel had coached Elam on how to calm and train the young horse. Instead of forcing the collar onto his neck, Nathaniel instructed Elam to simply hold it for the horse to investigate and play with. They did the same with the harness. When Elam had hooked the colt up to the small cart for the first time, he'd been jittery.

"Talk to him. Let him hear yer voice behind him. Sing to him if ya have to," Nathaniel had gently instructed.

Elam had chattered and murmured low and the colt had calmed. Day after day, Elam would ride behind that colt, humming, singing, or muttering. There was work yet to be done before the animal could be trusted to pull a buggy. But there was a stark contrast between the now-peaceful creature and the jittery beast Nathaniel had met when he'd arrived.

At least he could train a horse to settle down and like him. If only he could do the same with Amy.

— Chapter Twenty-Four —

Sitting on the backless bench, Amy listened carefully to the bishop as he preached. Kirsten had offered to help watch the *kinner* outside, so Amy sat tucked in close to Ella's side. Some districts required members to sit according to age. Being New Order Amish certainly allowed for more freedoms, including Amy sitting anywhere she wished on the women's side.

"I hope that the council meeting don't take too long," Ella had whispered to her as they'd taken their seats. "It's harder for me to sit here than it used to be."

Two hours later, the meeting was just beginning. There were only a few issues that brought any discussion. It seemed it would be over in almost record time.

But a hand raised near the front. With a nod, the bishop gave the man permission to speak.

"I heard there was some trouble in our community," Joseph Beiler, Lucas's father, began. "My nephew was attacked and beaten by some men who visited the Amish Country Market. It worries me how we have allowed the world this access to our community. It's one thing to sell goods to passersby, like we have always done. But it's quite another to be such a tourist stop."

Amy sat rigid in her place, but her eyes darted to the quiet, calm form of her father. He didn't raise his hand or make a move to respond. Just sat waiting.

None of this was shocking. The Millers had long known Joseph didn't approve of their business. He'd always considered them "on the fence" for the way they lived and worked and socialized with Englishers. But to be called out like this after Nathaniel's attack...

Arguments in support of the market filled Amy's mind until Ella's wrinkled hand landed gently on her knee. Immediately Amy quieted. Ella's watery blue eyes fixed on her face.

"I'd like to speak to that, if I may."

Amy jolted. She knew that voice.

Nathaniel.

When had he gotten back from Middlefield?

He rose now and walked from the back of the room, stopping next to the bishop and turning to face the people. His bruises had faded some. His eye was no longer swelled shut. The cut to his lip was barely visible. He stood there for a long moment, letting the people stare at him.

"I was attacked several weeks ago," he began. "But thanks be to God I am healing well. Three men entered the market after closing time. I'd neglected to lock the door right at six o'clock the way I should have." Amy wanted to protest. They often didn't lock the door right at six. At least, they hadn't right before the incident. There were always rugs to shake out or the porch to sweep off or small display items that needed to be brought back in. In any case, the sign had been flipped to closed right at six. She'd done that herself.

"They taunted and threatened me, but when I wouldn't engage in their little game, they threw a few punches and left." Nathaniel shrugged. An almost invisible blush colored his cheeks, but Amy saw it.

"Jesus said, '*In this world you will have trouble. But take heart, because I have overcome the world.*' I don't think it should really surprise us when we encounter darkness like the kind I saw that evening. Those men had a presence about them. They cared more about terrorizing me than they did about stealing anything.

"They weren't there because I was Amish. They were there because I am a Christian. I've been working at the market for several months now, and I've seen firsthand many of the English tourists ya mentioned,

Onkle. It's true they get a chance to see us, our handmade goods, and ask questions about us. But I also think this work gives us a chance to shine a light.

"Jesus said we were the light of the world and that we shouldn't be hidden. I think the market and many of our other businesses are great ways to shine that light."

Nathaniel finished his speech and slowly made his way back down the aisle to the back row, where he had been sitting. Amy heard the stirring around her but only watched Ella's hand as it lightly tapped her leg, then lifted back to her own lap.

⸙

"Oh, I am mighty glad to see ya!" Caleb declared as Nathaniel stepped through the back door of the market late on Monday morning.

Nathaniel grinned broadly, closing the door behind him with a solid snap.

"You are here to work, right? You're not quitting or something, are ya?" Caleb asked, the fear on his face evident.

"*Nee*, not quitting," Nathaniel confirmed with a shake of his head. "Is yer *daed* here?"

"*Jah*, I'll get him," Caleb offered in relief.

Nathaniel surveyed the back room. It was mostly in order, but there were several things that hadn't been done. At least, not the way he would do them.

"Nathaniel, *wilkum* back!" Daniel boomed.

"*Denki*," Nathaniel replied as he met Daniel's outstretched hand in a firm shake.

"We'll be glad to have yer help again. When do ya think you'll be ready to come back to work?"

"Today," Nathaniel answered decisively.

Daniel's eyebrows shot up in surprise. "Oh! If you're ready, then we are ready to have ya. But I don't want to push you."

"No one's pushing me," Nathaniel quietly insisted.

"*Nee.* I've noticed you aren't that kind of *mann.*" Daniel smiled.

"I brought the replacement handle for the cooler," Nathaniel said, tapping the box tucked under his arm. "Thought I would start by working on that."

Daniel nodded. "*Jah,* that's a *gut* idea."

⦿⦿⦿

Why was her pulse thrumming so hard she could feel it in her head? For the first time in weeks, it was shaping up to be a normal day. Nothing new or out of the ordinary. Just a regular old afternoon. Customers shopping. Sally chattering up a storm. Nathaniel working in the back room.

Nathaniel.

Her dad had at least had the courtesy to touch her gently on the shoulder and murmur that Nathaniel would be working today.

Of course, Amy had seen him at church on Sunday. She had wanted so much to speak with him. But the men had surrounded him after the meeting, and he had been so deeply engaged in conversation that she hadn't been able to get close to him.

Now he had been in the back room for nearly two hours, completely alone, but uncharacteristically she'd stayed in the storefront.

"How ridiculous," she whispered under her breath. Amy forced one foot in front of the other, leaving Sally to ring up the next order.

It's just Nathaniel. I need to check and see how he's doing. It's what a good storeowner would do.

She pushed through the door and stopped in surprise. The wood floor gleamed. The large heap of boxes that had cluttered the far side of the stockroom was gone, all broken down into a neat flat stack and waiting by the loading doors. The worktables were all tidy, the new items cataloged and ready to be shelved.

It took a minute for her to take it all in. But where was he? Her eyes caught on a figure standing in the corner, stock-still, mop in hand. His head was bowed, and he looked to be leaning on it.

"Nathaniel?" she said tentatively, her feet moving toward him.

His head snapped up then, and he straightened.

"Are ya okay?" Amy asked as she neared. Closer up she could see the slight frown on his face.

"*Jah*, I'm fine," he said quickly, then started the mop back in motion across the small patch of dry floor around him.

Amy stopped awkwardly several feet away from him. She was standing too close and too far at the same time. Had she imagined it? He'd seemed off-kilter, somehow, for a moment. But now he was mopping much the same as he often did.

"I'll just…um…"

"Make sure ya tell me when you're ready to lock up," he said as her words drifted to silence.

"*Jah*. I will." Her throat closed a bit. She would do anything to keep him from ever being hurt again. His bruises were almost completely gone, but she remembered them. The mere picture of his battered body that morning after the attack was seared into her memory. Judging by the slowness of his movements, she began to wonder if mopping was perhaps causing him more pain than he wanted to let on.

"Nathaniel—I—I can do that—the mopping, I mean. For now," she offered. His back was turned to her, but she saw him freeze for a moment.

"*Jah*," he said, clearing his throat. "I, uh, need to check the temperatures on the cooler anyway." He turned his whole body in such a way that he didn't twist, then handed her the handle for the mop. She took it and began working it across the floor.

Amy watched out of the corner of her eye as Nathaniel crossed to the coolers. He checked the thermometers and logged the temps on the clipboard beside the door. Yes, there was something a bit different about the way he was moving. He was hiding it well enough, but she could see it.

She could *pretend* not to notice anything different, though. She owed him that much.

⁓৩৫ ৯৬⁓

Nathaniel stood near the swinging door that led to the storefront. Amy had told him she was locking the front doors, and he'd made sure all the doors in the back were also sealed tight. If the attackers came back, he would be hard-pressed to make much of a stand. Another beating like that one, and he probably wouldn't survive. He couldn't stand to think about what that would mean for Amy.

Business had been good today, which meant Sally and Amy had spent the entire afternoon helping customers and ringing up purchases. He'd done his best to stock shelves. But all the bending and lifting had taken its toll. He hadn't really realized before just how much twisting his body did each day. Often he would find Amy suddenly beside him, kneeling down to pull jars out of the box and hand them to him so he could set them on the shelf.

Sally had left nearly an hour ago, and Nathaniel and Amy had been busy finishing up the day and going through the closing routine. He peeked through the small window in the swinging doors and saw Amy carefully sweeping each aisle. Her lips were moving. Was she talking to herself? He nudged the door open just barely and listened.

Her voice floated through the small gap, sweet and pure, lifting in gentle melody.

For a few moments, Nathaniel merely listened. He'd heard so much singing in his lifetime. Most Sundays were filled with songs, both at the church service and at the youth Singings in the evening. He'd heard his *mudder* and *schwesders* singing as they did chores around the house. He'd trained numerous horses by singing to them as he taught them how to tolerate bridles and pulling machinery or wagons.

But nothing like this. Nothing he had heard had ever sounded quite this beautiful.

There were no solos in Amish communities. Only the select few who happened to hear Amy singing as she worked would ever know the incredible beauty in her voice. They were the only ones who would ever hear a song just exactly the way it was meant to sound.

He pushed the door open farther and quietly stepped through. There was something about Amy's song that drew him forward. But Nathaniel only managed a step or two before she stopped abruptly and turned to him.

"Don't stop," he insisted before she could speak.

Amy's head immediately dropped. She stared at the pile of swept-up debris at her feet.

"I like hearing ya sing," he admitted.

She turned slightly, almost away from him. He thought she would just continue sweeping in silence.

But ever so quietly he heard her pick up the song again, not a note out of place:

> *"Softly and tenderly, Jesus is calling,*
> *calling for you and for me;*
> *See, on the portals He's waiting and watching,*
> *watching for you and for me.*
>
> *"Come home, come home,*
> *you who are weary, come home;*
> *Earnestly, tenderly, Jesus is calling,*
> *calling, O sinner, come home!"*

For several moments, Nathaniel busied himself in the storefront, straightening objects on the shelves that really didn't need straightening, just so he could listen. Did she even realize how beautiful her voice was? He doubted it. Amy seemed sure of nothing except her ability to run the market.

Tentatively Nathaniel hummed with her—so quietly he was sure she couldn't hear. His voice was nowhere near as good as hers, but he could carry a tune fairly well. Not wanting to disrupt her song, he stayed as quiet as he could.

> *"Oh, for the wonderful love He has promised,*
> *promised for you and for me!*
> *Though we have sinned, He has mercy and pardon,*
> *pardon for you and for me."*

When Amy finished sweeping, she stopped singing and turned to face him.

"I'm just going to double-check the locks," he said as he passed her. He'd triple-checked them already. But he would not take any more chances—not where her safety was concerned.

"Looks *gut*." He nodded as he turned back. "Let me drive ya home."

"Oh. Well, I rode my bike."

"Let's put it inside the back room so no one takes it," he suggested. He was already moving that way. The weather was pleasant enough for her to bike home, but he was looking for any reason to spend time with her.

"Okay," she quietly agreed.

It was strange, the way she had softened toward him. She'd been far nicer, far warmer, and far more considerate toward him today than she had been before the attack. It was a good change. A promising one. And hopefully one that didn't fade away anytime soon.

— CHAPTER TWENTY-FIVE —

On Sunday, Amy stood in the Beilers' yard, feeling the warmth of the morning sun on her shoulders. Kirsten stood at her side, attempting to keep Grace from running off. The space was filled with the sound of quiet conversations. The creaking of the buggies intermingled with the huffing breaths of the horses, all set to roam in the pasture.

"Did Ella ride with the Shetlers?" Kirsten said in surprise.

Amy's head snapped up and followed her sister-in-law's gaze. Sure enough, Ella was being helped out of Nathaniel's buggy. She must have flagged him down rather than waiting on a ride from one of her many grandchildren.

With a tottering but steady gait, Ella made her way to the house. Amy hurried over and took her friend's arm with gentle firmness. The elderly woman accepted her help without comment. Just a simple smile. They waited while the men filed into the home. Not every house was large enough to host church, but the Beilers' was. The partitioned walls had been moved aside, and two groupings of benches filled the space. The men sat on the right, and the women followed and sat on the left.

"I'll just sit with you, *jah*?" Ella said quietly as they made their way up the stairs and into the home.

"*Jah*," Amy agreed. Ella had taken to sitting with Amy more and more often lately. But Amy surely didn't mind. If Ella wanted to sit with her, she was more than welcome to do so.

The singing was always slower in church than at the youth Singings in the evenings. Beside her, Ella's scratchy voice lifted in an age-worn warble. Tears pricked at Amy's eyes as she listened to Ella sing. Such unwavering faith for so many years. It was beautiful to behold.

Finally, the service drew to a close. Kirsten rose stiffly and rubbed at her lower back.

"You would think I would be used to all this sitting," her sister-in-law mumbled quietly.

Amy winked. "Maybe ya would be if ya weren't pregnant all the time."

Kirsten rolled her eyes and smiled.

Ella's hand wrapped around Amy's arm, and Amy turned to face the elderly friend. But Ella's eyes were scanning the crowd around her.

"So many young people," Ella wondered. "Do ya go to the Singings, Amy?"

Amy tried not to stiffen. She was sure she and Ella had talked about this before.

"*Nee.* I don't," Amy answered. She searched for more words, an acceptable excuse, but came up with nothing.

Ella seemed to understand. "Maybe one day ya could try it again. You have such a lovely voice."

Amy's eyes widened a bit. No one had ever commented on her voice apart from her mother so many years ago when she was just a little girl, still learning the unwritten tunes to the various hymns.

"Too bad it's not just about the singing," Amy muttered, sure Ella couldn't hear her in the steadily growing noise of the crowd.

"The other parts might be okay, too," Ella argued, much to Amy's surprise.

No. Amy wanted no part of the drama that accompanied Singings. She remembered all too well the crowds of people watching to see who would pair up with whom. At one point, it had been a sorry source of pride—something she regretted now—especially with the way things had ended with Lucas.

"You have so much courage. I'm sure ya could handle it just fine," Ella finished.

Amy did not respond as she led Ella to a group of elderly friends. Courage? Well, yes, perhaps she did have courage. She had courage to work in an environment where outsiders questioned her lifestyle nearly every day. She had courage to run the store on her own. She had courage to choose to remain single. She didn't think courage applied to chasing after *buwes*. To Amy, that seemed more of a weakness. It had taken such courage to go on with her life, to keep living in the community, after Lucas had ended their relationship.

A toughness that was so different from the naïve, foolish love she'd felt for him.

⋅৽ල ৯৵⋅

With one snap of fabric, the air filled with a fine mist. Were it not for the warm sun on her back, Amy would be cold. But a sunny day was just what she needed to get this laundry hung out to dry in the fresh air.

With a firm thrust, Amy slid the clothespin down over the shoulders of Ella's navy-blue dress. Her mother would surely be glad to do Ella's laundry, but this was something Amy took upon herself. Mary had enough to do—enough other people to care for. Amy wanted to take care of Ella as much as she possibly could.

Of course, Ella had argued last year when Amy first suggested she could help with her laundry. She tried to not notice that Ella was letting go of more and more responsibilities lately.

Pinning up the last dress, she moved on to hanging up the white flowered sheets she'd pulled from Ella's bed earlier that morning.

The sound of a buggy rolling down the long driveway had Amy's head turning. What was Nathaniel doing here?

"*Gut mariye*," he called as he stepped easily down from his buggy. He certainly was moving around better these past few months. He'd even taken the mop from her hands a few weeks ago at the market, his smile crooked and slightly chagrined.

Amy stood, staring stupidly for several moments. His long strides across the grass were purposeful, his gaze locked firmly on her.

"What…" she stammered, attempting to shake herself from her stupor. "Why are ya here?"

His lopsided grin as he stopped just feet away and stared down at her didn't help her concentration.

"I wanted to see yer *daed*. I stopped at the market, but Caleb told me he was home today waiting on a foal to be delivered."

Amy glanced over her shoulder to where her dad was indeed holed up in the horse barn.

"*Jah*, he is. I can get him for ya," she offered as she set a pillowcase down in the laundry basket at her feet.

"*Nee*, I'll go to him," Nathaniel insisted. "You're busy enough," he added, with a nod to the long line of laundry billowing softly in the breeze. She saw his eyes land briefly on the undergarments flapping on the last line.

"I'm just getting these done up for Ella," she blurted out.

His gaze flitted back to her and he nodded.

"What do ya need to talk to *Daed* about?" she pressed. Somehow, she had to distract herself from his intense gaze.

He shrugged. "Just an idea I had for the market."

"What kind of idea?" she asked, her brow crinkling with worry. When Nathaniel had ideas, things changed.

"The *gut* kind." He grinned. With a wink, he turned and headed off across the grass toward the horse barn.

Amy worked her jaw, but no sound came out.

⋅⊚❦ ❦⊚⋅

"This doesn't feel right," Kirsten said as she stared down at the box on her kitchen table. Amy couldn't help but agree. Silas and Nathaniel stood nearby, all four of them peering almost worriedly down at the thing sitting on the polished surface.

With a wordless shake of his head, Silas drew the box cutter through the clear packaging tape. Kirsten drew in a deep breath and pulled open the flaps. Amy couldn't help but lean over to get the first glance. Layers of plastic and Styrofoam covered the small item inside. Kirsten's hands slid in and lifted it out of the box, shedding bits of packaging as she went.

A computer.

Amy still didn't understand how Nathaniel's "*gut* idea" had spiraled into this. How had he gotten Silas to jump on board? How had he convinced her father this was necessary? How had he persuaded the bishop to give him permission to take this step?

Kirsten reached out a slim finger and poked a practically invisible button. That was another wonder—how Kirsten had known which computer to buy. Amy had never realized how many choices there were until she and Kirsten had taken that trip to the library to use the public computers to order this small laptop.

Almost silently, the machine flickered to life, the bright glow from the screen harsh in the dimly lit kitchen.

Glancing behind her, Amy could see Silas and Nathaniel both wearing confused but curious expressions. All three of them watched as Kirsten sat down and her fingers flew over the keys. She followed the commands, moved the arrow on the screen while touching a small square beneath the keyboard. Soon she had them logged on to the brand-new internet connection that had been installed just days ago in Silas's woodworking shop. That was where the laptop would ultimately live out its days—in the office off to the side, where Kirsten kept all the financial records for Silas's woodworking business and the market.

"I'm amazed that ya know how to do all this," Silas said quietly, his long-fingered hands finding Kirsten's shoulders as she sat in front of him.

"I guess it's a bit like riding a bike," she laughed. "We'll be able to file paperwork, receive custom orders, advertise, and even do our books on here if we want to."

"Couldn't we do all of that without this thing?" Amy asked with a frown.

"*Jah*, we could," Kirsten agreed. "At least, we could for *now*. But the world is moving on and using less and less paper. Some of the paperwork I have to do can't even be done as a hardcopy anymore. I was spending several hours a month at the library or at my mom's house just to get through it."

"I didn't know all that," Nathaniel commented. "One of the English customers just asked me last week why we weren't on Facebook. I had no idea what he was talking about until he told me. Sounded like a good chance to let others know about the market."

Amy just sat in awe as Kirsten typed faster than she could even read.

"What are ya doing now?" she asked her sister-in-law.

Kirsten laughed. "Something I thought I would never do again—signing us up for our very own email account."

Amy was too embarrassed to admit she didn't even know what an email account was.

— Chapter Twenty-Six —

The Arabian stallion stamped his feet in the empty pasture. Nathaniel stood just inside the fence, wondering why he had agreed to take on this challenge. Then Isaac Troyer's pleading face came into his mind.

"I heard you're *gut* with horses. I have one I need some help with," Isaac had said on Sunday after church. The next morning, Storm had arrived in a bouncing trailer that shook from the anger of the horse inside. "Anything you can do would be a great help to me," Isaac had sighed dejectedly.

Truthfully, Nathaniel had never worked with such an angry horse. They had put him in a large stall, far from the other animals. Even so, the stallion had stamped and kicked violently at the sturdy wooden walls around him.

It had taken weeks for Nathaniel to simply walk into the pasture without fear of getting trampled to death. But Storm was no longer kicking at the walls of his stall, no longer stamping whenever Nathaniel neared, and no longer pricking his ears forward when Nathaniel sang to him. Which was often. Hopefully in a few weeks, he'd be able to slip the traces on over Storm's head and lead him around a bit.

"Are ya sure that's a *gut* idea?" Amy's voice called to him. He turned to see her standing at the edge of Ella's yard, which stretched along the pasture.

"He's calmer now," Nathaniel reassured as he turned and made his way over to the chest-high fence.

Amy frowned. "You sure about that?"

"He's as gentle as a kitten now." Nathaniel grinned as he leaned his forearms on the rail.

Amy's eyes darted between him and the horse.

"I doubt it," she breathed.

"Well, maybe not a kitten necessarily," Nathaniel allowed with tip of his head. A bead of sweat rolled down his back. Did she have any idea how alluring she was, standing there in the warm summer sun? The way the apron tied off at her tiny waist, giving her curves in all the right places? The way that particular shade of blue made her eyes brighter? The way the breeze blew those few strands of her blond hair against her long, slender neck?

"Nathaniel," she gasped. It took him a long second to tear his eyes away from her parted lips to glance behind him and see Storm sauntering toward them.

"He's okay," Nathaniel said quietly as he turned around to face the beast approaching them.

"Are ya sure about that?" she muttered again.

Sure he was sure. Maybe. Somewhat. Not really.

"He's just coming to see who I'm talking to," Nathaniel said, his voice low and calm. "Hey Storm," he continued. "Are ya curious?"

The horse snuffed loudly, and Nathaniel could have laughed.

"He says ya make him nervous," Nathaniel teased over his shoulder.

"The feeling is mutual," Amy admitted.

With a tentative hand, Nathaniel reached out and brushed a palm against the horse's neck. He let his hand travel down the neck and then up over Storm's shoulders and onto his back. Long, slow, smooth strokes.

"Looks like you've got him well in hand," Amy said, surprise registering on her face.

"He must like ya." Nathaniel grinned with his back to her. *That makes two of us*, he thought. "You'll have to come around more often." He smiled as he turned to Amy, his fists jammed into his pockets.

An uncertain smile flickered across her beautiful face, her eyes still dancing between him and Storm.

"Enjoy yer day with Ella," he called to her as she turned and walked away.

"Enjoy yer day with Storm," she retorted over her shoulder.

Spending the day with Storm was okay if it made her fret over him a bit.

⋅෴⋅

"Hullo, Ella," Amy called as she entered the house. It wasn't like Ella to not meet her at the door. Maybe she had seen her out talking to Nathaniel and wandered away from the window. The soft shuffle of feet sounded from the living room and Ella appeared, coming around the table and into the kitchen.

"Amy," she said, her voice as scratchy as ever, but warm and welcoming. "I'm glad you're here." Ella reached for her. Amy stepped into the old woman's arms and hugged her back, gently but tightly.

"Me too," she answered.

"Shall we get started?" Ella asked.

Amy spied the assortment of ingredients sitting out on the counter. There were the necessities of course: flour, sugar, salt, yeast, butter, milk. She tried to guess what they might be making as she washed up at the sink and dried her hands on one of Ella's embroidered towels.

"What are we making?" she asked loudly enough so that Ella could hear.

Ella smiled. "Cinnamon rolls."

Amy's hands trembled a bit. She'd asked so many times if they could make cinnamon rolls, and Ella had always said they would do it another time, another day, later. Why now? The question clanged around in her head as she forced a nod.

Ella stood right beside Amy as she dumped the ingredients into the bowl. First what looked like about three cups of flour. Then salt, yeast, sugar. Next, she mixed butter and eggs into warmed milk. Wet ingredients combined with dry ingredients. Amy focused intently, praying she could remember all these steps when she went to write them down in her book.

"Do ya know why I don't measure it all out?" Ella asked gently.

"No, why?" Amy was curious.

"Every time things are different. Every batch has its own day, its own conditions, its own air, its own temperature. I've made them so many times, and there have never been two batches that were the same," Ella replied. "In colder seasons, they need extra time. But in warm ones it will surprise ya how quickly they grow. Don't be afraid of it. Turns out in the end they are worth all the mess and all the trouble and all the work."

Amy felt a sting in her eyes. That felt like more wisdom than a cinnamon roll recipe required.

"Okay, add more flour. Enough so you can hardly mix it," Ella instructed.

Amy slowly added what seemed like four more cups of flour, stirring with all her might until her arms ached.

"That's looking about right," Ella said with a nod. "Now dump it out here and knead it around a bit."

Amy spilled out the dough, seeing that it was still too wet.

She winced. "Oops."

"Ah, that's just fine. This batch just needs a bit more flour."

Amy tossed another handful of flour onto the dough and began to knead it. Ten minutes later, Ella finally said, "*Jah*, that's enough. Back in the bowl it goes."

"Now what?" Amy asked as she covered the bowl with a towel.

Ella sighed. "Now we wait."

"You go sit down in the living room and I'll be right there," Amy said with gentle firmness.

Ella's shuffling gait drifted off across the floor to the living room. Amy turned and hurried to the basket she had brought with her and yanked out her notebook. A look through the basket told her she had forgotten to bring a pen. A desperate search of the kitchen and Amy found one in a drawer. As quickly as possible, she jotted down the measurements and ingredients she had just used. She could remember the steps, but the amounts were a different story.

When Amy made her way into the living room, Ella was sitting on the sofa, her eyes closed and her head drooped so her chin almost pressed against her chest. Strange. Ella didn't normally fall asleep during Amy's visits.

Amy lowered herself into the rocking chair and pushed it gently into motion. She had been careful not to make any sound, so she was surprised when Ella suddenly lifted her head.

"How has yer week been?" Ella asked, almost as if she hadn't been snoozing.

Amy made small talk with Ella, answering her questions and asking a few of her own.

"How long do we wait?" Amy asked after a long while.

"It's hard to know how long to wait," Ella answered. "We can check."

Amy stood and helped Ella get to her feet.

"I'll sit at the table this time," Ella said as they entered the eat-in kitchen. Amy settled the old woman into the chair and retrieved the bowl from the counter. She peeled back the towel and angled the bowl for Ella's inspection.

"Sometimes ya don't have to wait very long. And other times, ya have to wait a very, very long time," Ella explained as she examined the dough, poking it and pinching it between her fingers. "This one doesn't need any more time though. It's ready."

Amy's brow furrowed at Ella's words. Was she merely talking about the cinnamon rolls?

"You do so well baking, Amy," Ella said quietly as Amy prepped the dough on the table. "Ya listen well, and ya learn quickly. Ya know just what to do after you've done it a few times."

Amy swallowed the lump in her throat. She rolled the dough into a rectangle and covered it with melted butter, cinnamon, and brown sugar.

"Be careful when ya roll it up. Make sure ya get the roll nice and tight so it stays together when ya slice it," Ella coaxed.

"Now for the secret tool," Ella continued, grinning with a wheezy laugh. Amy's eyes widened as she looked down at the small pack of dental floss in Ella's hand.

"If ya use a knife, no matter how sharp it is, it will crush the soft dough. But if ya use the floss like so." Ella demonstrated, pulling the string under and then over until the ends crossed. She tugged it tight.

"Then ya get a perfect little slice." Sure enough, there on the table lay a perfectly cut cinnamon roll.

"There are times ya can be a bit rougher with the dough, and times ya need to be very gentle." Ella nodded as she picked up the roll and placed it gently in the baking pan.

Amy sliced the rest with the floss, nowhere nearly as neatly or easily as Ella had. But in the end, there were two dozen cinnamon rolls, each snuggled into a pan—one of which was Ella's precious and ancient cake pan.

"We cover them and wait a bit again," Ella said.

"Waiting isn't easy," Amy laughed and then abruptly stopped.

"*Nee*," Ella agreed. "Waiting can be very difficult."

Images of Hank passed through Amy's mind. She couldn't imagine sharing a life with someone, sharing children and grandchildren together, weathering all of life's ups and downs, and then watching them slowly fade and die.

"I miss my Hank," Ella said, the sadness bringing tears to Amy's eyes. "He was such a *gut mann*. Waiting to be with him again is not always easy. But I am glad for the time we've had."

"He was a *wunderbaar mann*," Amy agreed.

"That's what I want for ya. I want for ya to find yer own *wunderbaar mann*."

"I don't think that will happen," Amy choked. Once she had been so certain she had found her forever. But Lucas had left, shattered the vision of the future she had held and broken her heart into so many pieces. The years of avoidance after rejection had taken their toll. She'd forgiven him at least a hundred times over.

"Oh Amy, I hurt for you so," Ella said with such gentle sorrow that Amy could only bow her head and let the tears slip down her cheeks. Ella's frail hand gripped Amy's own with a tight squeeze. "I pray you will find someone who wants to cherish and treasure ya the way ya deserve."

The lump in Amy's throat would not go away as the tears fell. Deep down in her heart, so deep down that she could barely admit it was there, she wanted the same thing. But the problem was she would have to swim in that fearful place where her heart was vulnerable. And if she found she could not touch solid ground, then she would drown.

For a long while, the two women just sat together, staring out the window and listening to the sounds of summer wind. An hour later, Amy wandered back into the kitchen. The rolls were ready to bake. The smell of the finished treats was beyond anything she could have described. A layer of icing and Amy could tell just by the sight of them that they would be incredible.

"You take both pans with ya," Ella said as Amy stood to go.

"*Nee*, I don't need to do that," Amy insisted. "Caleb will be spoiled rotten."

Ella smiled and hoisted herself to her feet. "Well, maybe ya could find someone else to share with then."

Amy lifted a startled gaze to Ella's face, but the old woman was concentrating on shuffling through the kitchen, one hand sliding along the countertop as she kept her balance. Perhaps Amy was just reading too much into all of Ella's words. But everything she said today felt like she was saying more.

Amy set the two pans next to her basket and turned to Ella. Her friend's arms were waiting, and Amy soon found herself tucked in close, Ella's wrinkled forehead pressed against hers. "You are a treasure," she breathed. "I love the time I spend with ya." Amy could only attempt to swallow. "I'll be going home soon, Amy. And I want ya to know that I am ready to *geh*, that I've had a beautiful life, and that I want ya to have a beautiful life, too. You are loved, so very loved. You can trust in that." Ella's hands tightly gripped Amy's arms as she softly spoke. "I love ya so."

"I love ya too, Ella," Amy choked as she felt the elderly woman gently release her. She didn't want to leave her. This goodbye felt different from the others. "I'll bring yer cake pan back soon," Amy promised.

Ella merely closed her eyes for a long moment and then nodded. Amy looped her basket over her arm and scooped up the two pans of rolls. Ella stood in the doorway, the breeze blowing her skirt, as Amy snapped the reins and drove the buggy off the yard.

CHAPTER TWENTY-SEVEN

The new addition on the house stood tall, more than doubling the size of the original home. That extra space would be nice. As Nathaniel's siblings continued to grow, there would be less and less room for all of them. If the right piece of property came on the market, he would certainly consider buying it and having a place of his own. It would be nice to plant his own roots and get settled on a little acreage for himself.

"You did a nice job on these floors," Elam said as he stared down at the pine boards stretching the length of the giant kitchen and dining room.

"I only helped a little," Nathaniel muttered.

Elam smiled. "For a plain kitchen, it's not going to be very plain."

Nathaniel could only nod his head. Silas and Caleb had spent the better part of the past two days installing a bank of cabinets that stretched a long way along the outside wall, as well as a massive kitchen island. Nathaniel's mother would finally have the kitchen of her dreams, and she was practically quivering with excitement over it. But then again, the surprise guests who had shown up late last night had not done anything to lessen her delight.

Without so much as a word to anyone but Becca, Elam and Miriam had arrived after dark. Nathaniel was glad to see his friends, but a bit confused as to why they were there. Elam had declared Nathaniel looked a whole lot better than he did before, which was true enough. Miriam had simply stood near her brother and shyly smiled. Maybe she hadn't gotten the message several months ago. He'd been clear, almost brutally so, when he'd told her of his new home. Of course, he still had no relationship to show for all the time he'd spent with Amy at the market since then.

Becca and Miriam were in the completed living room, studying a quilt Becca was working on. Nathaniel and Elam were trying to be helpful to Silas and Caleb while simultaneously staying out of their way. Silas, of course, never seemed put out by anyone who was underfoot. Caleb, on the other hand, was constantly telling Nathaniel to quit lazing around and do something useful. It was a joke, but Amy would have smacked Caleb and the thought made Nathaniel smile.

The sound of a knock on the door startled him. He hadn't heard anyone pull up in the yard, but Silas was making plenty of noise with the cordless drill.

He turned around and pulled open the door to see Amy standing on the threshold, two pans in her arms. Had it been just yesterday he had seen her at Ella's? Her light lilac summer dress, one of his favorites, whipped fiercely about her as her bonnet strings flapped across her cheek.

"Hullo, Amy." He smiled warmly, backing up and waving her into the large new mudroom.

She drew in a deep breath and smiled. "Smells like fresh lumber."

"*Jah.*" He grinned.

There was a massive thump followed by laughter, then the whir of the cordless drill sounded behind him.

"And it sounds like *mei bruders.*" She twisted her mouth to the side.

"Finishing up the cabinets today hopefully."

"Well, I brought some coffee treats to tide ya over until yer kitchen is done," she said as she handed him the two pans.

"I'm sure whatever it is will be *wunderbaar,*" Nathaniel replied as he followed her into the kitchen.

She stopped abruptly at the sight of Elam and Becca and Miriam.

"It's about time ya brought us some treats," Caleb exclaimed loudly. He tossed her a playfully exasperated look and took the pans from Nathaniel's hands.

"Those aren't for you," she said sternly.

"Why not?!"

"You get enough at home," she sighed.

Caleb turned to Elam and motioned with a wave of his hand. "This is my *schwesder*, Amy. She's bossy."

Amy's eyes popped open wide as she glared at Caleb.

Nathaniel wanted to laugh, but Amy would never forgive him for it. He coughed into his fist instead and tried to hide his smile.

"Hullo. I'm Elam and this is my *schwesder*, Miriam. We're friends of Nathaniel's from Middlefield." Elam stuck out a hand and Nathaniel watched with a pang of jealousy as her long, thin fingers slid into Elam's hand.

"*Wilkum*," Amy replied warmly. After all these months with Amy at the market, Nathaniel knew there wasn't a person on earth Amy could not talk to. Still, something uneasy flickered in his stomach.

Miriam had never been close to Becca. Everyone knew she had come to see him and him alone. The realization hit him fully when he turned and saw the way she was gazing at him. He had done his best to let Miriam know where he stood. But it hadn't changed whatever hopes and ideas had been in her own mind. Miriam's eyes held such warmth and affection it was impossible to miss.

A glance at Amy's face said she realized the same. The smile that had graced her lovely face when he'd let her in had disappeared.

"Can ya bring the pans to work tomorrow?" she asked, turning to him. Any warmth that had been in her eyes was now gone.

"*Jah*, I'll make sure to do that."

She nodded, then turned away from him. "It was nice to meet ya," she said to Elam and Miriam. Her words were hospitable and kind, but he didn't miss the stiffness in her shoulders as she turned and walked back through the mudroom.

Was she jealous? How could that be? For her to be jealous she would have to feel...something for him.

Nathaniel followed mutely. What could he say when Miriam was just feet away? What could he say that would let Amy know how he felt about their visit? What could he say to this girl he was falling in love with, but who held him at arm's length?

He stepped close behind her and reached the door handle before she did. Her fingers touched his and drew back as if burned. That wasn't a good sign. He needed to slow her down—find time to say something to make her look at him again. For a long moment he stood near her, his chest nearly touching her back. With deliberate slowness, he twisted the knob and pulled the door open.

This wasn't the time or place to have this conversation. Tomorrow at work it would be different. He would be able to explain, to tell her this was not a visit he had planned, requested, or even known about.

Amy slid around the edge of the door and stepped over the threshold.

"I'll see ya tomorrow," he promised.

She walked away without even a nod.

☙ ❧

Daniel sat at the head of the table, lingering over the dessert Mary had set in front of him many minutes earlier.

"I miss Caleb, but it was nice to have just our *maed* home for supper tonight." Mary smiled across the table.

"More food for us," Shelby muttered under her breath.

"I'm sure yer *bruder* will see to it that any leftovers get cleaned up," Mary said cheerfully.

Amy picked at the strawberry pie in front of her. Any shred of appetite had disappeared after her visit to the Shetlers. The sight of Miriam standing in Nathaniel's house, looking so comfortable and at home, didn't sit well. Why, she couldn't say. Amy had felt awkward—like an intruder. She hadn't missed the way Miriam's eyes lingered on Nathaniel, the way she blushed slightly every time he looked her way, or the way she curiously studied Amy as though she couldn't understand why she would be there. Standing in the presence of the beautiful and petite young woman, Amy hadn't been at all sure why she was there either. Then Nathaniel's guilty expression had said it all.

"We are having a family meeting this weekend," Daniel said as Shelby and Anna took the dishes to the kitchen to wash up.

"What for?" Amy asked, trying to reel in her thoughts and focus on anything other than Nathaniel and his visitor.

"Some things yer *maam* and I have been talking about lately." Daniel shrugged. "Future plans for the market."

"Oh," Amy said with growing interest. Yes, focusing on the market would be a welcome change. She had lots of ideas about the future of the store. Maybe tonight she would start jotting some of them down. Better to discuss it together than having surprises because Nathaniel got a wild notion to do things differently.

"You do a *gut* job working there, but sometimes I worry it is too much for ya," Daniel said, his voice sounding strangely uncertain.

Amy studied his face while a frown of confusion covered her own. "Too much for me? I can't imagine how that could be." She shook her head. "I love my work there."

Her father merely nodded. "*Jah*. I know ya do."

— CHAPTER TWENTY-EIGHT —

Nathaniel sucked in a deep breath and pushed open the glass doors. This was not at all how he'd envisioned spending his day. But Miriam, with Elam's agreement, had insisted on seeing the market where Nathaniel spent so much of his time.

He'd had other plans. Plans to find a time to talk to Amy. Plans to explain the surprise of their visit. Plans to somehow let her know he only thought of Miriam as a friend and nothing more. But that was going to be much more difficult to do now.

"Oh, how charming," Miriam said delightedly.

Nathaniel was too busy scanning the storefront for Amy to respond. There she was—helping Bethany Schrock with some fabric selections. Amy's eyes lifted and landed squarely on Nathaniel. He offered a tight-lipped smile and noticed the minute her eyes shifted and saw his guests.

He didn't know how, but the polite smile she had been wearing for Bethany never once faltered.

Practiced. Professional. Polished.

He didn't want to think too much about how she had gotten that way. After being dumped by Lucas, she'd grown tough as nails. She could wear that smile in almost any circumstance.

Miriam was already wandering the aisles, Elam trailing in her wake and Becca close behind. If Becca had wanted to see Elam and Miriam, she could have just said so. Nathaniel would have invited them for a visit.

But of course, Becca didn't know about the conversation Nathaniel and Miriam had had just after the attack. She couldn't have known Nathaniel was looking for a little space from Miriam. He'd never wanted space from Miriam before…before Amy.

Nathaniel took the opportunity to make his way over to where Amy was cleaning up the fabric table. She bent and stretched across, folding the black material neatly back onto the bolt. He tried not to notice her long lean lines, the way not even the modest cut of her dress could hide her figure. But he was stopping himself from noticing her.

"*Gut mariye*," he said to her quietly. Bethany had wandered away and it was just the two of them.

"Giving a personal tour?" she asked. Her words were not spoken harshly, but there was a strange new wariness in her eyes—much like the look she'd had when he'd first started working at the market. One he hadn't seen in a while.

Nathaniel shrugged nonchalantly. "They wanted to see it. Becca thought it would be fun."

"Feel free to join them. Yer shift isn't for another twenty minutes." Her tone was all business. And yet, she knew the exact amount of time before his shift started. Interesting.

"I think they'll do just fine on their own. I'm going to get started in the back room."

She shrugged. "Suit yerself."

It took forever for Becca, Elam, and Miriam to clear out. The guests from Middlefield would be leaving first thing tomorrow morning.

At the end of the day, Sally left just after the front doors were locked.

Nathaniel quickly set aside his broom and went in search of the one person he wanted to spend time with today. She was standing at the counter, counting the cash in the drawer. He made his way over and stood in front of her, the counter between them.

"Can I talk to ya?"

Amy's eyes flicked up and then down to the bundle of money in her hands.

"Hm?"

"About my friends from Middlefield…"

That caught her attention. Amy's gaze flew up to his eyes and back down again.

"They aren't here for me," he explained quietly.

She huffed a laugh. "If they are yer friends, I think they are."

"I didn't invite them," he insisted.

"Then they must care about you a great deal to come all this way without an invitation," she said, still not looking at him.

"Amy," he said firmly.

Her eyes rose then, and what he saw there threw him a bit off balance.

"Elam is a good friend, and for a time Miriam was, too," he explained. He couldn't handle the way the space between them made her feel so far away. Slowly, he began to circle the counter around to where she stood. "But that was over for me when I met you."

She didn't turn to face him, and he closed the few steps between them, bringing his hands up on either side of the counter beside her. "I know ya don't want to date around or risk getting hurt again. I can understand that. But I think ya should know that I want to court ya. You've been my friend for months. We've spent so much time together. We know each other's families. I get you, Amy. And I'm asking for a chance."

His heart thundered in his chest. Amy stood frozen in front of him for a long moment and then she spun around to look up at him.

Her expression was skeptical—as if she worried he was making fun of her somehow. But when she saw his face, his serious expression, her eyes filled with fear.

"*Nee*. I can't do that," she gasped.

"Why not?" he asked calmly. Though he'd hoped she would say something else entirely, he had expected this.

"I—I—can't…"

Her words came out a whisper and his heart ached for her—for the fear etched into her features.

"I'm not asking for anything more than the chance to prove ya can trust me."

"I trust ya," she protested weakly.

"You trust me with the store. What about…other things?"

"What…other…things?"

"With you. Give me a chance, Amy," Nathaniel begged, his voice low.

Her eyes scanned his face almost frantically. As if she wanted to believe him but couldn't quite bring herself to do it.

At that moment, Sally appeared. "I forgot my…oh! I apologize," she said too loudly into the quiet space.

Nathaniel backed away as Amy practically knocked him over in an effort to put some space between them.

Amy hurried back to the storeroom at the speed of light.

"Sorry." Sally winced in embarrassment. "Rest assured, my lips are sealed!"

Nathaniel laughed, doubting that was even possible.

— CHAPTER TWENTY-NINE —

Amy snapped the reins, urging Sal to go faster. Caleb could not be trusted with the baked goods she had left cooling on the table after an entire day of baking.

Thursday wasn't a normal day for her to visit Ella, but Amy had promised to return her beloved cake pan with its precarious lid as soon as possible. At least Nathaniel had returned it to her promptly. His eyes had been wide with praise of the cinnamon rolls. Surely he had shared them with his family and his friends from Middlefield.

She still didn't know what to make of Elam and Miriam's visit. One look at Miriam told Amy everything she thought she needed to know about her relationship with Nathaniel. But Nathaniel had not wasted much time in explaining his side of the story to Amy.

She sat frozen solid in the swaying buggy as she remembered his words.
I want to court ya.

Had she imagined it? She hadn't intentionally done anything to encourage his attention. Perhaps he'd mistaken her friendliness after the attack at the store as more than a coworker's concern. He'd proven to be a *gut* worker, and she would hate to lose such a diligent employee. Perhaps a bit of guilt had caused her to send him the wrong message.

She hadn't come right out and said no though. She'd stuttered and stammered around like an addlepated schoolgirl. With a brisk shake of her head that sent her bonnet strings swinging, she straightened her spine and lifted her chin. There was nothing he could say that would change her mind.

And yet, the memory of him standing so close…

Sal swung into Ella's driveway almost without command. He sauntered to a stop and Amy stepped out, swinging the reins over rail of the high fence. On the far side of the large pasture between Ella's house and the Shetlers' property, she could see a familiar frame leading that angry horse. She pretended not to notice when his brim lifted and his eyes landed on her.

With a busy-looking tug she pulled the basket of Ella's clean and pressed laundry out of the buggy, placing the cake pan on top. It was one of the first days of almost summer-like warmth, and the yard was peaceful and serene and lovely.

Amy could not spare a hand to knock so she simply turned the knob on the door and let herself in. Inside, the house was dark. Not a lamp was burning. Poor Ella's arthritis was probably bothering her, and she hadn't wanted to try to light one.

Amy stepped in and set the basket down in the entryway, closing the door behind her. Drawing in a deep breath, she exhaled a sigh of relief to be out of Nathaniel's line of sight.

But something was off. Ella's home was always peaceful and quiet in its own way. But this was too quiet. There were no shuffling footsteps. No warbled, scratchy greetings drifting from other rooms. Not even a tick from Hank's beloved grandfather clock in the living room. Absolute silence.

"Ella?" Amy called, her voice trembling a bit.

No answer.

"Ella?" she tried again, much louder this time.

Still nothing.

She couldn't make her feet move any farther into the house. It was like a hand was holding her back from stepping into the kitchen or the back hallway that led to Ella's bedroom—she could not take another step.

No.

Amy whirled around and grappled for the doorknob with trembling hands. She yanked it open and let the door fly too far ajar. Without bothering to close it she stumbled down the two cement steps and flew over the yard.

"Nathaniel!" her voice rasped out of her, too quiet. She tripped on her own feet and lifted her frantic eyes to the pasture ahead of her.

He'd stopped, and his attention had snapped instantly to her.

"Nathaniel!" she practically screamed.

He was running toward her. She kept stumbling her way toward the fence and watched as he vaulted over it. Sliding to a stop, his hands gripped her upper arms and steadied her, his eyes intently searching her face.

"Ella...I don't think...she didn't answer me when I called...something's wrong," Amy gasped as though all the oxygen in the world was gone.

Nathaniel stared at her for a moment, then nodded. "I'll *geh* check. Just stay here," he commanded, his voice quiet but firm.

Amy tried to swallow, but the lump in her throat would not let her do more than choke. Nathaniel released her, and her arms felt impossibly cold where his hands had been. How long he was in Ella's house, she didn't know. It felt like hours but was likely only minutes.

When he at last stepped outside and closed the door, she knew. She knew and yet she watched him walk across the yard toward her.

"Ella's gone," his voice was low and calm.

"No," she gasped, though she knew it was true.

༺❀ ❀༻

Nathaniel watched as Amy trembled, knowing there was nothing he could do to ease this pain for her.

"I should have come by this morning." Her voice cracked.

"*Nee*, there's nothing ya could have done," he soothed with as much gentleness as he could muster.

"Is she—was she—"

"She passed peacefully in her bed."

Amy's hand came up and pressed against her trembling lips. Agonized tears ran down her cheeks, and she pinched her eyes tightly shut.

The desire to pull her into his arms and hold her was almost over-powering. Nathaniel ached to provide her any comfort he could, but he also knew she wouldn't welcome an embrace. Not now. Not yet.

He stepped past her as she silently cried and murmured quiet instructions to Gideon, who had been standing at the fence, knowing somehow he would be needed.

Gideon merely nodded and then dipped his head toward Amy. Over his shoulder, Nathaniel saw she had lowered herself to sit in the grass. As Gideon left, Nathaniel turned back and lowered himself down next to her.

It was a long, silent stretch before the police officer pulled into Ella's driveway. When the officer stepped out of the car, Nathaniel rose and told him what he had found. It was a different man than the one who had questioned him after the attack. This one was older and seemed to know just exactly what to do. Nathaniel turned and went back to Amy as the officer made a call and stepped up to the house.

It wasn't until the officer stepped inside that a sob finally tore loose from Amy. When she buried her face in her hands, Nathaniel could no longer sit silent beside her. Stretching one arm across her shoulders, he pulled her close and listened to her grief as it poured out. She didn't fight him, just leaned against him.

"Time to *geh* home," he said, after several long minutes. She didn't need to stay until Ella's body was removed.

"Will someone…"

"They'll stay with her," he promised.

He stood, pulled her up, and helped her into her buggy. Sliding in next to her, Nathaniel picked up the reins and drove off the yard.

— Chapter Thirty —

Morning sunshine poured in through the window as Amy pinned her hair. She pulled the bonnet on her head and reached for her apron. She tied the strings too tightly behind her. It would be a gloriously beautiful early summer day.

And a terrible day.

She carefully descended the wooden staircase and moved almost robotically to the dining table. Mary had the plates sitting all in a stack on the table, waiting for Shelby or Anna Mae to put them in their places. With steady but cold fingers, Amy picked up the plates and set each one gently in front of a chair.

"*Denki*, Amy," Mary said with a gentle smile as she carried a plate of pancakes to the table.

Amy merely nodded once.

Caleb, Shelby Jo, Anna Mae, and Daniel all filed in, their voices quieter and more subdued than usual. Amy purposefully kept her gaze on the glasses of milk she was filling on the table as they took their places.

Amy wasn't related to Ella in any way, shape, or form. The sympathetic offers and condolences would go to Ella's children, grandchildren, and great-grandchildren. As they should. But Amy's family knew and understood how much Ella had meant to her. And the gentleness with which they had treated her these past few days was almost more than she could bear.

The sooner today was over, the better. Funerals were never fun, but this one would be easily the most difficult Amy had ever attended.

"Did ya get the sign put up on the door at the market?" Mary asked Daniel as they all piled in the buggy.

"*Jah.* Closed today for funeral."

Mary's head merely bobbed in acknowledgement.

Ella's son, Ephraim, would host the funeral. With ten *kinner* and over twenty-five grandchildren, his home was the biggest in the family and would be large enough for the gathering.

Amy stayed silent and kept her head down as she waited to go inside. But she didn't cry. She didn't cry when she sat next to Kirsten and felt her sister-in-law's hand squeeze her arm. She didn't cry when her mom sat so close beside her, like she would hold her up if need be. She didn't even cry when she filed past Ella's body, dressed in the black dress Amy had just washed and pressed—the one that had been folded so carefully in the basket of clean laundry she had delivered that day…

She'd known, of course, that it would happen someday. Someday someone would discover Ella had passed. She'd even known the likelihood it would be her. And when the time came, she hadn't been able to face it.

But Nathaniel had.

He now sat on the men's side, watching her with concern as if he was waiting for her to crumble again.

No, she'd cried and mourned already. Too much of it in his presence. He'd driven her home in silence and walked her right up to the door. She'd distantly heard him tell her mom that Ella had passed away. She hadn't seen him since, her mom had insisted she take the day off yesterday. It was a wise move. Amy would not have wanted to break down and cry at the market.

Ella was undoubtedly in a better place. Her time of waiting was over, and she was with Hank again. The thought had comforted Amy greatly in the past several days. Hank, healed and whole, had been there to welcome her with open arms. And Ella would have laughed that same wonderful, wheezy laugh at the sight. Amy had great peace about where Ella had gone.

The song leader lifted his voice in a long note while the other voices drifted in to join him in the closing song:

"What a friend we have in Jesus,
All our sins and griefs to bear!
What a privilege to carry
Everything to God in prayer!
Oh, what peace we often forfeit,
Oh, what needless pain we bear,
All because we do not carry
Everything to God in prayer!"

Amy could practically hear Ella singing the words of this beloved hymn. Ella's scratchy voice struggling to hit all the notes but singing every word nonetheless.

"Have we trials and temptations?
Is there trouble anywhere?
We should never be discouraged—
Take it to the Lord in prayer.
Can we find a friend so faithful,
Who will all our sorrows share?
Jesus knows our every weakness;
Take it to the Lord in prayer."

Ella would have been right beside her, closing her eyes and singing every line from memory. Tears now pricked the back of Amy's eyes.

"Are we weak and heavy-laden,
Cumbered with a load of care?
Precious Savior, still our refuge—
Take it to the Lord in prayer.
Do thy friends despise, forsake thee?
Take it to the Lord in prayer!
In His arms He'll take and shield thee,
Thou wilt find a solace there."

Solace, a shield, arms wrapped about her. That is what Amy had found in Ella. Ella had wrapped their every moment in God's love. She had been a refuge to Amy when others seemed to despise and forsake her. And undoubtedly Ella had taken Amy right to the Lord in prayer. She knew it in her heart, the way she knew Ella had loved her, too.

> *"Blessed Savior, Thou hast promised*
> *Thou wilt all our burdens bear;*
> *May we ever, Lord, be bringing*
> *All to Thee in earnest prayer.*
> *Soon in glory bright, unclouded,*
> *There will be no need for prayer—*
> *Rapture, praise, and endless worship*
> *Will be our sweet portion there."*

The tears welled and spilled over, running down Amy's cheeks and her neck and into the neckline of her dress. Hot, scorching tears. The picture of Ella standing in that glory was a joyful one—so beautiful and full of so much hope and promise. But there was also the reality of the empty home. No Ella standing in the doorway to welcome her, skirts blowing around her legs. No one shuffling through the small kitchen. Nobody pressing their forehead against hers and holding onto her tightly. Ella was healed and whole again, reunited with Hank and her Savior. But Amy was left behind, feeling more broken than she had ever felt before.

⁂

Watching Amy cry had been difficult. No, it had been excruciating to see the tears pour down her cheeks as the People sang. The way her mother and Kirsten had leaned almost imperceptibly closer to her—to offer the comfort of their presence, the acknowledgement of her pain—had caused his own eyes to well. Amy was always so strong and so confident, but it was all a mask. She had a hard shell around her heart, but the love inside it was deep and strong and steadfast. She wasn't the impenetrable rock she imagined herself to be. Strong? Yes. Indestructible? No.

But you would never know it by the way she was acting today. It was a flawless performance. He could see that now. The way she would smile at friends, neighbors, customers when they asked her a question or as she rang up their purchases. The way she moved with perfectly straight shoulders and lifted chin. The way her voice was smooth, commanding, and so composed.

He doubted even she knew when her eyes betrayed her. There wasn't a shadow of the tears she had shed yesterday, but a strange, fierce determination. Like she was resolved she would not break, crumble, or show the slightest hint of vulnerability. So strong yet…fragile.

After the longest six hours of his life, she finally flipped the sign to closed, and he watched as she locked the doors.

She lifted her head and saw him standing there, watching her. There was a long pause.

"Do ya need something?" she asked, her voice all business. As if he hadn't just sat with her while her world had fallen apart. As if he hadn't even been there on one of the worst days of her life.

Nathaniel cleared his throat. "I, uh, wanted you to know I'll be a bit late tomorrow. I already cleared it with yer *daed*, but I wanted you to know, too."

"Oh." The word was flat but there was curiosity in her eyes.

"I have a meeting. A closing actually. I'm…buying Ella's place."

Her eyes widened slightly, and he saw her try to process that new information. After several long, silent minutes she swallowed.

"What time do ya think you'll be in?"

"Should be here by two."

"No problem," she replied coolly.

"I appreciate yer flexibility. I'd be happy to come in earlier the day after to make it up," he offered.

"That's not necessary," she said robotically.

He studied Amy for several more minutes. Anyone else would fall apart after holding themselves together like this. But she was as stoic and composed as a statue.

"I'll finish up in back," he said as he shoved his hands in his pockets, still not taking his eyes off her. *I know you're in there, Amy. I know yer heart is broken and ya feel everything and nothing at the same time.*

"Please do." She nodded professionally.

I'm not falling for this act.

But all he said was, "Let me know if ya need anything."

"Likewise."

I won't let you hide in that shell forever.

◦◦ᎦᎦ◦◦

Such a small key but such a big step. Nathaniel stood at the door he hadn't walked through since that awful day.

He'd been in Ella's house a time or two before, unbeknownst to Amy. Ella was frequently waving him over to the fence to chat or even into the house for an impromptu coffee time. Gideon certainly never complained and even lingered in the field or pasture, just hoping for one of those invitations.

It was on one of the times without Gideon that Ella had first mentioned looking for someone who might be interested in buying her property. None of her children or grandchildren were interested, since it was such a small place. An acreage with enough room for a large garden and a few outbuildings. The house itself was on the small side for an Amish home. Only four bedrooms and two bathrooms.

But it was a solid, sturdy, well-kept home. With a few small improvements, it would be the perfect place for him to make a start.

With a twist of the knob, he pushed open the door and stood inside the small entryway.

Everything had been cleared out by the family in the past day or two. All the furniture and household goods and personal belongings were gone. So much of Ella's home was gone. It was sad for him. He couldn't imagine what Amy would feel if she saw it in this state.

He made mental notes of the changes he would like to make as he moved through the rooms. Ella's family had offered to let him buy any of the furniture he would want for himself, but Nathaniel had decided to wait for the mud sale they would have in just a few days. Starting over fresh sounded more appealing to him. Having Ella's home filled with Ella's belongings would be too strange—like he was a guest in her home. No, he needed to make this *his* home now.

Time for a new beginning. Just as Ella had said to him when he'd told her he would be interested in buying her place. She'd nodded once. "Jah, that's *gut*."

He hoped it would be.

⚬⊙ ⊙⚬

"Not much of a mud sale when there's no mud," Caleb muttered as he walked along the road next to Amy.

She swallowed nervously.

"Mud sales are for spring or winter when there's lots of mud. Not such a hot day in June," he grumbled as little dust clouds puffed up beneath his boots.

Amy merely followed him as they walked past the countless buggies lining the road.

"I'll go check in and get a number," he said as they made their way toward the bustling yard.

There were tables stretching in long rows, all holding most of Ella's worldly possessions.

She wasn't going to come. She had planned to work. But her mom had insisted she go with Caleb. Had insisted there would be small things here or there Amy might like to have to remember Ella.

Seeing the tables, Amy wondered over all the items she had really never seen before. Were these all Ella's things? She had never gone through all the closets. But when her eyes landed on the table with kitchen things, she recognized some of them. Yes, some of those things she might like to have. She might bid on those. And there, all in a row, were Ella's cake pans. Shining like they were brand new. (They were, of course.) Looking like they had never been used. (They hadn't been.) All those cake pans Ella had never once cared for, sitting on display.

Ella would have wheezed a laugh. Amy only winced.

But where was the one she loved? Amy scanned the table up and down. Surely, they hadn't…

Off in the sun she noticed the table that sat by itself. *Free.* These were the items they didn't intend to auction. These were the things they didn't think anyone wanted. With rushed footsteps, Amy made her way to the table and there…there it was. The scratched, worn, overused metal cake pan with the horribly cracked and repaired plastic lid. Ella's favorite. She grabbed it up and clutched it close to her chest.

The one thing Ella had loved most, and there it was in the rejected pile.

No one had realized…

No one knew…

Just her.

Amy hugged it to her chest as if it were her dear old friend. So many lessons, and every one had been taught using that pan.

All the stuff on the tables behind her paled in comparison to this prized possession.

Tears flowed down her face as she pressed the metal against her chest. Without a doubt, Ella would have wanted her to have it. She knew that. Perhaps that is why she had insisted Amy take it with her, cinnamon rolls and all, that last time they were together. She had tried to say goodbye then and Amy hadn't realized.

"*Denki*, Ella," Amy whispered as she clutched this last gift.

Quickly, before anyone could notice she had been there, Amy turned up the driveway and hurried home.

⋆⋅☆⋅⋆

Nathaniel spotted Caleb looking confused and concerned as the crowd gathered for the auction. Ella had held loosely to things of the world. That much was evident by the small collection of goods to be auctioned off.

"Looking for someone?" Nathaniel asked as he came to stand beside Caleb. Caleb was half a head taller than most everyone around him. If he couldn't find someone, then Nathaniel wouldn't be that much help.

"*Mei schwesder.* Amy was here and now I don't see her." Caleb frowned, eyes still searching the crowd.

"I think she left," Nathaniel said in a low voice.

"She did?" Caleb turned his frown on him.

"*Jah.* I think it was too much for her," Nathaniel continued quietly, hoping no one would overhear him.

"Oh," Caleb said in understanding. "She was pretty quiet on the way over."

Nathaniel merely nodded. He'd seen it all. The brief minutes she had spent surveying the tables of kitchen items, the instant she had spotted the free table, the way she had grabbed that one old pan and clutched it to her chest. And then her quick escape. The mask had been gone, and he'd seen the grief.

"She doesn't bake anymore," Caleb whispered after several moments.

"I noticed."

The table of baked goods had been woefully empty all week.

"I'm afraid to tease her about it," Caleb confessed. "Afraid to even ask her about it."

"Give her some time," Nathaniel counselled. "She'll get back to it when she's ready."

"I hope so!" Caleb said, his hand pressed against his stomach.

Nathaniel managed a crooked smile.

The auctioneer took up the microphone, and the chatter died away as the bidding began.

⚬⚭⚬

Amy stared at the empty table. Her parents had gone to work together today—their usual day at the market—and her usual day to stay home and bake. But here it was, nearly noon, and not a single thing to show for it aside from six loaves of cinnamon bread. It wouldn't be long before her dad and Nathaniel were tempted to replace her baked goods table with something that actually brought in money. She wouldn't blame them.

A knock sounded on the door and she started. She hadn't heard anyone pull up in the yard, and she'd been standing here for several minutes.

With wooden steps, Amy moved to the door and pulled it open. Nathaniel, his hair wind-tousled and almost in his eyes, stood on the porch holding a large box.

"*Gut mariye.*" He smiled softly.

Was it a good morning? Amy didn't really feel that way. She ducked her head and frowned. How long she stared down at the ground she didn't know, but he cleared his throat and she snapped her attention back up to him.

"I, uh, brought something for ya," Nathaniel said, dipping his head at the box in his arms.

She quirked an eyebrow and stepped aside, letting him into the house.

"The cinnamon bread smells *gut.*" He smiled as he turned to her after setting the box on the empty table.

"*Denki,*" she said, her voice barely above a whisper.

"I was at Ella's sale, and I got some things I thought ya might like to have."

Amy stared at him in surprise. Gifts. He'd bought them…for her? Who did something like that? She crept toward the box and peered inside. A mixing bowl, the one Ella had used for everything. Her rolling pin. A set of measuring cups she doubted Ella had ever used. A set of embroidered tea towels that always hung, one at a time, on Ella's oven door. A few items Amy had had in her mind to get. Not everything, but she had never hoped to have everything.

"I know it was probably hard for ya to be there—to watch her things being sold." He shrugged. "I didn't know what you would want, exactly, but I figured she would have wanted ya to have some of her things."

Why would he do this for her?

She stared down into the box and fought back yet another wave of tears.

"I've got to get to the market," he said after several long moments.

She heard his firm footsteps moving to the door.

"I lost it," she blurted out, bringing his footsteps to a halt.

She turned, facing him, but looking down at her twisting hands.

"My notebook with all her recipes. It's gone," Amy choked. "I had it the day of our last lesson, that day I brought ya the cinnamon rolls. But I don't know what happened to it. I can't find it anywhere."

When she raised her eyes, he was standing there, hands in his pockets, calmly considering her.

"It's all gone, and I don't remember..." she broke off, trying to make him understand. The only recipe for anything she sold at the market that was her own was the cinnamon bread. Ella's recipes were the key to everything else. Now all of it was just a tangled mess of ingredients and measurements in her mind.

"Maybe they will come back to ya," he gently suggested.

"Maybe. But things usually don't."

Chapter Thirty-One

Doing normal things felt good. It had been three days of good, solid work at the market since the day of Ella's sale. Three days of greeting customers, ringing up their orders, and answering their questions. Three days of feeling a little more normal.

Waves of sadness still swept through Amy now and then, but less often when she was busy working. It was on those drives home where she passed Ella's house or when she would have stopped to check on her that she felt it most—the grief.

But today had been mostly good. That, at least, was a relief.

She slid the dollar bills through her fingers, counting as she went, and logged the number in the book to give to Kirsten later that week.

The sound of Nathaniel clearing his throat lifted her gaze. Thankfully, he was on the other side of the counter this time and not behind her.

"I got ya something," he said, his voice strangely uncertain. His hands were tucked behind his back and his eyes were wary.

Something more?

"Something from the sale?" Amy asked with a frown. He needn't buy her so many gifts. She hadn't properly thanked him, but those items from Ella were a priceless treasure to her.

"*Nee*," he said, shaking his head. "But…maybe something to go with it."

She stood transfixed as he moved his arms. In his hands was a small black notebook. Her heart gave a skip, but then settled into disappointment as she realized it was not *her* black notebook. Not the one with all the recipes. Not the one she had lost.

"You said ya lost yer notebook. I know this isn't the notebook itself with the recipes inside, but I thought maybe ya could use this one—to try again," he suggested as he held it out to her.

Amy stared at the gift for several long moments. Try again? How could she *try again*? Every measurement, every ingredient…it was all gone.

"I don't remember—"

"I know ya think that's true. But I'm wondering if maybe, deep down… ya do," Nathaniel said as he looked at the notebook in his hands. He held it out to her again.

She considered his words for several long moments. *Did* she remember? Some things were obvious, of course. Cinnamon rolls had cinnamon and sugar and flour and butter. She didn't know how much of each but…

Her fingers reached out and touched the black cover.

"*Mei maam* knows a lot of recipes by heart because she's made them so many times. And it made me wonder if maybe ya know some of Ella's by heart." He shrugged.

Amy frowned. "I don't know…"

Nathaniel nodded seriously.

"But it might be worth a try," she hedged.

He set the notebook in her hands and smiled, at first tentatively and then a bit brighter.

"*Denki.* For this and for the things from the sale," Amy murmured.

"*Yer wilkum,*" he replied.

Then she watched him saunter away, hands shoved in his pockets, looking like he didn't have a care in the world.

⁂

Mary had her enormous extension table set with as many plates as it would hold and, there was still another table set up next to it for the older *kinner*.

"Yer *bruders* and their families will be here soon," Mary announced as Amy kicked off her shoes in the mudroom.

"Do ya need any help?" she asked as she stepped into the kitchen.

"*Nee*," her mother answered as she stirred a large pot of gravy. "Everything is done or cooking. Nothing left to do but get it to the table," she said with a cheerful smile. "How was the market?"

"*Gut*. Not as busy as yesterday but still a *gut* day."

"Lots of tourists?" Mary pressed.

Amy nodded and grinned. "*Jah*. 'Tis the season."

"Summer is always busy with English customers," Mary said knowingly.

The sound of horses and buggies rolling onto the yard drifted through the open windows. Amy watched as David helped all his children out and then Sarah. Silas and Kirsten came next, Grace bounding out of the buggy and skipping up the sidewalk to the porch and Benjamin toddling as quickly as his little legs would carry him. Kirsten stepped out carefully into Silas's waiting arms. The smile she beamed up at him was so warm Amy stepped away from the window and moved to the door to greet Grace.

Michael and Deborah were not far behind, and soon Shelby Jo and Anna Mae were busy helping their mother get all the food on the table.

"You didn't start eating without me, did ya?" Caleb called as he banged through the door.

Amy rolled her eyes.

"You live here and you're still late for supper," Amy teased him.

"Hey," he protested, a hand placed firmly against his chest. "I am a hard-working *mann*, I'll have ya know."

"Funny," she replied with a smart tilt of her head. "I've never seen it."

He narrowed his eyes in challenge. "Ask Silas how hard I work then."

Silas considered his brother with a raised eyebrow and nodded slowly. "Caleb works hard enough."

A look of delighted satisfaction flashed across Caleb's features.

"But he also got off work two hours ago," Silas finished in total seriousness.

Caleb froze, his eyes widened in what Amy was sure he thought was an innocent expression.

"I had other…things to do," Caleb said with a shake of his head.

"Like visit Rachel Shetler?" David asked as he took his place at the big table.

Caleb's head whipped to his oldest brother and his eyes grew round.

"Well, that's interesting," Amy muttered wryly.

"I think *Maam's* ready for us to eat," Caleb suggested hopefully.

Mary laughed and agreed. Every seat at the table was filled, and at Daniel's intake of breath they all bowed their heads in silent prayer. With his unspoken amen, the chatter instantly erupted. Platters and bowls were passed, and plates were filled. Michael made sure to monitor the portions on Caleb's plate, much to Caleb's loud protests. Conversation flowed from how the crops were doing to how gardens were growing to weather and reports from the most recent quilting frolic.

Amy drank it all in. After a full day of work, being surrounded by these people was a welcome bit of entertainment and energy. She would always be grateful her older brothers had chosen to live so close by—all of them within miles of the home they'd grown up in. Family dinners were commonplace. There was almost never a week where Amy didn't see every member of the family at least once. Not all plain families were that way, but somehow her parents had raised children into adults who were still a close-knit unit. Deep down, Amy knew she'd always have them. And that when she really needed them, they would be there.

⊰❊⊱

Gallons and gallons of paint, brushes, masking tape, and sandpaper. Nathaniel heaved a sigh as he surveyed the massive pile of supplies sitting in the entryway of his house.

His house. Even though he owned it now, he still thought of it as Ella's house.

"Where shall we start?" Becca asked dubiously as she surveyed the pile with him.

"The kitchen will be the most work," Gideon offered. "I'll start in there."

"I'll help ya," Rachel offered.

The two of them grabbed masking tape, drop cloths, and one of the five-gallon buckets of paint.

"We could get this room finished quickly," Becca said as she surveyed the nine-foot-square room.

Nathaniel nodded and the two of them got to work taping off the windows and doorways.

There was nothing wrong with Ella's house. He could have moved right in and been just fine. But he wanted to give it a freshening up. A little paint would do the trick. Or a lot of paint. Paint in every room. This could take a while. Fortunately, Becca, Rachel, and Gideon seemed eager to help him.

The smell of paint wafted up at Nathaniel as he stirred the full bucket and dumped it in the tray. With a few long, steady strokes, he pushed the roller up and down the wall. Only after several minutes did he step back and take a look.

"Painting is so satisfying," Becca sighed as she stood beside him, surveying their work.

"*Jah*," he agreed. "Do ya think the color is okay?"

She cocked her head and studied it. "Well, what matters is whether or not *you* like it."

Nathaniel glanced at her and then back at the wall. It looked fine to him. But then, most things on those paint cards did. The lady at the store had recommended neutral colors. He wasn't totally sure what that meant, but he'd bought what she had suggested. He and Caleb had loaded it into the truck and then unloaded it into the house.

"I'm not too picky," he admitted.

Becca nodded. "I think it looks very nice."

Nathaniel sighed in relief.

They continued on with their work, Becca easing paint around all the trim boards with a brush while Nathaniel rolled broad strokes onto the walls.

"How long do ya think it will take finish this place up?" Becca asked as she stretched up to swipe the paint across the top of the window trim.

"I don't know exactly," Nathaniel confessed. If he really buckled down and focused on just the house, it might take him just a week or two. But working at the market and helping his dad with the farm meant he wouldn't be able to just focus on the house. "Maybe a month?"

Becca was silent for a long moment. "Did Elam talk to ya about us coming to visit him for their barn raising?"

The question gave him pause. He knew, of course, they were having a barn raising later this summer. But Elam had never said anything to him about another trip to Middlefield.

"*Nee*, he didn't."

Out of the corner of his eye he saw Becca's shoulders sag.

"Were ya hoping to *geh*?" Nathaniel asked after another awkward minute.

Becca shrugged. "Maybe."

"You could take the train like I did," he reminded her.

His sister straightened up and looked at him as she bit on her lower lip.

"It's not difficult," he reassured as he took in her uncertainty. "You just have to get on the train and ride all the way to yer stop. Then Elam will be there to pick ya up."

She seemed to consider that, blushed a bit, and dropped her head. "*Jah*, maybe I could do that."

Interesting she had only mentioned Elam's name—not Miriam or any of her old friends in Middlefield. Just Elam. Maybe *that* was why Elam had shown up. To Nathaniel it had been an unannounced visit. But Becca had known. And how had Becca known? Pieces of the puzzle started to fall into place.

Becca could certainly do a lot worse than a guy like Elam. He didn't feel any need to protect her from anything he knew of his friend and that was a relief.

"Do ya think Elam would ever...move here?" Becca asked, interrupting his thoughts.

Nathaniel's head snapped to her face, but she was resolutely focused on the paintbrush in her hand.

"I don't know," he answered. "He's a hard worker. I doubt finding a job would be too hard for him."

Becca did not respond, but that seemed to answer all the questions she had about his friend. How had he missed all this happening right under his nose? Had he been that distracted? He laughed silently to himself as the answer flitted through his mind.

Jah, maybe he had been.

CHAPTER THIRTY-TWO

The piles of paper surrounding her father at the table were not an unfamiliar sight. Daniel had always done the paperwork and bookkeeping after supper while Mary washed the dishes.

Amy watched as he scrubbed a hand down his face, rubbing his eyes and stroking down his beard. He looked tired. More tired than she and he had only worked at the market until one o'clock today. Daniel never stayed long after Nathaniel arrived.

"Can I help with anything, *Daed*?" she asked as she approached the long extension table.

His somewhat bleary eyes peered up at her through his glasses and held her gaze for a moment.

"*Nee.* I'm almost finished," he sighed.

Amy nodded but sat anyway. "What are ya working on?" she asked as she looked down at the papers, notebooks, ledgers, and file folders in front of him.

Her dad signed and dated a form and slid it into a manila folder.

"This is all the business side of the market," he replied with a wave.

Amy stayed, hoping he would show her in more detail all the things he was working on—all the things he had worked on to keep the market going.

"You mentioned having a family meeting about the market," she reminded him. She'd been collecting ideas of her own to present at that meeting. Strangely, her dad had not said a word about the store when all her brothers and sisters had been together for supper just a few nights ago.

He set down his pen, closed the folder, and placed his elbows on top of the papers. His fingers steepled in front of his bearded chin as he considered her observation.

"That was before Ella passed away," he said quietly.

What did that have to do with the market? The question must have been written across her face.

"I know how hard her passing was for ya," Daniel said, turning gentle eyes on his daughter. "I thought it would be best to wait until ya had had some time to work through some of yer grief."

Amy blinked at the sudden, unexpected sting of tears. He had known. She'd thought she'd hidden it so well—at least from everyone except Nathaniel. He'd seen her well up far more often than she'd intended.

"Yer *maam* and I are getting older," he said with another sigh. "In the past several years, you have done a wonderful job stepping into yer mother's shoes. You run the storefront with great grace, hospitality, and wisdom. You are personable and capable, and the customers appreciate yer calm, gentle ways. We are both very pleased with the *gut* work ya do."

Amy felt her face flush with his praise. She'd known they appreciated her, but to hear it said aloud was a reassurance she could hardly have ever expected to hear.

"It's becoming time for me to step aside and let someone take over my role as well," he continued.

Amy's eyes shot to his face and searched for some clue as to what he might be suggesting.

"I've talked with each of yer *bruders*. None of them, Caleb included, have an interest in taking on my role. And sensibly so. They've all found their own paths—their own work. I asked them more as a courtesy, but I expected their polite refusals. So that leaves me with the question of what to do next."

Amy's mind was blank as she watched her dad rub his temple. *What to do next?* What could that mean?

"I—I could…" she stammered.

Daniel's smile was gentle, but he shook his head. "When yer *maam* and I were courting, it was our dream to open a store together. One where Amish goods by our craftsman could be offered for sale to the community and the outside world. It took us years of working hard to finally open the doors at the market. We worked tirelessly for so long to make it profitable—make it something that could support our family and be a blessing to everyone connected to it. I could never have done it without yer *maam*. She could not have done it without me. We were a team. The business is too much for one person alone."

The room felt suddenly overly warm.

"You are very *gut* at what ya do. You love it, and I would never take it away from ya. But I am considering selling the business."

"Selling the business?" Amy gasped, blinking rapidly in disbelief.

"I would like to train someone to do what I do, both at the store and behind the scenes."

"Who?" Her voice was barely above a whisper.

"I have not figured that out yet," Daniel said with a deeply furrowed brow.

Amy's head swam with questions and arguments. How could they dream of selling the family business? Who would they sell it to? No one else would be able to run the store the way her father did.

"There's no real hurry. We are still thinking about it. And praying. Lots of praying," he gently reassured her.

"But ya won't give it to me?" she finally choked out.

Daniel's eyes filled with such gentleness and love that Amy had to blink back tears.

"I know how ya love it. Yer *maam* and I have enjoyed watching ya grow to love yer work there. And you will always have a place there—I will see to that. But putting that burden on yer shoulders, it is not something I would do to yer *maam*. And not something I would do to ya, *dochder*. I know the burden of owning and running that store, and it would totally overtake yer life, leaving no room for *familye* or any future dreams that might come yer way. I can't take that away from ya." Daniel's large, calloused hand rested lightly on Amy's forearm.

Amy couldn't bring herself to respond. There were too many words, too many emotions. The shock of his revelation overwhelmed her. She needed somewhere quiet to process it all.

"We'd appreciate yer prayers and advice, *dochder*," Daniel said, squeezing her arm as she made to stand. Maybe later she would be able to reach the part of her heart that appreciated the gentleness in his words tonight. But right now…

Right now, she needed to escape.

ഇരുഭ

So many loaves of cinnamon bread covered the baked goods table. Truth be told, Nathaniel was growing a bit tired of it. Memories of lemon bars, whoopie pies, chocolate chip muffins, cream de menthe brownies, and snickerdoodle cookies floated through his mind, making his stomach growl. It was obvious Amy still wanted to bake—still loved to do it. But he'd seen nothing but cinnamon bread for weeks on end now.

He turned to where she was rewinding a bolt of burgundy fabric.

He grinned. "How's the notebook?"

Amy heaved a sigh. "Empty," she confessed.

"You know you could bake something else—something other than one of Ella's recipes. At least until ya remember them," he gently suggested.

"*Jah, Maam* said the same thing." Amy nodded. "I just can't bring myself to do it. Ella's things were all so good. Everything else just pales in comparison."

He seriously doubted he would reach the same conclusion.

"Have ya tried yet? To remember?"

"*Nee*," she whispered.

"Maybe ya should."

"Maybe," she murmured, sliding the bolt of fabric back onto the shelf.

"I think it might come back to ya if ya just give it a try."

Amy lifted her eyes and stared at him. "That never happens with me."

Nathaniel grinned despite her annoyed expression.

The bell above the door jangled, and his eyes widened in surprise as he spied Essie Beiler stroll in with a few of his cousins. As far as he knew, the Beilers never shopped here. A quick glance at Amy confirmed his suspicion.

For several long moments, Amy just stared in silence as Lucas's younger sisters walked along in Essie's wake. They quietly whispered to each other over items on the shelves. Nathaniel had never seen Amy frozen in shock at the sight of a new customer. He quietly cleared his throat and that seemed to startle her awake. Her wide eyes swung to him.

Nathaniel gently tilted his head in the Beilers' direction, and Amy's gaze turned back to the group of young women. With a single determined nod she jerked into motion and set off for the group.

"Can I help ya find anything?" Amy asked, her voice that perfect combination of softness and composure. He just couldn't quite figure out how she always did that.

He purposefully busied himself with straightening the rows and rows of homemade jams and preserves. These were his cousins and he intended to say hello. But Amy needed to be the one to help them find what they were needing. She had nothing to prove, but he wanted them to see her in this place, doing what she was so good at. He wanted them to know she wasn't the person Lucas had known—wasn't the same girl who had been so broken and rejected. Amy had found herself here at the market, and he wanted them to see that.

⋅◈⋅ 𝔊 ⋅◈⋅

The door was locked, the cash drawer had been counted, and the money was safely tucked away in the safe. It was still light outside—would be for several more hours—and it cast the aisles in a warm glow.

Amy grabbed her dust cloth and moved to the side of the store dedicated to Silas's handmade furniture. Few of his pieces spent enough time in the store to gather dust, but she'd always made sure all of it looked impeccable.

Amy stopped in front of the long extension table that stretched ten whole feet. All twelve chairs were all perfectly crafted to match. It was a striking set. No surprise Essie had stood and stared at it for several minutes. But she hadn't come in for furniture. She'd come in for fabric. A very *specific* kind of fabric. The kind of fabric women bought when they were expecting a baby.

As Amy swiped the cloth over the polished surface of the table she sang quietly.

> *"Abide with me: fast falls the eventide;*
> *The darkness deepens; Lord, with me abide.*
> *When other helpers fail and comforts flee,*
> *Help of the helpless, O abide with me."*

When the Beilers came, Nathaniel had not disappeared into the back room, though she was sure he had plenty of work to do there. He could have approached the girls, his cousins, and been the one to greet them. But instead he had silently offered her that chance.

> *"Swift to its close ebbs out life's little day;*
> *Earths' joys grow dim, its glories pass away.*
> *Change and decay in all around I see.*
> *O Lord who changes not, abide with me."*

Amy had been able to see the slight swelling of Essie's stomach beneath her dress. And it only made sense. Babies came soon after marriage for many Amish couples. Lucas and Essie had been married for many months now.

It wasn't jealousy that she felt. No, she truly was glad for Lucas and for Essie—that they had found such happiness with each other. But there was the secret pain that throbbed within her—that this was a path she would never walk.

> *"I need your presence every passing hour.*
> *What but your grace can foil the tempter's power?*

> *Who like yourself my guide and strength can be?*
> *Through cloud and sunshine, O abide with me."*

She heard the gentle thump of the swinging doors as Nathaniel stepped through to the storefront, mop and bucket in tow. The water softly splashed as he lifted the mop and rung it out before he set it on the floor.

Essie had been kind, if not a little shy and quiet. There had been no gloating or pride shining in her eyes. Neither had there been any kind of judgment, condescension, or combativeness in her words. She had been as friendly as any other Amish customer. She had treated Amy as she would have treated any other member of the community. Something had eased in Amy's chest at that.

Despite Nathaniel's presence, she kept singing.

> *"I fear no foe with you at hand to bless,*
> *Though ills have weight and tears their bitterness.*
> *Where is death's sting? Where, grave, your victory?*
> *I triumph still, if you abide with me."*

Nathaniel's mop made a gentle swooshing sound as she ran her dust cloth over the backs of the chairs. Maybe it was time to set down that whole saga with Lucas. She hadn't intentionally carried it, but there were times when she felt weighted down by it. Almost as though people remembered what had happened to her and wouldn't let it go—wouldn't let her forget that embarrassment. But if Essie could get past it, then surely anyone could. And Amy could learn to simply move on—to accept it had happened and *move on*.

> *"Hold now your Word before my closing eyes.*
> *Shine through the gloom and point me to the skies.*
> *Heaven's morning breaks and earth's vain shadows flee;*
> *In life, in death, O Lord, abide with me."*

She didn't miss the way Nathaniel sang quietly along with her.

— Chapter Thirty-Three —

Long, lean legs spilling out of the buggy door onto the dirt floor of the barn—that's how she found him.

Amy cleared her throat loudly—authoritatively.

Caleb lifted his blond head and looked out at her.

"This better be good," he mumbled.

She waited a minute while he finished ratcheting away at something inside his buggy.

"Okay," he groaned as he sat up. "What is it?"

"I need yer help with something."

He looked at her warily.

"I'm going to try to recreate Ella's recipes, and no one has eaten quite as many of them as you." She smirked. "So I was wondering if you would eat them and tell me how close I am to getting them right."

Caleb studied her seriously. "Is this a joke? I feel like ya might be teasing me."

Amy shook her head. "*Nee*. No joke. I want to try while I still have hope of remembering them. Before I get them mixed up with other recipes that aren't Ella's."

Caleb sighed deeply. "I'd ask what's in it for me, but I think that's pretty obvious."

"I might fail a few times—get some stuff wrong. So you'll have to be…nice," she warned.

"I hate to tell ya this, but *fail* is a highly subjective term, and I doubt it will apply to anything ya bake. But I can tell ya when it tastes good," Caleb offered.

"*Gut*. Let's get to work then," Amy said with a sharp nod.

°⋅⊙⋅⊙⋅°

Ella would have wanted her to try.

All those years of baking lessons and time spent together—Ella wouldn't want all of that to be set aside now she was gone. She would want Amy to honor the memories of all the things she had taught her. That thought had kept her in the kitchen until late last night. Caleb, true to his word, had sat at the table reading and sampling every single item she placed in front of him. Finally, he'd begged her to stop. Surprisingly, even Caleb had a limit. The progress had been good. Not perfect, but good.

Baking was not the only thing Ella would have wanted Amy to keep at. No—Ella had encouraged her time and again to at least try going back to Singings, though everything in Amy rebelled at the idea.

"I'd like a ride to Singing tonight," she said to Caleb. Even just the words tasted like ash in her mouth.

Caleb was clearly stunned but had not teased her. She was wishing he'd talked her out of it as the buggy rattled onto the Eshes' yard. Buggies already lined the driveway. Horses wandered the pasture. The sun had not yet sank too low, and the heat of the summer day lingered.

Amy peered through the buggy window at all the young people who had gathered. She'd likely know most of them. Unless someone had family visiting, there wouldn't be any surprises.

She followed in Caleb's wake, his long legs carrying him far faster than she cared to walk. They both moved toward the volleyball nets that had been set up in the yard. Amy scanned the space for friends. There were only a few women her age left, of course. Most of them had married in the last several years.

"Amy!" came Becca Shetler's cry of greeting.

Amy's head snapped over to the farthest volleyball game and to Becca's wildly waving arm. Caleb had already joined in, no doubt hoping to catch Rachel's eye. Amy began walking toward them, but Becca met her halfway and towed her right onto the court.

"I'm too short to play this game," Becca laughed. "We need some height on our side."

Amy was not tall compared to any of her older brothers. Curiously, she glanced to the other side of the net, where Caleb and Nathaniel stood. Another look at those on Becca's side proved her friend's words to be true. No one, not even Isaiah Troyer, stood taller than five-foot-six. Amy's five-foot-nine height seemed like a definite advantage. She swallowed nervously. Volleyball was not a sport she had ever really learned to play. It had always been Lucas's game, and she'd always been content to watch and cheer him on. It had looked simple all those years ago. Maybe it wouldn't be so bad.

She turned back to the net and gulped down her fear. Her eyes rose to Nathaniel, who held the ball near the back line. With an easy toss, he lobbed it into the air, gave it a solid slap, and sent the ball flying.

Amy stared up at the ball as it came careening down, directly at her. Frozen stiff, she waited, laced her fingers together, and held her arms in front of her. With a dull thud it struck her arms and stuck.

Why hadn't it bounced up the way it did for the others? She stared down at the ball as it rolled harmlessly out of her arms and onto the grass.

The sound of muffled laughter hit her first. Her face was burning before she even lifted her eyes to see the lopsided grins on the faces of the *buwes*.

"Good try!" Becca cheered as she scooped up the ball and sent it back over to Nathaniel.

Amy did not dare look at him. Whether his eyes showed his amusement or an apology or pity, she did not want to know. She straightened her arms, laced her fingers together even tighter, and readied herself for the next serve. He'd served it directly at her last time, so he was clearly skilled enough to place the ball anywhere he wanted. Why wouldn't he do the same again? She was obviously the weak spot on the court.

Nathaniel lifted the ball, tossed it perfectly, and sent it flying over the net once more. But this time it went far to her left—nowhere near her. Her teammates, short as they may be, fielded the ball well and sent it back over. She watched it bounce back and forth between sides before Caleb finally blocked a shot without even jumping off the ground.

The game went on for what felt like a miserable eternity. Amy missed at least half a dozen balls that were supposed to be hers. She outright caught two of them in her arms, and the three she managed to hit barely rose above her shoulders. A complete disaster. Her arms stung where the ball had slapped her. Her fingers ached from the way she had clutched them together so tightly.

When it was over, she turned to follow Becca and Rachel into the barn.

"Looks like I've finally found something ya aren't good at," Nathaniel's voice said quietly behind her.

Amy whirled, her back ramrod straight, to where Nathaniel stood, grinning at her.

The shame burned on her face.

"There are lots of things I am not very good at," she retorted a bit too sharply.

He tilted his head. "I haven't found that to be true."

"Apparently ya know how to do everything," she sighed in frustration.

Nathaniel smiled then—almost a secret smile. "No, not everything. But I *do* know volleyball," he said as he tossed the ball and caught it with one hand. "Here, hold yer hands like this."

He tucked the ball under his arm and reached out for her. Long fingers curled around hers, and instead of lacing her fingers together he simple folded one of her hands into a fist and curled her other hand around it. His hands were so warm her skin tingled.

"Now, when the ball comes toward ya, just wait a little bit longer. If ya go too soon, you'll connect at the top of yer swing and miss the chance to use yer momentum," he said as he gently guided her arms down and then up.

Amy would not lift her eyes from his hands.

"With a little bit of practice, you'll have it all figured out."

"What makes ya think I want to practice?" she bit back, lifting her chin defiantly.

Nathaniel's eyes were gentle and calm, despite the fire she was wrapping around every word. He merely shrugged.

"It's a good chance to socialize," he said easily.

"It's a good chance to embarrass myself is more like it," she mumbled. It wasn't easy to keep snapping at him if he never snapped back.

Nathaniel only gave her a lopsided grin and shook his head.

"Don't tell me ya didn't hear people laughing at me."

His grin faded as he settled his gaze on her face. He looked at her so long she dropped her eyes and swallowed uncomfortably.

"Does that matter?" he asked finally. "For what it's worth, they weren't trying to be mean. When the ball hits someone in the head, it might make a few people laugh. But no one was making fun of ya."

He could defend them all he wanted. It hadn't felt quite so innocent to her.

"Looks like it's time to *geh* in for singing," he said with a glance over her shoulder.

Amy turned and noticed most of the young people had drifted toward the barn or were already inside. All those people had seen her finally work up the courage to go to a Singing, only to watch her put on a shameful display in volleyball. A wave of uncertainty crashed into her.

Nathaniel walked past her and headed toward the barn, the volleyball still tucked underneath his arm.

There was just no way she could stay and risk any more embarrassment. No way she could walk in there and not attract attention. No way she could wait around afterward only to ride home with her brother. Ella had been wrong. This was not the way forward.

Amy turned and took a few steps down the driveway.

"I wouldn't do that if I were you."

She stopped cold at the sound of Nathaniel's low, gentle voice. He was only a short way behind her—he must have been watching and followed when she turned to sneak away. She stood her ground, facing resolutely away from him, her back so straight and stiff it ached a bit.

Why not? she thought. *What does he know?*

"If ya leave now, it will only be harder to come back later," he murmured.

"Who says I'd want to come back?" Amy whispered, sure he could not hear her.

"The Amy I know is too brave and too confident to let a little thing like a volleyball game make a decision for her. She manages an entire store each and every day, helps customers, talks to Englishers, keeps the inventory organized, stocks shelves, and knows a whole business inside and out. Nothing scares her. She would *not* run away," he challenged.

Run away? That wasn't what this was. She would never run away from anything. She'd stayed away simply because she was tired of going to Singings. She was tired of the positioning and the hoping and the longing and the flirting that happened on these Sunday nights. No, she just wasn't one of *those* girls anymore. After all those years at the market, there was literally no one she couldn't talk to. She wasn't afraid of anything.

She spun back around to tell Nathaniel just that, but when she turned the driveway was empty. She hadn't even heard his footsteps crunch away on the gravel. The barn was glowing with warm light. The buzz of voices as the young people all found a place to sit drifted to her over the quiet, dusky farmyard. No one would know she had been tempted to leave. No one except Nathaniel. He knew she had wanted to run. That just wouldn't do either. She couldn't let him go on believing she had run away because she was afraid. *Nee.*

With a determined march, Amy walked quickly across the yard and stepped into the glow of the barn. Some had taken their seats, but many were just now moving to the rows of benches. A quick glance to the *buwes'* side and she saw Nathaniel conversing easily with Samuel Esh. She waited for a moment for his eyes to land on her, to see she was not afraid, but they didn't.

Becca was suddenly at her side, tugging on her arm.

"Come sit with me," Becca ordered. Amy blinked and once again allowed herself to be tugged along in Becca's wake.

With a rather ungraceful plop, Amy landed abruptly on the bench next to Nathaniel's sister. She sat in a state of surprise as girls, mostly younger but a few older than she, sat down all around them, their chatter dulling to loud whispers.

The *buwes* sat on the other side, facing the girls. Amy tried, really tried, not to notice when Nathaniel made his way easily to a seat, lowered himself, and lifted his head. His eyes immediately landed on her, and she watched in stunned silence as he grinned at her and winked.

৯৫ ৯৯

Maybe…just maybe…she had missed this. As the songs rang out, clear and full of harmony, and Amy lost her voice in the blend of the voices around hers, she felt a pang. Singing in church was one thing—but singing here, singing a little bit faster and a little bit newer material, singing right along with all those young voices, this was something special. This was what she had given up.

The last notes died away, and for many long moments she just sat and soaked it in. She might have to admit to herself it had been a mistake to stop coming to Singings. The actual singing itself was easily worth any of the other social games at play. Though she was not going to be playing volleyball again anytime soon.

People began to stand up and mill around—none of them in a real hurry to see the night end. These gatherings only happened every other weekend. It was one of the only times the young people got together without most of the adults present. Still, she should find Caleb and make sure he didn't forget and leave her here without a ride home. With his endless flirting, she had no doubt he wouldn't remember her until tomorrow morning when she wasn't there to help put breakfast on the table. She should have given him some kind of stern warning—perhaps threatened to never bake anything for him again. And yet, if he was going to ask to drive someone home, it might be good if he did forget her. That would be an awkward buggy ride, that's for sure.

She stood and scanned the crowd for her unnaturally tall younger brother, but he was nowhere to be found.

Amy tried, really tried, not to notice Nathaniel. She tried not to make note of the way he stayed seated, laughing with Ezra and Adam Troyer. Tried not to care about the way his eyes danced with delight at whatever story they were telling him. She forced her eyes to look anywhere but right at him, but frequently her gaze darted back over to where he sat. And never once did she see him looking at her.

Becca hauled Amy to her feet and dragged her over to talk with Irma, Sarah, and Susanna. She couldn't make herself focus on anything they were talking about, but she smiled and nodded and laughed in what she hoped were all the right places.

Movement at of the corner of her eye caught her attention. Her gaze shot to the *buwe* approaching. Jacob Stoltzfus was sauntering bravely over to their group. Her breath stuck in her throat. Surely he wasn't coming over here for her. But she'd didn't think he was involved with Becca, Irma, Sarah, or Susanna.

Amy's panic ebbed into embarrassment as he shyly asked Irma if she would like to get some lemonade. Irma ducked her head bashfully and agreed. Had everyone seen how nervous Jacob's approach had made her? If he had walked up to her in the market, she wouldn't have batted an eye. But here...here it was all so different.

"Come with us," Becca urged as Moses Yoder invited her to get some lemonade. Susanna and Sarah had already been invited by other *buwes*. No one had asked Amy. She could feel her cheeks burning as she shook her head. She would just *geh* find Caleb and go home. She lifted her eyes to look for him. How could such a tall, blond *buwe* disappear so easily?

People in the crowd moved a bit and she stood locked, absolutely frozen in place, as Nathaniel strode to her from the other side of the barn. His walk wasn't slow or fast—just measured and purposeful. His eyes were laser-focused on her. He was so intent she was almost taken aback. But then she saw the spark in his gaze. She'd seen that look before. How many times? So often at the store, she would meet his eyes and that look would be in them. How had she missed it? Had he been watching and waiting while all the other girls were chosen?

"Hullo," he greeted, as if he hadn't talked with her earlier that evening.

Amy merely swallowed, the desire to run out of the barn mysteriously disappearing.

"Did ya have a nice time singing?" Had he winked or was it just her imagination? But there was no mistaking the slight grin he wore.

"*Jah*," she croaked.

Now he smiled widely. "I thought it sounded better than usual tonight."

"I'm sure that had nothing to do with me," she protested quietly.

"I'm not." He tilted his head. "May I offer you a ride home?"

How long had it been since she'd heard those words from a *buwe* at a Singing? Lucas had been just a young boy. Nathaniel was certainly no young boy.

"Since Caleb left without me, I guess I need one," she grumbled, her mouth twisting off to the side.

"*Nee.* He's here," Nathaniel replied with a nod toward an open door just yards away, where Caleb was most certainly standing.

"Oh," she choked.

"May I still take ya home?" he asked, quietly enough that those around them could not hear. His voice was like rich, warm honey.

Her traitorous body allowed her head to nod—to agree. This had to be a mistake. She wasn't ready to play this game. She wasn't ready to risk her heart this way again. Just those few seconds of waiting for him to walk across the barn had wreaked havoc on her heart.

"Would ya like to get some lemonade first?" he asked, gesturing to the back of the barn. Amy glanced toward the crowded table and looked back at Nathaniel. His smile widened at her wide-eyed expression.

"*Nee.* Me neither," he agreed.

Somehow, Amy made her legs fall into step beside him. Nathaniel's hands were shoved into his pockets and his gait was slow and easy. He was in no hurry, apparently. She tried to shake the feeling that everyone was watching their every movement. Surely not. Surely they had better things to do than watch her get a ride home from a *buwe* for the first time in so many years. Surely they just wouldn't care.

Surely none of them would care to notice the way she was flushed and slightly shaky. None but Nathaniel.

⋆৩৩৩⋆

They'd ridden together before, of course. But not like this.

Nathaniel remembered the night of the attack. Pain had shot through his body with every sway and jostle and made it one of the longest buggy rides of his life. Still, there was the way she had leaned into him—so desperate for warmth and so filled with rage. He would never forget it. As painful as it had been, her presence had been comforting. Now she was safe and whole beside him.

Glancing over to where she sat, pressed far against the opposite side of the buggy, he had to grin a bit at the difference.

She'd not said a word over the last three miles. Merely sat rigidly straight and gripped the seat with what looked to be all her strength.

"Did ya miss it?" he asked into the quiet dark.

Amy's head turned toward him and then back to the front. "Miss what?"

"Going to Singings?"

"Oh," she paused. "Parts of it, yes."

Nathaniel nodded. "But not the volleyball, I'm guessing."

"No," she agreed emphatically. "Not the volleyball." She paused for several long moments. "I'm not very athletic," she confessed.

"You don't have to be." He shrugged. She was so slim and made so many amazing treats he wondered how she managed to keep her figure.

"Caleb will likely lecture me on all the things I did wrong," she grumbled.

"Caleb talks too much," Nathaniel sighed.

Amy's bubble of laughter surprised him. And delighted him. He looked over to see her smiling, her teeth white in the dark interior of the buggy.

"*Jah*, that's very true." She shook her head.

They fell silent as Susie trotted ahead of them.

"Do ya think you'll go back? To Singing, I mean?" Part of him was kicking himself for even asking. Had she heard the deep hope in his voice? He would find a way to see her, one way or another. But these Singing nights would be a powerfully good reason to spend extra time with her—time away from the market and the pressures and distractions of their work.

"Maybe," she answered quietly, after a long pause.

That was more than he had dared to hope for, especially after the disaster of her first volleyball game. He'd been shocked she hadn't run off the court and left after the ball hit her in the face that one time. He would have chased her down then, of course. But she would have left in a far more fragile state. Only Amy would pluck up enough courage to overcome all the fear and uncertainty of the past many years.

Why she had even decided to go to Singing tonight he couldn't imagine. His shock when Becca called out her name had to have been obvious. He wanted to ask her why, but to speak it aloud might call for answers she wasn't yet ready to give. Maybe answers she hadn't even admitted to herself.

Whatever her reason, he was grateful.

He'd taken the long way home. She'd know that. Even so, the Miller farmyard came into view sooner than he would have liked. In the last few miles, she had at least released her grip from the bench seat—though her posture was still rigid.

"Looks like we beat Caleb," he commented with a sly grin. He hadn't forgotten what it was like to be a seventeen-year-old Amish *buwe*.

"That's just fine with me," she said, her voice matter of fact.

Nathaniel reined Susie to a stop and turned to look at Amy. She was staring straight out the window.

"I know this wasn't an easy night for ya."

He could make out the way her throat bobbed when she swallowed.

"But I hope you'll try again," he continued lowly. He wanted to touch her hand, to uncurl the fist in her lap, to set her at ease somehow. But this was not the time to touch her—he could sense that.

"*Denki* for the ride home," she stumbled over her words which was so unlike her.

"I'm always happy to offer you a ride home," he confessed quietly.

She merely nodded and slipped out the door. He watched her until she had climbed the steps and crossed the porch to the door. Without a glance behind her, she turned the knob and entered the dark and silent house.

He knew he had pushed her. He only prayed it wasn't too far.

— Chapter Thirty-Four —

Amy stared down at the list again. That black notebook no longer looked quite as pristine and new. Flour was smudged on the outside cover from when it had sat on the messy kitchen counter. The page she was working on was dotted with drips of something—probably melted butter. But she could still read the list of ingredients.

Flour, sugar, baking powder, salt, cocoa powder, eggs, chocolate chips. Those were the ones she was sure of. And this one had some odd measurements in it—that much she remembered, too. Not just a cup of flour, but a three-quarters cup of flour. She noted the measurement. Oh, and that reminded her—three-quarters cup of chocolate chips. She used to simply set the measuring cup on the counter after the flour and pour in the chocolate chips. Yes, that was right. She circled it only when she was one hundred percent certain she had it right.

She turned back to Ella's mixing bowl and with a firm hand stirred the batter for the double chocolate chip muffins. She hummed under her breath while she worked the spoon. Tuesdays were always peaceful. With her parents at the market together, she was free to spend her day however she pleased.

Footsteps sounded on the porch just moments before the knock came on the screen door. Amy quickly wiped her hands on the towel and made her way through the mudroom, where Caleb and Daniel's many straw and black felt hats were lined up on pegs on the wall.

She swallowed back a strange thrill as she spotted Nathaniel standing on the other side of the screen.

Slowly, she pushed the door open and stepped out into the already warm air. Nathaniel's bicycle sat propped against the picnic table next to the house.

"*Guder mariye*," she greeted.

He nodded and ducked his hat-covered head, but she could still see his slight grin. "I assume yer *daed* is already at the market."

"*Jah*, he is."

"Can ya leave a message for him from me?" he asked, lifting his head so she could see his eyes, shaded beneath his hat.

For a moment, she forgot herself and simply looked up into his face.

"*Jah*," she exhaled abruptly, remembering his question.

"Let him know I can work those extra mornings he asked me about yesterday," Nathaniel explained.

"Okay," she answered a bit weakly. More time with Nathaniel. For some odd reason, it made her stomach flop.

Then Amy furrowed her brow and blinked in confusion, but Nathaniel had already started down the stairs.

"Ya know, we New Order Amish have cell phones. You could have called," she called after him.

"*Jah*," he answered. "I know."

Amy's face burned at the implication.

"Do ya have a minute?" she asked.

Nathaniel stopped halfway down the sidewalk and glanced over his shoulder.

"Sure."

Amy led him into the house, through the mudroom, and into the kitchen. She saw his eyes scan over the groupings of cookies scattered across the surface of the table.

"Did ya ever try the sugar cookies I used to bring to the market?" she asked.

"I may have tried them a time or two."

"*Gut*," Amy declared. "Close yer eyes and try to remember what they tasted like."

She watched the slow grin spread across Nathaniel's face.

"This is serious," she reminded. "You have to concentrate."

Nathaniel bit his lip, inhaled a deep breath, and sobered up.

"Open yer mouth," she instructed.

Nathaniel obeyed and before she could think too deeply about what she was doing she slid a third of a cookie into his mouth, her fingers barely brushing his lips. She pulled away as if he would bite her, but Nathaniel closed his mouth and chewed slowly, as though he were savoring every bite.

"Mm," he muttered, his eyes finally flickering open.

Amy forced herself to look away from his lips, away from his intense gaze.

"Was it the same?" she pressed hopefully.

"It was very, very good."

Amy shook her head. That wasn't what she was looking for.

"But was it the same?" she pushed.

He paused as he considered her.

"Does it matter? If it is delicious, it doesn't matter if it is exactly the same as Ella's. No one would notice or complain about a cookie that tastes that good," he insisted.

Amy considered that. Maybe he was right. Maybe it was time to blaze her own path.

"Can I have the rest?" he asked with a crooked grin.

Amy offered the rest of the cookie and watched him eat the whole portion in one bite.

"For what it's worth," Nathaniel said after he swallowed, "I'm glad you're trying."

Was there a double meaning to that? It sounded like it. She'd been doing plenty of *trying* lately.

Quick as a wink, before she could even register what was happening, Nathaniel reached out and brushed what was likely flour off her face—his thumb skimming across her cheek and down her jaw.

Amy froze in shock and watched as he slowly lowered his hand. His gaze was too intense, even though he was smiling a bit.

"See ya tomorrow," he crooned. If the room had been full of people, no one would have heard him. But the room was empty, and his words wrapped around her, even as he walked out the door, threw a leg over his bicycle, and pushed off down the driveway.

⋅౭ℜ ℜ౨⋅

His mother had certainly been busy. Nathaniel stepped into the kitchen just after work and noted the new space had been put to good use. The smell was incredible, and he was instantly ravenous.

"We're having the Millers over for supper tonight." Becca beamed as she moved a bowl out of the fridge and onto the counter.

That explained the picnic tables sitting in the shaded backyard.

Without another word, Nathaniel spun on his heel and hurried up the stairs. He doubted he had time for a shower, but at least a fresh shirt would be good. He slipped his suspenders off his shoulders and worked loose the buttons.

Amy hadn't said anything about a picnic tonight. He guessed it would be a surprise to her as well. He sent up a silent prayer that she would come, even after their full Friday at the market.

He combed through his hair, still trying to get used to the shorter, more modern style that was common here. Picnics with neighbors were certainly normal—especially on weekends and in nice weather. Though the days were awfully hot, the evenings were perfect. He'd planned to go over to his new house and do some more work. There was a long list of projects he wanted to tackle. But the picnic definitely sounded like more fun.

A sudden burst of footsteps and chatter from his youngest siblings signaled the arrival of their guests. He couldn't ignore the strange flutter of excitement low in his stomach. It hadn't even been a whole hour since he had seen her.

Nathaniel stepped out the door to a yard bustling with activity. When Becca had said "the Millers," he hadn't realized she'd meant *all* of the Millers. Silas and Kirsten, Michael and Deborah, and even David and Sarah were there, their many children already running around the yard. Daniel, Mary, Shelby Jo, and Anna Mae climbed out of their buggy. And faster than was necessary Caleb's buggy pulled onto the yard. Nathaniel smirked as he caught a glimpse of Amy's irritated look at her younger brother.

She hopped out of the buggy with another annoyed glance at Caleb and set off across the yard to the picnic tables. Nathaniel watched her from several yards away as she warmly greeted Becca and Rachel. She had changed her dress as well. Gone was the brilliant maroon she had been wearing all day. In its place was a pale pink dress he'd never seen at the market. She looked like a fresh summer breeze. He was not going to sit at any table other than hers.

One long table was filled to overflowing with food. Fried chicken, baked beans, potato salad, macaroni salad, broccoli salad, homemade rolls, meatloaf, casseroles, and more pies than he could catalog. There were few things he loved more than potluck picnic meals.

Just minutes later, at his father's call, everyone took a seat. Nathaniel watched as Amy perched between Kirsten and Becca. He quickly claimed a seat across the table, sitting between Gideon and Silas. Caleb managed to sit at the end of their table right next to Rachel.

After prayer and everyone's plate was full, the conversation flowed easily.

"Where did ya get all these picnic tables?" Amy asked Becca as her eyes scanned the long line of tables extending along the backyard.

"Gideon made them!" Becca announced with a tip of her head.

Gideon ducked his head shyly. Where Caleb liked being the center of attention, Gideon was just fine behind the scenes.

"Nicely done, Gideon," Silas commended him.

Gideon's head rose a bit, but he merely nodded.

"Gid, I gotta tell ya this," Caleb sighed dramatically. "You've got to stop all this working all the time. You make the rest of us look bad," he chastised playfully.

"The rest of us?" Nathaniel questioned with a raised eyebrow.

Caleb nodded even as Nathaniel caught Amy's amused glance. "That's right. Us *young* people. You *old* people are supposed to work hard."

Silas heaved a long-suffering sigh beside Nathaniel.

"What shall we do after supper?" Becca asked, a little too perkily.

"Definitely volleyball," Nathaniel answered as he shoveled a forkful of macaroni salad into his mouth. He didn't miss the way Amy's eyes shot to his face. She considered him seriously, but he only grinned back at her.

"Okay," Becca agreed, her eyes darting back and forth between Nathaniel and Amy. "Volleyball it is then."

"I like softball," Amy objected.

"Girls don't play softball," Gideon said in quiet surprise.

Amy leveled a warm but intense gaze on his little brother. "They do here," she insisted.

Gideon shook his head. "This I've got to see."

⊶⊰ ❦ ⊱⊷

The teams were divided as evenly as possible. They spanned all ages, even Daniel taking a spot on a side. The Millers made a big deal about keeping Caleb and Silas on separate teams. It didn't take long for Nathaniel to see why. Caleb stepped up as the opening batter. Just one pitch, and with a mighty swing Nathaniel watched the ball soar through the air and land somewhere in the pasture of his property. Zach went chasing off to retrieve the ball while Caleb trotted around the bases.

"That's the lazy man's way of playing," Amy called out from first base.

Caleb threw his hands in the air as if he couldn't help it.

Nathaniel watched as Anna Mae stepped up and took a turn batting next. With a perfectly lobbed pitch from Daniel she managed to hit the ball through the infield and past the third baseman. Nathaniel was up next.

Softball had never really been his thing. He preferred volleyball. But never had getting to first base mattered quite as much as it did now. Not when Amy stood there, waiting and watching. A bead of sweat rolled down his back as he pulled the bat back over his shoulder. Daniel was a good pitcher, and he had no trouble managing to get to first safely.

"Softball, huh?" he asked as he planted a foot on the metal plate that served as a base.

She merely shrugged. He let his eyes linger on her face for a few moments before turning his attention back to home plate.

"I like yer dress," he said quietly over his shoulder. With a glance behind him, he saw her duck her head shyly. A blush colored her fair skin and it made him smile.

The rest of the inning did not go as well. The teams switched places. Nathaniel took a spot at third base with Caleb offering to pitch.

Amy led off the batting order. Nathaniel found his heart pounding just a bit as she stepped up and took a practice swing. This was not the "unathletic" girl from the volleyball game. He could see that already.

"Be nice," she commanded as she pointed the tip of the bat at Caleb.

"Ha!" he laughed loudly in defiance.

But his pitch was fair, and she hit it solidly, sending the ball whipping past Nathaniel, faster than he could field.

Gideon stepped up to bat and managed a base hit. Zach was next, and everyone called out encouragement. Caleb shuffled inconspicuously closer while Zach took a few practice swings. The ball came soaring through the air, and Nathaniel watched as Zach widened his eyes and swung with all his might. The ball thudded off his bat and rolled harmlessly toward Caleb. But Caleb was busy pretending to swat away a bee. The ball rolled between his legs and the other children roared. Caleb immediately looked around his feet and bent over in half, comically peering through his own legs. Bending too far he summersaulted head over heels in the grass and came up looking just as confused. By now, Zach was safely on first base and everyone else was in stitches.

Silas stepped up to bat next with the bases loaded.

"Don't lose the ball, Silas," Amy warned.

Nathaniel didn't have time to wonder what she meant. With a lobbed pitch and a massive swing, the ball arched high into the sky. He watched in disbelief as the ball landed in Ella's...his own...front yard.

Cheers erupted from Silas's team and Nathaniel stared off behind him to where the ball had flown so impossibly far. It would be several minutes before Jacob would even be back with the ball.

"Thanks for not breaking a window, I guess." Nathaniel smirked as Silas jogged toward him.

"I held back a little bit," Silas admitted.

Nathaniel blinked as Silas patted him firmly on the shoulder, then stepped on the base and headed for home.

。◦◦。

Amy drew a deep breath of the cool evening air. The sun had sunk below the horizon a little while ago. The pitcher of lemonade had been passed, refilling all their glasses more than once. Her parents and married brothers and their families had all gone home an hour ago. But Caleb and Amy remained outside with Nathaniel, Becca, Rachel, and Gideon, listening to the droning of the cicadas and the chirping of the crickets.

"Well," Caleb sighed. "I was supposed to meet a few friends soon."

"Who?" Amy questioned.

"Some of the guys." He shrugged nonchalantly.

"I'll see her home," Nathaniel calmly interjected.

Amy's gaze swung back over to Nathaniel. All she could do was blink as Nathaniel and Caleb made arrangements for *her* transportation.

Caleb was off before she really knew what was happening. Where on earth he could be going at this hour of the night, she didn't know. The remaining five of them talked for a while longer, and the night sky grew darker, putting on an incredible star show.

"I can't believe I'm saying this, but I'm a little chilled," Rachel said with a shiver.

"It's getting late anyway," Becca agreed with a yawn.

Rachel smiled. "*Gut nacht*, Amy."

"We should do this more often," Becca added with a warm smile of her own.

"I'd like that," Amy admitted quietly.

Gideon followed his older sisters inside and left Amy sitting at the picnic table across from Nathaniel.

"Would ya rather ride home, or shall we walk?" Nathaniel asked.

"Oh, um, whatever you want," Amy answered. She truly didn't care. Strange. She always had an opinion about everything.

Nathaniel nodded slowly. "I wouldn't mind a walk. It would take me longer to hook up the buggy than it would to actually drive ya home."

"You won't mind walking home in the dark?" Amy worried as she stood to follow him across the yard and down the driveway.

She saw him smile. "*Nee*. I won't mind," he assured her. Something in the sound of his voice gave her goosebumps.

It was only a mile between their homes, but the thought of him walking along the road alone didn't sit well with her.

"So...how do ya feel about volleyball now?" he asked as they started down the gravel road, their steps crunching loudly.

Amy grinned, despite herself. They'd forced her into a volleyball lesson after the softball game had ended. Nathaniel had repeated his lesson on how to hit the ball, and she'd practiced volleying back and forth with Becca. The small bit of practice had helped her improve enough so she actually returned a serve when play began. Everyone in the game had applauded her success. To which she had rolled her eyes and curtsied.

"It helped there were other kids learning along with me," she admitted.

Nathaniel's teeth were white in the dark as he smiled.

"It's amazing what we can do when we feel the freedom to make a few mistakes," he agreed.

She blinked and considered his words carefully.

"Maybe Caleb needs to fear making mistakes a little more," she mumbled, her mind suddenly wandering to her younger brother. What kind of mischief might he be getting into tonight?

Nathaniel laughed quietly. "It's only *Rumspringa*. He's just enjoying life before settling down a bit more. I'm not at all worried about Caleb."

"I guess I'm not either," she confessed after a few long moments. "He's just...such a handful lately."

"He does make life interesting," Nathaniel agreed with another chuckle.

"I think he likes Rachel," Amy said quietly.

"Mm," Nathaniel hummed. "I think Caleb likes a lot of girls."

Amy sighed in resignation.

"It's okay for him to not know yet. He's young. He's got lots of time to figure out just which one he can't live without."

Caleb was seventeen. A bit older even than she had been when Lucas had ended their courtship. And she had been certain—absolutely positive—they were a match. It wasn't that she wanted Caleb to settle down just yet. He really was too young to be serious about anyone. But Amy genuinely liked Nathaniel's younger sister. She certainly didn't want to see her hurt by Caleb's carelessness.

"He made it pretty clear we were the old people tonight, didn't he?" she said as she shook her head.

"*Jah*, but that's okay with me."

Amy glanced over to see Nathaniel's smile turn softer in the moonlight.

"You don't miss being seventeen?"

He snorted. "*Nee*. Not a bit."

"Really?"

He grinned and shook his head. "I'm exactly where I want to be."

She fell silent at his response.

"How about you? Do ya miss *Rumspringa*?"

"No. Definitely not."

"None of it?"

Most of her *Rumspringa* was spent courting Lucas. She didn't miss that. She didn't miss the naïve, doe-eyed girl she had once been. But memories glimmered in the gaps. The laughing with her friends at Singing. The baking days she would spend with other girls her age in their mothers' kitchens. The way her friends would show up at her home for a visit in the middle of the day.

"Only a few small things," she said quietly. "The rest of it…" She waved a hand as if brushing it away like a pesky mosquito.

Nathaniel made no response.

Those first few years, before Lucas had begun courting her, she remembered the excitement of being young and unattached. She remembered what it felt like to have a *buwe* look a little longer at her than he had before. She remembered the nervous flutter when one of them would work up the nerve to finally talk to her. Then with a start, she realized she actually didn't *miss* all of that. She had it now.

"I guess if my life includes evenings like this one, it's hard to have any regrets or disappointments," she admitted.

Nathaniel touched her hand and pulled her to a stop.

She turned to see his face barely illuminated by the moonlight. But she could see his eyes, shining intensely at her.

"Please go to Singing this Sunday night," he said softly.

Amy swallowed. Two weeks ago, as she had struggled to get to sleep after he had brought her home, she had promised herself she was done. The day he had shown up and brushed flour off her cheek, she'd vowed not to encourage his attention. But now, looking into his eyes, she doubted all those convictions. His fingers gently curled around hers, and she tore her gaze from his face and stared down at their joined hands.

How had this happened? How did she keep finding herself in places where he was just what she needed and wanted? How was he this patient, when she so often tried to push him away?

"Okay," she replied quietly.

A pulse of fear wound through her. She couldn't go making these kinds of concessions—not if she wanted to protect herself. And she really didn't need him. She could do just fine without him. She'd proven that over and over again.

Over the past four lonely years full of a secret yearning.

Gently she pulled her fingers free from his and hugged her arms around herself. Nathaniel let her pull away and simply fell into step beside her as they turned into her driveway.

Right up to the foot of the porch steps. That's how far he walked her before his shoes scuffed to a stop.

"*Denki*. For walking me home," she said quietly.

"Anytime."

Amy turned and stepped up the stairs, her legs feeling strangely heavy. She watched him through the screen door as he turned and made his way back down the driveway.

It was entirely possible to live without him. She'd been doing that for years now.

Problem was, she no longer really wanted to.

— Chapter Thirty-Five —

The open-air courting buggy bounced along faster than necessary. Amy sighed from her spot next to Caleb. His new fascination with driving fast was less than amusing to her. She suspected he was spending his nights racing some of his friends, but she couldn't prove anything.

A shrill jingle sounded, and she jumped.

Caleb quickly fished a bright, shiny cell phone out of his pocket.

"What on earth is that?!" she demanded with wide eyes.

"Hullo, Syd," Caleb greeted, holding the slim device up to his ear and speaking into it.

Amy stared at his profile as he completely ignored her in favor of the electronic contraption in his long-fingered hand.

She rolled her eyes and turned them to the road ahead of them. At least one of them should be paying attention to the road.

Caleb finished his phone call and tapped the screen.

"This is called a cell phone," he explained. "I use it to make and receive telephone calls."

"I know what it is," she bit back. "I just don't know why *you* have one."

"I am a very in-demand guy," Caleb said matter-of-factly.

"You are supposed to be plain," Amy chastised. "Nothing about that thing looks plain."

"Just a plain old smartphone," he drawled.

Amy snorted. "Let me know when that smartness rubs off on ya."

"I'm really so very glad ya decided to start going to Singings again," Caleb sighed.

That shut her up. She wasn't so sure this time she had a lot of choice in attending. Not when Nathaniel had looked at her that way and begged her to come tonight. Not when the memory of how much she had actually enjoyed singing with other young people had followed her through the past two weeks.

It was slightly less terrifying this time. The rows of courting buggies didn't bother her nearly as much as they had two weeks ago. She left Caleb to tie up his horse and wandered alone toward the various groups of young people.

Irma fell into step beside her.

"Nice night for a Singing, *jah*?" Irma said as they walked along the yard, surveying the volleyball courts.

"It is," Amy agreed.

Irma was a few years younger, but that mattered little to Amy.

"Becca told me there was a fiercely competitive match going on over here between the *buwes*," Irma said with a nod and a lopsided smile.

"Sounds interesting," Amy laughed at Irma's chagrined expression.

"That's one way to put it," she giggled.

The two of them ambled toward the shouting and loud bouts of cheering. Sometimes the games were coed, sometimes not. But the boys tended to play a little rougher when there were no girls on the court. Amy was just fine with sitting down in the grass to watch rather than finding a game to join, even though she felt a bit more confident after the lessons at the Shetlers' farm.

A few of the *buwes* on the court were wearing shorts and t-shirts. But most wore the normal pants, suspenders, and button-down shirts.

Nathaniel stood at the net, laughing at something Lucas's younger brother, Levi Beiler, had said. There were too many people watching this match for him to notice her in the crowd. For many minutes, she watched as the young men served the ball and volleyed it back and forth, often jumping to block or spike the ball at the net.

At a break in the action, Caleb arrived on the scene. Amy twisted her mouth to the side as a chorus of greetings came his way. With easy strides, he reached the court and was immediately pulled into one of the teams. Amy was too far to hear what was being said, but she could see Nathaniel greeting her brother and slapping him firmly on the back.

Caleb easily stepped into place. Nathaniel stepped off the court and headed directly for where she and Irma sat in the grass. He stopped to talk to a few friends on his way, but his path never varied. She fought the blush that lit her face as he sat on the grass next to her. Apparently, she had been wrong about him not noticing her when she had arrived.

"Need a break?" she asked.

"I'm getting too old for this stuff," he moaned.

She laughed quietly and turned her attention to the game. Caleb was jumping and blocking shots no one else could reach. His shirt had come untucked and hung haphazardly around his suspenders. He threw back his head and laughed at something one of his teammates had said. Clearly, he was in his glory. She wasn't sure if she should hope he lost his cell phone or not.

Becca landed on the grass next to Nathaniel and something eased in Amy a bit. Now at least it looked less like he was sitting next to her and more like they were just a casual group of friends.

The games ended as the evening sky darkened. Everyone began to stand and slowly make their way toward the barn. There was no schedule here. When it seemed like they were all seated and ready, the singing would begin. Amy ambled beside Irma, Becca, and Nathaniel. She was profoundly grateful for Irma's companionship tonight. Maybe, Amy thought, she should make more of an effort to talk to her and get to know her better.

A short, bustling woman chattering nonstop to a friend blew by their group. Amy recognized Sally immediately and felt amusement bubble up inside her. She dared a glance back over her shoulder and caught Nathaniel's eye. The same laughter shone in his eyes, and she had to bite her lip and look away.

Nathaniel wandered away to the side of the barn where all the young men would sit facing the women's side. Irma and Becca sat down on either side of Amy, and she was soon lost in their discussion of Emily's new set of twin baby *buwes* who had arrived just a few days ago.

The sound of someone loudly clearing their throat hushed the chatter and a gentle silence fell. The leader sang out and the rest of the youth joined him. Amy added her voice to the group, but goosebumps covered her arms. She knew that voice. It had become more familiar to her than most. Despite all her reservations and fear, she knew him better than anyone else in this building, save Caleb.

It was Nathaniel.

Chapter Thirty-Six

"I can't tell ya how much I appreciate what ya did with Storm," Isaac said with wide eyes. "He's a different animal."

Nathaniel grinned and shook Isaac's outstretched hand. "I'm glad I could help." Truth was, he hadn't been sure he'd be able to handle Storm that first day. But an hour or two each day had made a world of difference.

"I plan to harness him up this Sunday when Katie is here to visit," Isaac continued as a slight blush crossed his face.

Nathaniel had met Isaac's fiancée once before. She was a lovely young woman with dark brown hair and glasses. And she had looked at Isaac as if he was the greatest person on the planet. The memory of it made Nathaniel ache a bit.

"Sounds like a *gut* idea," Nathaniel agreed. He'd already trained Storm to pull a buggy. In fact, he'd had Storm pull his courting buggy home from Singing on Sunday night. Amy hadn't realized it until they were a mile down the road. But Storm had behaved himself, and at the end Amy had been impressed. Nathaniel fought a smile at the memory.

"You sure do have a lot of nice things for sale here," Isaac said, interrupting Nathaniel's thoughts. It certainly wasn't Isaac's first time at the market, but he wasn't someone who shopped there all that often.

Nathaniel nodded. "*Jah*, we have a good inventory."

"Uh, I was wondering if you'd be interested in maybe selling some homemade baskets?" Isaac asked as he studied his shifting feet.

"Possibly," Nathaniel said.

"My Katie, she makes baskets," Isaac added a bit shyly.

Nathaniel grinned. "Does she have some we could take a look at? I'm sure Amy would like to see a few examples and talk to her about pricing."

"*Jah*, I'm sure she could do that. I'll have her bring some by on Saturday," Isaac said enthusiastically.

"Sounds *gut*."

Nathaniel saw Isaac out the door with a wave and stepped back inside. Sally had things well in hand with only one other customer, so Nathaniel headed to the back.

He found Amy in the back room with a quilt spread across the worktable.

"I talked to Isaac Troyer about…" Nathaniel's words trailed off as he noticed what Amy was intently studying. On the table lay one of the most extraordinary quilts he had ever seen.

He whistled.

"It was here early this morning—sitting outside the back door. No name. Just a note to donate the proceeds from the sale to the community fund again," she said, chewing her lip.

Nathaniel frowned. "We just sold the other one last week."

"I know. It's like she knows…"

"Somebody local then," Nathaniel concluded.

"Must be," Amy said as her fingers reached out and trailed over the surface of the brightly colored fabric.

"What's the pattern?" he asked.

"Pineapple log cabin, I think," Amy said quietly.

"What price do ya think you'll put on it?" he asked curiously. The other two mystery quilts had sold for well into four figures.

"I'll have to ask Deborah, but probably a little more than the last one. It's more complicated. The pieces are smaller," she said as she pointed to a few tiny squares.

"I know I shouldn't wonder, but I'm awfully curious who makes these," he admitted.

"*Jah*. So am I," Amy replied. "But it's such a humble way for this woman to help others."

He nodded in agreement. "And it's an honor she chooses us to let her do that."

Amy's eyes came up to his and held his gaze. After a bit, she dropped her gaze back to the quilt and smiled slightly. Her expression softened.

"It is."

༄༅༅༄

"What can I help you ladies with today?" Amy grinned widely as she approached Irma, Susannah, Sarah, and Becca.

"I'm looking for some fabric for a new dress," Irma said with a smart nod of her head.

"A dress that will make a certain someone sit up and take notice," Susannah giggled.

Irma rolled her eyes.

Amy smiled. "How are things with Jacob?"

Irma smirked in reply. "Well, I'm not planting any celery anytime soon."

"Why ever not? Seal the deal!" Sarah urged with a wave.

"We've only gone on a few rides together. There's plenty of time for getting serious…later," Irma declared with a flutter of her hand. "Let him stew a while."

"His favorite color is red," Sarah commented lightly, her eyes scanning the items on the shelves around them.

"I know just the thing," Amy said warmly.

"You have a good eye for fabric," Irma said several minutes later as Amy slid her shears through the expanse of brilliant burgundy cotton.

"*Mann* or no *mann*, a pretty dress is fun to have." Amy smiled without looking up.

Irma nodded. "That's why I like you, Amy. You have a good head on yer shoulders."

When the four friends left, Amy rewound the countless bolts of fabric they had been inspecting. True, Irma had needed fabric for a new dress. But a warmth spread through her as she thought through their visit. All four of them had come and spent time with her, had offered her gentle words of praise for the appearance of the store, and had asked her opinion on nearly every fabric option she carried. They'd found a way to come to her when her working hours didn't really allow her to go to them.

They were all a bit younger than her, truth be told. But that mattered less to Amy than it ever had before. These were the friends who were welcoming her in. Ever so gently, they were drawing her out and into their group. It felt…nice. Nice to be wanted and sought out. Nice to laugh with them and be listened to. Nice to have their friendly smiles and gentle teasing.

She was beginning to realize just how easy it had been for her to hide away at the market. Maybe her dad was right. Maybe she should think just a little bit more about life outside the walls of her family's store.

.⊷ఁ৯.

It wasn't all that often that Amy received invitations for supper. So when one came from Silas and Kirsten, she readily accepted. Of course, it seemed terribly innocent until she arrived at their house and saw Susie roaming in the paddock next to Titus.

The sound of voices reached her before she even hit the bottom of the stairs that led up to the wraparound porch on Silas and Kirsten's house. She didn't bother to knock tonight. Clearly, she was not the only person on the guest list.

"*Aendi* Amy," came the squeal just seconds before the force of little Grace crashed into her legs.

"Oof," Amy choked as another set of footsteps came slapping along in Grace's wake. Benjamin managed to toddle over on his own two legs but grabbed fistfuls of her skirt to keep his balance.

"Well hullo there, little loves," she crooned as she handed her dessert to Kirsten's waiting hands. Amy knelt down and pulled them both into her arms. Grace wrapped her arms around Amy's neck and Ben scrambled into her lap.

"We are having a supper party!" Grace announced with wide eyes.

"Pardeeee," Ben babbled.

"I can see that!" Amy laughed.

"Will ya sit by me?" Grace asked seriously.

"Oh, of course I will," Amy agreed, equally serious.

That was all the reassurance Grace needed. She released Amy's neck and went running off past the enormous dining room table to pounce upon her father's knee. Silas caught her easily and swung the girl up into his lap. Ben raced off after her and soon found himself scooped up next to his sister.

Nathaniel, Becca, Rachel, and Caleb sat on the sofas near Silas.

Kirsten shook her head. "Those two have more energy than squirrels."

Amy laughed and stepped into the kitchen to help with supper preparations.

"What's for supper tonight?" Amy asked, surveying the flour-dusted countertop of the long kitchen island.

"Homemade pizza. Not very Amish, I know," Kirsten answered with a wave of her hand.

Amy rolled her eyes but smiled at her sister-in-law.

"How many more years before us Millers can convince you that Amish people actually like pizza?"

Kirsten tilted her head this way and that. "I made the crust from scratch, at least."

"At this stage of the game, I'm thinking that was more than you should have done." Amy grinned as she considered Kirsten's swollen stomach.

"It was a good distraction. Kept my mind off the false labor I've been having lately."

Amy's smile grew. "Any day now."

Kirsten drew in a deep breath and let it out slowly. "*Jah.* I think we're ready."

"Shelby is ready to come stay a while."

"I should talk to Silas about that, shouldn't I? That would be a worry off my mind. Especially at night." Kirsten nodded as she pulled a tossed salad out of the refrigerator.

"Talk to me about what?" came the deep voice of Amy's brother.

"Several things," Kirsten answered with a grin. "But first I need you to get the *kinner* settled at the table. It's time to eat."

"We'll get these things on the table," Amy insisted, stepping into the kitchen and taking the salad out of Kirsten's hands. "You have done enough."

Amy began pulling the pizzas out of the oven. It had been a long while since she'd had pizza, and it smelled so good her stomach rumbled.

Becca was already placing the salad, breadsticks, and soda on the table when Amy brought over the first of three enormous pizzas.

"Well, I don't know what you guys are going to eat, but this looks great," Caleb said with wide eyes.

"*Onkle* Caleb! You share!" came Grace's outraged command

"Sare!" Ben echoed.

"Okay! Okay!" Caleb laughed, holding up his hands in surrender.

Amy lowered herself into the chair next to Grace, but when Nathaniel sat next to Amy, she felt her cheeks warm. She'd have to talk to Kirsten about her attempts at matchmaking.

The meal was a chorus of laughter and lively discussion. Grace and Ben finished their meal long before the adults were ready to leave the table and toddled off to the living room to play together.

When it was time for dessert, Amy waved Kirsten back into her chair and made her way to the kitchen to start the coffee and cut the peanut butter cheesecake she had brought along.

"Need any help?"

Amy jumped at Nathaniel's calm, low, steady voice.

"Oh, um, sure," she said, startled.

"What did ya make?" he asked as he stepped next to her at the counter.

She tried to keep her hand from shaking as she pulled the knife through the dessert.

"Peanut butter cheesecake," she answered.

"My favorite," he murmured.

She pulled a slice out and slid it onto a plate. Nathaniel picked it up and she watched out of the corner of her eye as he brought it to the table and set it in front of Kirsten.

"Oh my," Kirsten said in surprise.

Amy's heart warmed at the kindness in his small act. Kirsten was a young wife and mother. The times she got served first were few and far between.

She continued to plate the rest of the slices, and when it was the last one she brought it to the table and set it in front of Nathaniel's place.

Only Caleb would notice Nathaniel's piece was larger than the rest.

.ൟൟ.

Nathaniel's fingers curled around his third cup of coffee. For nearly two hours they had played a raucous game of Apples to Apples. Caleb's intermittent fits about no one choosing his outlandish cards were still ringing in Nathaniel's ears.

It became obvious the two married people had a distinct advantage. Silas and Kirsten always seemed to know each other's cards, sometimes breaking into quiet bouts of shared laughter.

Footsteps on the stairs sounded, and Nathaniel's attention was drawn from Silas's explanation of the finishing process he'd used on the new dining set at the market. Amy descended, the picture of poise and grace in the dim lantern light.

Silas paused, but Nathaniel only dropped his eyes to his coffee cup.

"Did they go down okay for you?" Kirsten asked as Amy lowered herself in the chair next to his.

"*Jah*, no trouble at all." Amy smiled softly across the table to where Kirsten now sat near her husband.

Nathaniel fought the urge to inch closer to her on the bench that stretched along their side of the table.

"They will probably sleep well with how energetic they were today," Kirsten laughed.

Silas grinned in amusement and drained the rest of his coffee.

"Is there anything I can help ya with these next few weeks? I could come over after my shift and help ya get the baby's room ready or cook or clean…"

"Oh, that's sweet of you, Amy," Kirsten said softly. "I'll need you most when the baby is born. You were so good with Grace and Ben."

Nathaniel sat in quiet consideration. Amy worked so hard each and every day, and yet she was offering to come here and do hours more work.

"I'll be here," Amy reassured. "Where is everyone else?" she asked suddenly.

"Caleb was getting restless. He took Becca and Rachel home," Nathaniel answered quietly.

"That *buwe*…why can't he be more like you were, Silas?" Amy sighed in exasperation.

"I courted an Englisher," Silas countered with a crooked smile.

"Okay, yes, but it turned out well. I'm talking about *Rumspringa*. You wore t-shirts every once in a while at home and learned how to drive. That was it. Caleb has a cell phone for goodness sake!"

Silas shrugged. "I have a cell phone."

"In the shop. Where it belongs. Caleb's is in his pocket. And he just seems…wild," Amy worried.

"Caleb is not wild," came Silas's quiet reply. "He's always been full of life. He's a *gut* kid. Just give him some time."

Amy sighed deeply, but Nathaniel could tell Silas's words had calmed her. No one spent as much time with Caleb as Silas did. They were total opposites in personality even though they looked so much alike.

"I should get ya home," Nathaniel murmured quietly to Amy. Almost the minute the words were out of his mouth her shoulders slumped a bit.

"It's later than I realized," she agreed.

Nathaniel stood and stepped over the bench, stepping back while Amy stood. It had been so comfortable while his sisters and Caleb had been there. But now, with just Silas and Kirsten, it seemed different. More like they were a couple. He had taken her home from Singings and on a few other occasions. But that didn't mean she considered him her beau.

What more could he do to convince her?

⊱⊰

Amy stood in the back room and peered through the small window in the swinging doors. Through the plastic she could see Nathaniel ringing up the order of some English tourists. His smile was genuine, warm, and friendly. He was calm and collected, easily chatting with them and answering whatever questions they might be asking.

She sniffed and turned away from the window. This late summer cold was not her idea of a small hardship. She couldn't very well be greeting customers and helping them with their orders when her nose was so red and runny. Hopefully in a day or two she would be back to her normal duties. But for today, Nathaniel had agreed to switch places with her. She would definitely be slower when it came to some of the heavy lifting, but at least she could do something helpful while he ran the front of the store with Sally's help.

Her mom had wanted her to stay home and rest. But Amy had assured her she would be able to get through the day just fine. And Mary was in no hurry to be tied down at the market when Silas and Kirsten's baby was surely just days away from being born. Shelby had moved in with them for a short time, so Kirsten would have nothing to worry about when the time came.

Amy picked up the baskets Katie Kinsinger had dropped off. They were fine pieces Amy had no doubt would sell well. And Katie had been smart enough to price them to sell but not too cheaply. Isaac had been thrilled with the arrangement. Anything to help his soon-to-be-wife feel like she fit into this community.

Nathaniel had done well to recommend the samples and that Katie meet with her.

Those first few days when he had turned her world upside down by making changes and moving things around seemed like a long time ago. Most of his changes had turned out for the better. The internet sales for Silas's business were beginning to come in at such a pace he was looking to hire additional carpenters to handle the workload.

No one else had ever come into the market as an employee and done so much for their business. Nathaniel was the ideal person to have on their staff. She doubted anyone else in the whole community would have loved and protected and defended the store the way Nathaniel had. No one else would have pushed for its success and promoted its growth, and certainly not with the respect he had shown for the many years of her parents' hard work.

Sally burst through the doors and interrupted Amy's thoughts.

"Well, it is time for me to get going. I sure do hope ya feel better tomorrow, Amy! Those summer colds are just the worst! I will never understand where they come from. Colds are for cold weather. My *maam* has some *gut* medicine for colds. Would ya like me to bring ya some tomorrow?"

Amy smiled but shook her head. "Oh, no thank you. I'm handling it just fine," she insisted.

"I am glad to hear that. Make sure ya get some good rest, though! I hope you are one hundred percent over it before Kirsten has her baby. They sure do have some lovely children, don't they? Grace is such a sweet child and that Ben looks just exactly like his *daed*. I'm sure ya enjoy babysitting for them every chance ya get."

Amy nodded and pressed her lips together. If she said anything, Sally would just have more to say in return.

"Well, I will see ya tomorrow!"

Sally slipped out the back door and Amy let out the breath she had been holding. Sally was a gift, too. But not quite the same as Nathaniel. While Sally's skills were welcome at the front, Nathaniel could work wherever he was needed most.

She peered at him again through the small window. He was sweeping near the front doors. The quiet sound of his voice filtered through to the backroom.

> *"He leadeth me: O blessed thought!*
> *O words with heavenly comfort fraught!*
> *What'er I do, where'er I be,*
> *Still 'tis God's hand that leadeth me.*
>
> *"He leadeth me, he leadeth me,*
> *By his own hand he leadeth me;*
> *His faithful follower I would be,*
> *For by his hand he leadeth me."*

Amy's lips mouthed the words along with him though her scratchy throat would not allow her to sing.

Then a stunning sudden realization crept over her.

Nathaniel should be the one.

If her parents wanted to find someone to buy the market, to run it the way they believed it should be run, to continue to make it the blessing it was to the people of their community and to the customers they served, then Nathaniel should be the one.

Of course, if he bought it, owned it, that would be…strange for her. Perhaps even too strange. He would be her boss, in a manner of speaking. That didn't seem to work in her mind. She respected him, but to consider him her boss was odd. They were just friends. Sort of. But if Nathaniel was indeed the owner, it would put them in a different place. Their relationship, if that is what they were developing, would certainly be challenged.

A part of her still wished the store could be hers. But she understood more now that it was simply too much for her to handle all on her own. If she let go of the dream of owning the market, would she also have to let go of the tiny hope she had for a relationship with Nathaniel?

If only there were instructions—a clear path—for all these decisions. But there were no recipes for life. And that was ultimately what she wanted—perfectly outlined details on what to do and how to do it. Follows these steps and this will be the end result. She craved that order.

But that was also precisely what she was most lacking in these days. She was still slowly learning this practice of surrender. It was so hard to let go, to loosen her grip and simply hold her hands open to see what God would place in them. It went against everything she had become used to.

Risking decisions in the kitchen was one thing. The worst that could happen there was a failed batch of brownies. Which Caleb would still eat. But here a failure would be far more painful and with bigger consequences.

The thing was, it was working in the kitchen. Many times, she would gather ingredients and a memory of baking with Ella would find its way into her mind. The measurements weren't always there, but she had learned to adjust. To add more flour or use another egg. To simply give herself permission to try and to set aside the fear.

Could she risk it here?

She knew Nathaniel would be the right choice for the market. She knew he would love it the way she would. He had been doing that since the first day he walked in the doors and rearranged the back room. Ultimately, he wanted what was best for the market. And so did she.

It was time to talk to her father.

— Chapter Thirty-Seven —

"Need a ride?" Caleb asked.

Amy turned to see him leaning on the doorway, one arm actually braced on the top of the frame. He was wearing clean clothes and his still-damp blond hair curled slightly about his forehead.

"No thank you." She shook her head and turned back to the window. Dusk was falling.

"Someone picking you up?" Caleb pressed.

Amy forced herself to swallow.

"Maybe," she admitted. She had also changed after supper. Tonight she was wearing her bright turquoise dress.

"Tell Nathaniel I said hi," Caleb teased as he strode past her and out the door.

Almost as soon as Caleb's courting buggy disappeared down the long lane, she saw another turn in. They didn't normally ride together in his courting buggy when it was still daylight. Dating wasn't really as much of a secret as it had been for her parents. Mary still liked to tell stories about how Daniel would show up and toss pebbles at her window to take her out for late-night buggy rides. Still…riding with Nathaniel in the dim light of evening…everyone would see and know.

Know they were…

What they were she didn't even know. But she knew what everyone would think—that they were dating.

She quickly made her way out of the house and down the stairs and waited while he pulled up. With an easy hop, he was out of the buggy and reaching out a hand for her. Amy slid her fingers over his palm and felt his hand firmly wrap around hers.

"Is that a new shirt?" she asked as she took in the crisp sky-blue shirt fabric showing beneath his black suspenders.

"*Jah, Maam* bought it for me yesterday," he said as he smoothed a hand down the buttoned front. "She's awfully happy to be allowed to buy shirts now."

"No store-bought clothing for ya in Middlefield?" she asked with a smile.

"Definitely not!" he answered with wide eyes.

"I like being New Order," she confessed quietly.

"I do, too," he agreed as he clicked his tongue at Susie and put the buggy in motion.

The Troyers' yard was filled with buggies and horses. Other Amish districts in the area had been invited to join in on the annual late-summer volleyball tournament. Their just-harvested hayfield was now filled with buggies and horses. Caleb was already here...somewhere.

She climbed out of the buggy while Nathaniel secured Susie to the rail.

"Are ya playing today?" she asked as they made their way toward the long line of volleyball courts. There had to be at least eight of them.

Nathaniel shrugged. "If someone wants me to. But I'm *gut* with just watching, too. What about you?"

Amy glanced over to see the slight smile on his face. It wasn't unkind, but she could see he already knew what she would say.

"*Nee.* I'm just here to watch," she said emphatically.

"Works for me."

As they slowly strolled by the courts, Amy could see some of the games were lighthearted and just for fun, but others were intense and very competitive. Caleb was on one such court. He enjoyed volleyball and was a popular teammate given his height, but she knew his real love had always been softball. Just like Silas. Just like her.

They sat and watched Caleb playing, his wavy blond hair blowing in the wind. There was no shortage of young women watching this game, Amy noted. Becca, Rachel, Irma, and Susannah found them soon enough and sat next to them. Games started and ended, and there was a slow selection of the best teams.

๛๑ ๑๛

"Let's get a drink," Nathaniel suggested as the court they were watching finished their play.

Despite the now-dark sky, it had been a very hot day. A cold drink sounded awfully good right now. So did some time away from all this craziness. Amy agreed with a nod and walked beside him to the refreshments table.

Minutes later, he had guided them away from the volleyball courts to a quiet area of the farmyard. Here and there around them were other couples, but no one close enough to really overhear them.

"These are my favorite," Nathaniel sighed after he took a long draw from the root beer float in his hand.

"Of course they are." Amy grinned as she shook her head and sipped at her own root beer float.

"What's yers?"

"My what?" she asked with a blink.

"Yer favorite thing to drink?" he asked, his head tilted to study her.

Amy considered the question for a long moment before her mouth twisted to the side. "You'll only laugh at me," she protested.

Nathaniel shook his head and raised his eyebrows. "*Nee*. I won't."

Amy sighed. "Once, I went to a gas station with Silas. It was so cold. I was freezing, so I got myself a French vanilla cappuccino out of one of those machines. Best thing I've ever had."

Nathaniel grinned widely and huffed a breath.

Amy whipped her head to him. "See! You're laughing!"

"*Nee*. I'm smiling," he argued.

"That's how laughing starts," she snipped.

"True. But I stayed with the smile and didn't move to the laugh."

"You made a sound," she accused.

"A breath! I was breathing!" he protested.

Amy pinched her lips together but didn't look convinced. There was no way she knew how beautiful she looked tonight. This dress that was a stunning complement to her skin and her hair. The way the slimmer cut of the women's dresses in their district set off her lovely figure. The way her eyes were a deeper shade of dark blue than anyone else's. He watched her fingers trail through the coarse grass beneath them.

"Those fancy drinks are too sweet for me." He smiled. Somehow, he just couldn't picture it—her with a fancy coffee drink in her hands.

Nathaniel was staring at her, but he couldn't bring himself to look away. They'd started this summer with her refusing to do anything social. But now…she had changed. She was still confident and independent, but he'd come to see the softer side to her.

"Have ya talked with my *daed* recently?" she asked, her brow furrowing as she stared out at the moonlit field of corn.

A strange question. There was something she wasn't telling him.

"Not recently. Why?"

Her shoulders merely pulled up in a small shrug.

"He was talking about making some changes at the market," she murmured.

Nathaniel's stomach flipped uneasily. He loved his job and was perfectly content with the current arrangement. He couldn't think of a single thing he would want to change.

"What kind of changes?" he asked with a frown.

"I don't know for sure what he'll decide to do. I just wondered if he had talked to ya," she answered cryptically.

"He hasn't," Nathaniel replied after several long moments. Judging by her expression, these weren't changes she was particularly excited about. And nothing made him warier than her unease.

Chapter Thirty-Eight

It had been hours since Silas had shown up in his large, new, and very nice truck. It had been time for an upgrade, he'd told her with a shrug. Amy already knew the rules for individuals in their district who owned vehicles. Silas imposed even more strict rules for himself. While other men were allowed to use their vehicles to reach worksites or haul supplies, Silas only used his truck for trips to the lumberyard and to deliver goods to customers beyond the limits of buggy travel. If it was possible for him to use a buggy, he did.

But this morning, he was on his way to town for lumber. Nathaniel had told her the other night on their way home he would be making the trip to town with Silas to get some needed supplies for the market. She hadn't even realized they were low on paper towels and floor cleaner. But a quick survey before he had arrived this morning confirmed they were.

Of course, Caleb was along for the ride.

"Such lovely baskets," the gray-haired English woman said as she set one of Katie's handmade woven baskets on the counter.

"Aren't they nice?" Amy agreed with a warm smile.

"I'm going to have to tell my friends about this place." The woman smiled as she set her large purse on the counter and fished for her pocketbook. "We might make a whole day trip out of it."

"That would be lovely." Amy nodded as she tapped the buttons on the cash register and rang up the items on the counter. "Yer total comes to $47.91."

"Who is the furniture maker?" the woman's husband asked as he peered over Amy's shoulder to the side of the store where all of Silas's pieces were on display.

"That would be my brother," she answered easily.

"Wonderful craftsmanship," the man murmured, his eyes still fixed on the items behind her.

"*Denki.* I'll pass along the compliment." She smiled as she handed the woman her change.

Almost reluctantly, the couple picked up their purchases and moved to the doors.

"Oh! That quilt!" the woman suddenly gasped.

Amy's eyes followed their gaze though she already knew what had drawn their awestruck attention.

"It's stunning," the woman breathed.

Amy had to agree. She'd heard no less than a dozen similar comments just this morning. Even the Amish shoppers had stopped to stare up at it.

"We just got that in a few days ago," Amy explained. Nathaniel had hung it just minutes before he had left that morning.

"Who is the artist?" the woman asked, her eyes still glued to the brilliant piece hanging above their heads.

"It's a mystery," Amy admitted. "Every once in a while, we receive one of these amazing quilts with a note to donate the proceeds to our community fund."

"No one knows who it is?" the man asked with a shocked frown.

"*Nee.* Nobody," Amy answered in quiet consideration.

"Oh, I will definitely have to bring Evie and Nancy back here!" the woman exclaimed. "Wonderful little store!"

Amy could only smile as they pushed through the glass-paned doors into the bright sunshine. It was another scorching hot day.

As she stood at the glass, watching the couple climb in their shiny, expensive-looking SUV, Silas's large white truck pulled onto the lot. He parked near the loading dock but didn't back up. That load of lumber in the back was headed for the woodshop at his place. One day, it would sit in the showroom behind her as a table or a hope chest or a bedroom suite.

"They seemed like nice people," Sally gushed as she stepped up to gaze out the glass doors with Amy. "And they are right—that quilter is an artist. But ya know what I like? I like that she leaves just one tiny mistake in each piece. That's a lovely touch. I think she could make a perfect quilt without a stitch out of place, but she chooses to leave a flaw. As though she's saying only God can create perfection. You know I like to sew, but I make lots of mistakes. I guess most of my sewing just goes to show how much better God is at making things than I am," Sally laughed.

Amy stared at her in affection and amusement. Sally was a delight. A chatterbox, but a true delight.

"*Gut nammidaag*, ladies," Nathaniel called as his long legs carried him through the back room doors to where they stood at the front. "Busy day?" He smirked.

"Actually, yes," Amy informed him. Even though the two of them were standing there staring out the window and there were no customers in the building, it had been a busy morning.

"Glad to hear it." He nodded as set down the carrier of drinks in his hand on the counter. He pulled out one tall cup with a plastic lid and handed it to Amy.

"What's this for?" she asked in surprise, her fingers curling around the warm cup.

He winked. "For you."

She swallowed and blinked in response.

"One for Sally, too," he said as he handed another tall cup to Amy's small, smiling coworker.

"Oh! What on earth is it? Is it coffee?" Sally gushed.

"French vanilla cappuccino," Nathaniel answered easily, his eyes swinging to Amy with a glimmer of amusement.

Sally peeled off the plastic lid and let the steam waft into her face. She sucked in a long, deep breath and closed her eyes. The smile on her face was nothing short of pure joy. It almost made tears prick Amy's eyes, that Nathaniel had thought of Sally, too.

Amy was so busy watching Sally and taking her first sip that she jumped as Nathaniel stepped up close to her and leaned to whisper in her ear.

"I figured it would make for a fun afternoon," he breathed. "You know, see what happens when Sally gets a strong dose of caffeine."

Amy choked on the laughter that bubbled up as she attempted to swallow.

"Oh my," she gasped, her eyes watering with suppressed laughter. "It's still too hot," she choked, fanning her face with a hand.

Nathaniel's eyes glimmered in silent laughter. "*Jah*, it really is," he agreed. "Be careful with that stuff, Sally," he said almost sternly. Only Amy knew his warning had nothing to do with the temperature of the drink.

Sally spun around at his words.

"Oh, I surely will be! I'll never forget the first time I drank a cup of coffee when I was just terribly little. I didn't know to go slow and I just gulped it down. *Mei maam* says my eyes went larger than the cup. Couldn't taste anything for a whole week! That was frightful! Why do they make these drinks so hot, I wonder? I suppose it's so they stay nice and hot for people on a long drive. But when I'm on a long drive, I like to have something ice cold. Like coca cola."

Amy watched, trying desperately to hide her smile behind her cup, as Nathaniel walked backward all the way to the swinging doors, the grin on his face stretched wide as he listened to Sally's never-ending narrative.

⊱∾⊰

It was just after lunch when Caleb came strolling in the doors of the market. Nathaniel waved a hand in greeting from across the storefront, and Caleb nodded distractedly back. A frisson of worry wound through Nathaniel. Caleb was never this serious and focused.

He watched as Caleb spotted Amy at the fabric table and immediately set off for her. Amy's eyes flickered then shot back up to watch Caleb's approach. Nathaniel was several yards away but could hear the worry in her voice.

"What is it?" she asked.

Caleb grinned softly. "Just came to give ya the news…"

"News," Amy whispered.

"Kirsten had her baby an hour or two ago," he announced.

"Oh!" Amy clapped her hands. "What did she have?"

"I just told ya! A baby!" Caleb threw up his hands in playful annoyance.

"Caleb!" she warned.

"Okay, okay. She had a girl. Naomi Rose."

Nathaniel could see Amy's eyes welling with tears. Her fingers pressed against her lips as quiet joy stole over her features.

Clearly, she was happy at these good tidings of a new niece. Nathaniel felt a measure of joy himself for Silas and Kirsten and their family.

But there was something more there. When Caleb bid his goodbye and walked out the door, a little more calm and sober than he normally was, Nathaniel's gaze focused again on Amy.

"Was that *gut* news for Silas and Kirsten?" he asked when he approached her.

"*Jah*." Amy smiled, her eyes indeed shining up at him with tears. "A healthy baby girl," she beamed.

"I can see you're very happy for them," he murmured quietly.

Amy merely dropped her gaze and ducked her head.

"I'm happy for them, too," he told her. "It's *gut* to see such a great *familye* blessed with healthy *kinner*."

"What they have…" she paused, shaking her head. "It's the dream."

Throughout the day, she kept busy helping customers. But many times, he saw her catch her breath and blink back tears, that tentative smile hovering but with a touch of strain.

Nathaniel tried to give her space. He certainly didn't want to pry or to make her cry. But he stayed somewhat close…just in case she broke unexpectedly.

It was for that reason that when the doors had been locked, the sign flipped to closed, and Sally had made a quiet and gentle departure, Nathaniel stood near the doors to the back room, listening for her.

Amy's voice began with an unsteady warble—so uncommon for her.

"Why should I feel discouraged,
Why should the shadows come,
Why should my heart be lonely,
And long for a heav'n and home…"

Her voice trembled but grew in strength.

"When Jesus is my portion?
My constant friend is He:
His eye is on the sparrow,
And I know He watches me;
His eye is on the sparrow,
And I know He watches me."

There was a pause, and he wondered if she would just stop there, wondered if she was crying and unable to continue. But a glance through the small window and he saw her draw in a deep breath and lift her chin.

"I sing because I'm happy,
I sing because I'm free,
For His eye is on the sparrow,
And I know He watches me."

Nathaniel blinked against the burning in his own eyes. He forced himself to swallow the lump that had gathered in his throat and pressed a hand against the ache in his own chest.

"'Let not your heart be troubled,'
His tender word I hear,
And resting on His goodness,
I lose my doubts and fears;
Though by the path He leadeth,
But one step I may see;
His eye is on the sparrow,
And I know He watches me;

His eye is on the sparrow,
And I know He watches me.

"Whenever I am tempted,
Whenever clouds arise,
When songs give place to sighing,
When hope within me dies,
I draw the closer to Him,
From care He sets me free;
His eye is on the sparrow,
And I know He watches me;
His eye is on the sparrow,
And I know He watches me.

"I sing because I'm happy,
I sing because I'm free,
For His eye is on the sparrow,
And I know He watches me."

Nathaniel stepped through the swinging doors and simply stood there, letting the last notes echo in the storefront. He stuffed his hands in his pockets to keep himself from reaching for her.

She knew he was there. But she hardly turned her head when she gently wiped beneath her eyes with a long, pale finger. She set the dust mop behind the counter and turned to him.

"Ready to *geh*?" he asked, his own voice gravelly and rough.

She nodded once. "Ready."

Nathaniel waited and followed in her wake as she strode past him, through the back room and out the back door.

— Chapter Thirty-Nine —

Amy dumped the cup of flour onto the blob of dough in front of her and sank her fingers into the soft lump. With gentle but firm movements, she pushed and pulled at the dough. Just the way Ella had taught her. *This* she remembered. *This* was easy and good.

If these turned out, she would deliver them to Silas and Kirsten. To Grace and Benjamin. And take some more time to snuggle precious Naomi Rose. Born with hardly a trace of hair, just like Benjamin. It seemed Naomi would favor her father's hair coloring rather than her mother's. By the contented glow on Kirsten's face, she was just fine with that. Of course, the joy that also shone on Silas's face was impossible to ignore. It made Amy's heart glad to see her brother so filled with happiness. Their road hadn't been easy. There had been moments when she herself had made it even harder. But last night they had been the picture of gratitude and blessing.

Amy continued pulling at the dough, folding it over and pushing it down. She could practically feel Ella standing right next to her, peering at her over her shoulder.

Naomi was the picture of perfection. God really was the ultimate artist. Her tiny hands, her itty-bitty lips, her delicately formed ears. Beautiful and lovely—just as all her nieces and nephews had been. She'd not really recognized the wonder of it until Grace. Grace had broken open some part of Amy's heart she hadn't even known was there. Broken it open and filled it with laughter and love. Just about as soon as Amy had lost Lucas, there had been Grace.

Amy kneaded the dough one last time, then placed it in Ella's big mixing bowl and covered it with one of Anna's hand-embroidered flour sack towels. Perhaps…all the things she thought she had lost had never really been hers. Perhaps God had better things in store for her.

Would that include her own children one day? She desperately hoped so. Would it include meaningful work she enjoyed with all her heart? She prayed it would. Would it include someone with whom to share her life?

Her mind wandered over the events of the summer. She'd lost Ella, of course, but only for a time. She'd lost her recipe book, but she might be able to recreate it. She'd also lost the loneliness. Irma, Becca, Rachel, Susannah, and even Sally had become dear friends when she had felt so left behind by all the other women her age. Gone were her days of self-imposed exile. Gone were her days of hiding in plain sight at the market.

For years she had told herself she didn't need to socialize when she had the store. And truth be told, there was social interaction there. But conversations at the market were not deep and almost never about things that truly mattered. It was hard to make a strong connection to someone in just a few minutes here and there.

Instead she'd had a summer of Singings. Nathaniel had given that to her. He'd given her the courage to try again. He'd given her the space to be herself. He'd given her hope.

Memories of their time together drifted through her mind. Before she realized it, an hour had passed. She stood and peered in at the dough. It had not doubled in size, but it was rising. *Hm.* What would Ella have her do? Ella would not give up. That much she knew. Ella would put it in a warmer place and wait a bit longer. Amy tucked the cloth back over the bowl and set it in a patch of warm sunlight on the table.

More time.

Was that all she had needed? Just a little more time in a warm place?

Once she had wanted so much and would not have hesitated to give God a list of her requests. But when He'd said no, she'd stopped asking.

Yet she knew, knew that just because He had said no once didn't mean He always would. It frightened her to ask Him now. She'd rather sit here, clutching all of hopes in her own hands. To hold her dreams in an open hand before Him—that was terrifying.

But that was faith.

Could she dare to hold the dream of a life with Nathaniel in an open hand? Was there love in her heart for him? These past many years, the only thing she had asked God for—contentment in a life lived alone—He had not given to her.

Maybe it was time to trust He had good plans for her.

Amy peeked in again at the dough. Two hours now. It'd had double the amount of time to rise, warm, grow.

The cinnamon rolls were ready.

⁖୧୨⁖

Amy seemed different today. Still herself and yet…not. The sadness was gone. He had been relieved to see that. There was a quiet peace about her.

Twice now he'd seen her laughing with Sally. All out throwing her head back, eyes dancing, hand braced on her stomach laughter. The sound of it was almost as beautiful as her singing.

Never as long as he lived would he forget the sound of her song that night after Naomi had been born. He'd heard her sing so many times before—her voice always pure and rich and strong and beautiful. But that night…it had been different. The song had come from her soul.

Nathaniel swallowed the fear that had been welling up inside him for the past several days since Daniel had stopped to see him. Days and long nights of prayer had been the only path since then.

He couldn't put it off any longer.

— Chapter Forty —

Amy made her way to the back room, shutting off the overhead lights as she went. Nathaniel was standing with his back to her, staring out the back door. He'd been awfully quiet the past few days. He had smiled less often, and when he did it was subdued. Worry gnawed at her.

She grabbed her sweater off the small shelf at the back but simply hung it over her arm. He held the door open for her and she stepped through. She watched as he pulled the door closed and locked it securely. Again, she wondered...how had she missed it? That night when he had been so brutally beaten and she hadn't even noticed his injuries? That seemed like a lifetime ago.

Amy climbed up into his courting buggy and waited. This was their new routine. He'd eventually stopped asking if he could drive her home and she'd stopped feeling awkward about it.

Nathaniel climbed in next and she felt him sink down next to her, his thigh brushing against hers. Even that seemed familiar and normal now.

He picked up the reins but paused. "I, uh..." He cleared his throat almost nervously. "I've been working on Ella's house. I was wondering if ya would like to see it."

Amy waited until his eyes shifted to hers. Why was he worried? She could see the lines pinching the corners of his eyes. "*Jah*, I'd like to see it," Amy replied, trying to be reassuring.

Nathaniel nodded and swallowed. It only took a few minutes for them to travel from the market, across the highway, and onto the gravel road. He pulled Susie into that familiar drive and Amy's heart thudded. She hadn't been here since the day of the mud sale—hadn't set foot inside the house since the day…

Nathaniel stopped and tied Susie to the small hitching post Amy had used countless times. He helped her out of the buggy but didn't release her hand. Instead, he wound his long fingers through hers and looked at them for a long moment. With a firm grasp, he held on and led the way to the house.

Amy could practically see Ella standing there in the doorway, apron and skirt billowing softly around her.

Nathaniel unlocked the door, opened it, and stepped inside. She followed him up the cement steps into the little entryway. Then memories came flooding back to her. Ella's tottering gait down her galley kitchen, on her way to meet Amy at the door. Ella's wheezy laughter at Amy's stories. It felt so strange to be standing here and not see her there.

The entry was both the same and different. On the floor was a giant rug Ella would not have allowed for fear of tripping. The walls were no longer off-white but a calm, pale gray. The hardwood floors gleamed as though they had been recently refinished and polished to a high shine.

Amy felt her eyes welling and closed them for a moment, imagining Ella was still here.

"If it's too much we can do this another time," Nathaniel offered, his voice calm, low, and gentle in the mostly empty room.

"No," Amy protested. "I'm okay."

She stepped into the kitchen, a long wall of cupboards down each side. Light poured in through the curtainless windows above the sink. The cabinets were painted a lovely shade of dark gray. The walls here had been painted a fresh, crisp white. It was amazing how much brighter it seemed.

"I might have Silas make some new cabinets someday," Nathaniel said. She could see him behind her, watching her intently. Amy knew Silas's work better than just about anyone, apart from Kirsten and Caleb. There was no doubt that whatever he made would be beautiful. But these cabinets held memories. Amy wanted to tell Nathaniel to keep them. But those were her memories. Not his.

The dining space next to the kitchen was empty except for the built-in cabinet along the back wall. That he had painted to match the other cabinets. The giant picture window over the table looked out onto the yard—Nathaniel's yard. The apple trees dotting the landscape were growing heavier with fruit.

"I'll probably need Silas to build a table, too," Nathaniel muttered. She saw him run a hand through his hair, then rub it along the back of his neck. Amy smiled a little.

She wandered past him into the large living room. This space was also sparsely furnished. One lone rocking chair sat in front of the fireplace. Ella's corner cabinet, her two rocking chairs, her sofa, and her grandfather clock were all gone now.

"It seems so different," she murmured, almost to herself.

"It's a bit empty yet," he admitted.

Clearly Nathaniel had painted every single wall. The windows Amy had always washed twice a year were now crystal clear. He'd been busy. As different as it looked—and as much as it pained her to admit it—Ella's house had never looked quite so good.

"You've done a wonderful job," she said, turning to Nathaniel.

His gaze was fixed on her.

"Ella would be pleased."

Nathaniel ducked his head then. "I have one more room to show ya," he said quietly.

Amy hesitated. She knew there was only one more room on this floor besides the bathroom. Hank and Ella's bedroom.

No. She really didn't want to go there. Ella had died in her sleep, in her bed, in that very room. It would be too much. Amy couldn't stand in there knowing it was the last place…

"Trust me," Nathaniel said, his hand stretching out to her.

For a long moment, she stared at his hand—at the long fingers that had not thrown any punches that awful night because he knew taking the beating would be more protection for her.

Amy tilted her head down and blinked against tears. She forced her hand to reach out for his and found her trembling fingers enveloped by his own strong ones.

Nathaniel led Amy purposefully down the small hallway until he stood before the door. Gently, he turned the knob and pushed the door open. Amy stared at the scene before her. Standing in his bedroom would have been a bit strange and possibly a bit inappropriate. But this was not his bedroom. This was…an office. A large desk sat in the middle. Two bookshelves lined the wall behind it. A beat-up old office chair was pulled up to the desk, which displayed a small tin can filled with yellow pencils and a desk calendar.

It needed more—much like the rest of the house. But the bright blue walls of Ella's bedroom had been painted a soft gray, giving it a sense of calm and peace.

"Is yer room upstairs?" she asked, her question blunter than she intended.

Nathaniel nodded. "I haven't done much up there yet."

Amy had rarely been upstairs in Ella's home, but she knew there were several bedrooms there.

"There's something I wanted to give ya," Nathaniel continued, clearing his throat. "Ella's grandson brought it over yesterday."

He opened the desk drawer, pulled out a manila envelope, and handed it to Amy. She took it, feeling a familiar weight.

"He said they found it going through some of her things," Nathaniel explained. The look on his face was gentle and calm.

Amy held it, stared down at it, and shook her head. Surely this couldn't be her notebook.

"They weren't sure who it belonged to. That's why he stopped here—wondering if I would have any idea."

Amy couldn't speak. Her hands and her heart knew without opening the envelope what she held. All the recipes returned.

Nathaniel smiled softly. "I should get ya home before yer *daed* thinks I locked ya in the cooler."

Words had deserted her. Amy merely turned and walked back through the house and out the door, then climbed into the buggy. Nathaniel followed wordlessly in her wake.

"I'm sorry you've been through all that work to try to remember those recipes," he offered as he neared her driveway.

"I'm not," Amy answered, her voice sounding surprisingly steady.

Nathaniel smiled and nodded as he pulled into the long lane. He stopped beside the Millers' house. The lights were just now making the windows glow a rich, warm yellow. Mary would have supper on the table and Daniel would be sitting in his rocking chair, reading.

"There's one more thing," Nathaniel said. "Yer *daed* offered to sell me the market." His eyes searched hers, but of course Amy already knew. It would have been more of a shock had she not told her dad to ask Nathaniel.

Nathaniel must have seen the knowledge in her eyes.

"He said ya wanted me to be the one to buy it."

She dropped her eyes to her lap but managed to nod.

"The thing is, Amy, I don't want it without ya," he said as his fingers wound around hers.

Amy's head snapped up and her gaze flew to his face, dim in the evening light.

"What?" she breathed.

"I don't want it all on my own. It was never meant to be owned and run by just one person," he insisted. Her father had said the same to her on more than one occasion. She'd come to realize it, too. Evidently, so had Nathaniel.

He turned to face her.

"Amy, I only want what I can share with you."

Amy was suddenly aware of just how close he was. Buggies were tight spaces—something she was certainly used to. But it felt even smaller now.

She stared at Nathaniel, his face so close in the fading light.

He cupped her jaw with his hand. "I know you aren't sure. I know you're scared and don't want to get hurt again." He leaned forward, but instead of kissing her he simply pressed his forehead against hers. Just the way Ella had for all those goodbyes.

The familiarity of the action struck her, leaving her breathless.

"Amy, all those recipes are in yer heart. Look and see if ya find me there, too," he whispered.

꧁ ꧂

Amy sat on her bed and opened the old, worn notebook. She already knew what she would find—recipes that had been slowly returning to her. Caleb had nearly eaten himself sick this morning on the bounty of what she'd made the night before. Nathaniel hadn't known that she'd spent hours not just trying to remember, but successfully recreating every recipe. He hadn't known she had already searched her heart.

Her fingers brushed over the cover of the notebook he had given her. For the most part, it matched the old one. But inside there were instructions like Ella's—fistful of flour, pinch of salt, sprinkle of cinnamon. Gone were so many of the exact measurements, down to the smallest fraction.

Nathaniel was right. All of the time she'd spent making bars, cookies, muffins, breads, and cinnamon rolls before Ella died, before she'd lost this notebook, had been stored up in her heart, where they would not leave. It was her need for perfect instructions that had let her down.

But not anymore.

She thumbed through all the old pages, really seeing for the first time the girl she had been.

But her scanning stopped as she paged through. Shaky, almost messy handwriting that was not her own lay scrawled across a previously blank page. Amy's vision blurred with tears.

She had never expected to hear Ella's words again.

Oh, my dear girl,

These years with you have been such a treasure to me. How I loved getting to spend time with you. You have brought joy and peace to my heart. I only hope God used me to do the same for you. We don't always understand His ways, but they are always for our good.

Sometimes, a recipe will steer you wrong. Be brave enough to live without them.

Love,
Ella

— Chapter Forty-One —

Becca fidgeted beside him, checking and double checking for something in the bag on her lap. Nathaniel shifted slightly in the black vinyl chair next to her.

"Tell me again how I'll find him," Becca asked, her eyes not moving from the two hands that gripped the handle of her bag.

"It's very easy," Nathaniel reassured her. "When the train gets to Middlefield, ya get yer bag and get off the train. Go into the station. There's a waiting area there, much like this one, and he'll be there waiting for ya."

"You're sure about that?"

Nathaniel glanced at her face to see her lips pinched tightly together.

"*Jah*, I'm sure," he calmed her as he tried to resist the urge to smile.

Becca drew in a deep breath and nodded.

"What if he's not there?" she breathed.

"He'll be there," Nathaniel promised. No one knew Elam as well as he did.

"What if he doesn't want to see me?" Becca worried.

This was the real question. Truth be told, as well as he knew Elam, he did not know how Elam felt about Becca. Elam had always been kind to her. He was friendly to her whenever he came over to see Nathaniel. Then again, the fact Elam had invited Becca to the barn raising said something.

Nathaniel shrugged. "Sometimes all ya can do is tell someone how ya feel and see what happens," he answered quietly.

"*Jah.* You're right," she sighed. "*Denki* for staying with me while I wait."

"*Yer wilkum.*"

He glanced at the clock on the wall. At this rate, he'd likely be a little bit late for work, but he'd called Daniel very early this morning to let him know. What he would find when he got to the market he couldn't even begin to imagine.

⸙❦⸙

Amy set the last of the packaged baked goods on the table. It was absolutely covered—nearly overflowing. There were only a few more minutes until it was time to open. Daniel was in the back doing paperwork of some kind. Amy looked down at the whoopie pies, chocolate frosted brownies, sugar cookies, cinnamon bread, and cinnamon rolls with a sense of satisfaction.

Footsteps sounded behind her as Daniel moved to the front doors to unlock them. But they stopped, and she turned to see not her father standing near her, but Nathaniel.

His eyes scanned the table and flicked up to her face. The happiness there was almost more than she could take.

"Did ya get Becca to the station already?" she asked.

"*Jah.* Yer *daed* was in a hurry to get to David's this morning," Nathaniel answered, tilting his head to the windows where Daniel's buggy was indeed quickly leaving the parking lot.

"I see ya found yer returned notebook helpful." He smiled gently.

"Actually, I didn't use it," she told him, her eyes never leaving his face.

"Oh?"

Amy returned his smile "I'll cherish it always, of course. Especially with the note Ella wrote to me inside. But I like my new one better."

"Why is that?" His voice had dropped, and he took a step closer to her.

"It's less detailed, less structured, less…safe. It gives me room to adjust and adapt." She tilted her head back and forth. "You were right," she breathed. "They were all there."

Nathaniel took another step. "Now ya know you can trust yer heart to guide ya. You don't have to be afraid of what ya feel. There are important lessons and memories there—people who would never let ya down."

"You," she breathed, her eyes fixed on his.

Nathaniel stilled, swallowed, and closed his eyes. When he opened them, she saw her own hope mirrored there.

"Can ya trust me with yer heart? Believe that the depth of my love for ya would be far greater than any hurt I would ever cause ya? Believe that even if I saw the very worst of ya, I would still see ya as the best person I know? Believe that even if I failed ya, I would still lay down my life for yers?" he asked.

"We've already been through all that." Amy shook her head. "It's not hard to believe when you have proven it over and over." She took a step, closing the gap between them.

Nathaniel's arms slid easily around her waist, as if that was exactly where they belonged. She peered up into his face as her fingers twisted into his suspenders.

He smiled crookedly. "Might be risky."

"Might be worth it," she whispered with her own answering smile.

Nathaniel's head lowered then, and as his lips brushed against hers, she felt a thrill chase through her. But it wasn't fear. She wasn't afraid anymore. God had brought them together and given her more than she could have asked or imagined.

"I have something for ya," she murmured when he pulled away, his arms still warm and solid around her.

She opened her hand to reveal the small key in her palm.

"I want ya to have this."

Nathaniel released one of his arms to take it from her. His eyes searched her face.

"You know I only want this place if it is ours together," he said, looking intently in her eyes.

"Then it's a good thing we'll always be together," she answered.

Softly came the sound of a car pulling into the gravel parking. With a last quick kiss, Nathaniel grinned widely and backed away.

"Save me some of those cinnamon rolls," he said as he made his way to the glass doors.

Amy couldn't stop the laughter from bubbling up inside her. Every day with him. There wasn't anything better she could ask for.

Amy stood in the kitchen and surveyed the scene before her. Every drawer was pulled out and every cabinet door hung wide open. As far as she could tell, there was absolutely no rhyme or reason to how he had organized his few belongings. At least there wasn't much to rearrange. Less than twenty minutes later, she had pulled Ella's mixing bowl out of one of the many boxes in the living room and pulled open the cupboard where it had always been kept. On the wooden shelf was a ring where the base had left its mark over the decades. Amy slid it back into place and smiled. She knew, deep in her soul, that Ella would be pleased.

"I can see you've been making yerself at home," came the low morning voice of her husband.

Amy blushed as she watched him carefully buttoning the cuffs of his still-untucked white shirt. His hair was so much darker when it was wet. It was less than twenty-four hours since they'd been pronounced *mann* and wife. There was so much that was new. She hadn't anticipated feeling so utterly changed. She turned away from him, feeling shy.

Nathaniel's hands landed on the countertop on either side of her, effectively caging her between his arms. She felt his chest press against her back and bit her lip to hide the smile on her face.

"Here I thought I had done such a *gut* job of arranging the kitchen, only to find Mrs. Shetler doesn't approve," he rumbled, his lips brushing her ear.

Amy spun in his arms to face him.

"Hm," she hummed as she placed her hands against his chest. Had it really been a year since she'd almost fallen on the front deck of the market? "Mr. Shetler doesn't always know best when it comes to arrangements," she quipped playfully.

The crooked smile on Nathaniel's face held a knowing, but curious look. "Is that so? Then maybe I should ask Mrs. Shetler for a tour." His eyebrow quirked but his hands stayed firmly in place on the counter behind her.

Amy gave up on fighting the blush. There was just no way to act normally after...

"I think ya have enough new territory for now, sir. You just leave the kitchen to me."

Nathaniel's answering smile blazed across his face.

"New territory," he laughed.

"What would ya like for breakfast?" she asked, desperate for a subject that wouldn't make her face burn.

"There are just so many choices," he said in mock consternation.

"Cinnamon rolls. Cinnamon bread. Cream cheese muffins. Chocolate chip muffins. Bacon. Eggs. Toast. Pancakes."

Nathaniel's brows rose. "Yes." He lifted his palms from the counter, slid them around her waist, and pulled her against him. The touch made her stomach flip.

"Yes to what?" Amy laughed.

"Yes to all of it," he answered with a mischievous grin.

"All of it?! I can't make *all* of it. That would take a lifetime!"

Nathaniel's answering grin melted her. "Well, good thing we have a lifetime then."

"*Jah*," Amy whispered.

"I better *geh* check on those horses. They're probably very jealous of you and all the attention you've been getting," he said as he bent to kiss her.

"Come back soon," she called to his retreating back.

"Why, Mrs. Shetler, ya sound like a lovesick newlywed," Nathaniel declared in mock surprise as he placed his hat firmly atop his head.

Amy giggled. "Well, maybe that's because I am."

Nathaniel smirked. "*Jah*. Me too. Good thing God brought us together." He winked and pulled the door shut behind him.

She leaned to watch him out the window as he strode across their yard to the horse barn. Later today, she would make a homemade white cake in Ella's trusty old cake pan, whose broken lid still held together after all these years.

It had been broken into so many pieces, but Ella had just kept taping it back up. Cracked and beaten but mended and still useful—still wanted and loved by someone wonderful. Nathaniel and Ella, they had that in common.

— Second Epilogue —

Sally pulled in a deep breath as she smoothed her hands down her apron. A day at the Amish Country Market with Nathaniel and Amy was markedly different from a day at the market with Mary and Daniel. She looked over her shoulder to see that Mary was deeply engrossed in conversation with Nathaniel's mother, Leah Shetler, and Rachel Stoltzfus. They'd been talking for the past several minutes, leaving Sally to handle all the rest of the customers this cold December morning.

With a quick tuck back of her shoulders, she cheered herself to greet the English couple stepping up to the checkout counter.

Sally reached for the jar of homemade jam Beth Kauffman had made.

"Oh, I think you will enjoy this a lot!" she said warmly as she slid the jar across the wood counter toward her register. With one hand, she punched in the keys on the keypad. This, at least, was something she knew she did quicker than Mary. The cash register was added several years ago, when Amy began working at the market full-time. Mary still sometimes complained about the machine but made a good faith effort to use it properly.

"My friend makes this jam, and she has the very best recipe in the district. They grow their own strawberries in their yard every summer. You should see it! Their patch is bigger than our whole garden. Her strawberry jam is my favorite, but one time she made dandelion jam.

Now *that* was interesting!" Sally gushed as her fingers flew over the keys, adding up all the other items the couple placed on the counter.

Sally smiled at their wide-eyed faces. "Yer total is $43.19."

They wordlessly handed her a plastic credit card, which Sally quickly swiped through the small reader next to the register. With a quick tug, she yanked out the small tape and handed them their receipt.

"*Denki* so much for stopping! Come again!" she bubbled as they grasped the twisted twine handles of the small brown paper sack.

Another glance told her Mary's conversation was still in full swing. Near the sewing notions section, she spied Becca Shetler patiently waiting. Sally tossed a glance around the storefront and hoped she could help Becca with whatever she needed before the next customers were ready to check out.

"*Gut* morning, Becca!" Sally greeted her friend as she rounded the long table where they measured and cut yards of fabric. "An awful cold day out there, isn't it?"

"*Jah*, it is that," Becca agreed with a smile.

"What can I help ya with today?" Sally asked, her eyes darting over Becca's shoulder to where the other customers appeared to be still busy shopping.

"Could I get a couple yards of this emerald cotton?"

"Of course," Sally said, the scissors already in her hands. "Making a new dress? The new one ya wore to Nathaniel and Amy's wedding was especially lovely! I know Amy special ordered that fabric, and it looked so striking on ya. I love seeing all the new clothes at weddings, don't you? I don't think I will ever forget how lovely Amy looked that day. Or the happiness on Nathaniel's face."

Becca smiled gently. "*Nee*. Me either. They both seemed very happy."

Sally heard a strange note of wistfulness in Becca's voice but chose to let it pass without comment. She unrolled the bolt onto the table and measured two yards.

"This shade of green will be just the most beautiful thing on you! What a lovely choice! I think it would be so nice to see some green in the middle of this cold, cold winter. I'm really not sure if spring will ever get here. But then again, I tend to think that every year. I don't mind a little snow, but I'm not sure my *bruders* can pile the snow much higher at the end of our sidewalk," Sally continued as she eased the sheers through the length of dark green material.

"I'm tired of *schnee*, too," Becca admitted. "I was hoping to *geh* to Middlefield this weekend, but with the storms they are predicting…"

"Middlefield! You were just there, weren't you? I guess that was a few months ago already. I imagine ya still have many friends back there. It can't be easy to move to another state and leave all those loved ones behind ya. *Mei daed* is from Pennsylvania, but he moved here when he was just a young *buwe*. Even so he still thinks our bonnets are a funny shape. He's always teasing my *maam* that she should make a heart-shaped bonnet like the ones his *maam* and *schwesders* wore."

Sally saw a woman making her way to the checkout counter. With quick hands, she folded up the yards of fabric and handed the bundle to Becca.

"Will ya excuse me for a bit? I sure do miss Amy. Nathaniel too, of course. Don't get me wrong, Daniel and Mary know how to run a business. But Nathaniel and Amy are a well-oiled machine when it comes to running this place."

Leaving Becca behind, Sally rushed to the register and began punching in the few items the woman placed on the counter.

"I must be too late in the day for your baked goods," the English woman said with a disappointed frown.

"Oh! Well, truth be told, we don't have anything fresh this week because the baker of those yummy treats just got married and is on her wedding trip. You come back next week and I'm sure you'll find a wonderful selection to choose from. Her cinnamon bread is good, but my favorite is definitely her cream cheese muffins. Yer total is $13.59." Sally slid the items carefully into a paper bag and waited while the woman fished the bills out of her wallet.

"I guess I'll be back next week then," the woman said as she handed the bills to Sally.

"Well, we will look forward to seeing ya again soon!" Sally cheered as she slid the coins out of the drawer and into the woman's hand.

It wasn't until after Becca and Leah had left that Mary came to the register.

"I think I'll head to the back and see if there is anything I can help Daniel with," Mary said with a smile and a nod.

Sally rather thought it was Daniel who should take a step out of the back room and come see if there was anything they needed help with. But instead she merely returned Mary's smile and nod. As the swinging doors closed behind Mary, Sally closed her eyes and drew in a deep breath. She wouldn't exactly wish Nathaniel and Amy's wedding trip was over, but she did desperately miss them this morning.

The bell above the door jingled slightly and Sally took a moment to calm her heart before she launched into action.

"*Guder mariye,*" came a quiet voice.

Sally's eyes flew open to find Noah Esh standing on the other side of the counter. Noah was not tall and thin like Silas or Caleb or Nathaniel. He was shorter and stockier but still taller than Sally. His green eyes were bright beneath the brim of his stocking hat.

Sally beamed. "Noah! *Wie geht's?*"

A light blush covered his face, though that could just as easily be from the cold.

"Fine, *denki.* You?"

Sally drew in a deep breath and let it out. She could tell him how busy they had been, tell him how stressful the whole morning had been, but instead she just smiled brightly. "Well, I'm doing just fine. I'm mighty glad I don't have to *geh* out in the cold today, that's for sure. Is there something I can help ya with today? Or I'd be happy to get you a warm cup of coffee from the back, if ya like."

Noah merely shook his head at her offer of a hot drink. "I've been working on some of the outdoor furniture pieces Nathaniel asked for and thought I'd drop off what I got done."

"Oh, certainly! Nathaniel isn't here right now. He's on his wedding trip. But I'm sure he would be just fine with ya leaving the new pieces here where he stores the rest of the seasonal outdoor items. I could show ya if ya like," Sally offered.

Noah merely nodded.

"I sure was sorry to hear Ira is not doing well. But I am sure he is greatly relieved his business is in such capable hands!"

Noah made no response as he followed in her wake.

"Okay. This is our seasonal storage room. We have all kinds of things, as ya can see. You are welcome to put whatever ya want in here. Feel free to move some things around if ya need more space. Amy and Nathaniel are mighty particular about where things go when it comes to the storefront and the storage room. But this room they don't seem to care about as much. At least not yet. You just never know when that Amy is going to get a bee in her bonnet about straightening something up. It's a good thing she has Nathaniel..." Sally trailed off.

Noah was merely watching her as she talked.

"*Denki*," he finally said.

"Yer most *wilkum*. I would offer to help ya, but I don't really know how much help I would be. I'm guessing whatever ya brought is too heavy for me to lift. And ya look more than capable...of lifting...heavy things." Sally stopped abruptly. She felt her face flame and she quickly looked away. Usually, the more she talked the more she felt like she made sense. But somehow her words had gotten wildly out of control.

Noah cleared his throat and grinned. "I'm sure I can handle it from here."

"*Jah*," Sally croaked. "I'll just make sure to get you a receipt for what ya dropped off. Nathaniel likes to have record of everything our suppliers drop off. He's very particular about that sort of thing. I'll just be in the storefront, but I'll keep an eye out for ya. For when you're finished unloading, I mean." She quickly snapped her mouth shut again.

Noah nodded and Sally whirled and made her way over to Nathaniel's desk in the corner. He did most of the bookkeeping for the store at their home, but some paperwork needed to be done onsite. She pulled out the receipt book and filled it out. Keeping inventory was important to the market. Making sure none of the things people dropped off were lost or unaccounted for was something Nathaniel and Amy took very seriously. Perhaps she should keep a better inventory of her words, Sally thought. At least when she was around Noah.

By the time Noah stepped back inside, Sally had the receipt in her hand.

"There ya go," she said a bit too cheerfully as she handed him the slip of paper. "I'm sure glad ya brought those over today. The weather for tomorrow doesn't sound very pleasant. But since it's all outdoor furniture, I suppose it wouldn't have made too much of a difference. Even so, it would have been no fun to unload all of that in the rain."

Noah waited a beat and then smiled. "*Denki*, Sally."

"*Yer wilkum*," Sally quietly answered.

Noah's steps were slow and measured as he walked back to his wagon. He'd said her name. The sound of his voice saying her name echoed in her mind. For some reason, it sounded different when he said it. Different from anyone else.

᠃ᐤᑫ ᑫᐤ᠂

The basement of the Miller home was packed. Not surprising given how everyone seemed to love Caleb Miller. Caleb had an easy way with people. He could flirt with girls but never hurt their feelings. He could tease the boys but then laugh at his own mistakes and misadventures. He was a friend to everyone, and Sally counted herself a beneficiary of Caleb's kind nature and good-humored attention.

As the Singing drew to a close, the smell of freshly popped popcorn wafted down from the main floor. Sally's stomach growled quietly, and her mouth began to water. Just as the last song was finished, down came the giant bowls of popcorn, plates of cookies, and trays of bars.

"I'm surprised ya eat popcorn," said a quiet voice from behind her as she grabbed a handful of still-warm kernels out of the bowl.

Sally turned to see Noah standing behind her.

"*Mei bruders* grow it. I would guess this is actually their very own popcorn. They sell it at the market. They also sell it online. Kirsten helped them make a webpage and everything. They've actually even started to talk about trying some other varieties. Funny how people get all excited about the purple and the blue and the red popcorn, even though after it pops it's all the same color. I personally like the baby yellow popcorn the best," Sally said. Then, to stop herself from saying anything more, she popped some of the kernels into her mouth and started chewing.

Noah reached out and scooped up his own handful. "They do good work."

Sally giggled. "Most of the time, *jah*, that is true. They can be a mischievous handful at times, but their popcorn business has certainly taken off. I'm glad. It gives them something to do and keeps them out of the trouble they might find if they had more time on their hands. It's good to have something to do."

Noah shook his head. "I don't have younger siblings." Sally knew that, of course. "I imagine all of yer *bruders* and *schwesders* keep ya on yer toes."

"That's one way to put it! They sure are a busy lot. We all watch out for each other, but since I am the oldest it means I do most of the watching. I can only imagine being the youngest in a *familye*. Must be nice to have some peace and quiet every once in a while..." Sally's voice trailed off. She was most definitely *not* a source of peace and quiet in Noah's life these days.

He smiled crookedly. "*Jah.* I get plenty of peace and quiet. But I don't mind a little...conversation."

"One evening at my house would cure ya of that, I am certain." Sally shook her head with wide eyes.

Noah grinned and shook his head, staring down at the few kernels left in his hand.

"When you're ready to *geh*, I could give you a ride home," he said quietly.

For a minute, Sally wasn't sure she had heard him correctly. Had he really just offered her a ride home? No one had ever done that at Singing before. No one. Not once.

"Really?" she squeaked.

Noah nodded slowly. "Whenever you're ready," he said again.

"O-okay," Sally stammered.

Noah turned and walked easily away, so Sally forced herself to go and talk to her friends. She'd never had to *force* herself to talk before. But her attention was firmly focused on the young man on the other side the room. The one who would glance her way every now and then. As time passed, she began to wonder if perhaps she had misunderstood. Or perhaps Noah had misunderstood. Perhaps he hadn't realized her brother, Fletcher, was here and planning to give her a ride home. Perhaps Fletch had plans to drive a girl home and had asked Noah to take her. That would be a possibility, were it not for the fact Fletch did not seem the least bit ready to consider dating.

But sure enough, as the crowd began to thin and the Millers' basement began to empty out, she saw Noah move in her direction. His steps were slow and measured but purposeful.

"Ready?" he asked.

Sally merely nodded and followed along after him. She could feel the eyes of a great many of the youth staring after them. It certainly wasn't unusual for *buwes* to ask to drive a girl home after a Singing. That was the way things went in the Amish dating world. But it had never happened to Sally. And truth be told, she wasn't sure it had ever happened to Noah. She wracked her brain as she followed him. They'd lived in the same community, belonged to the same church district, for their entire lives. As she had grown up, Sally had seen his older siblings marry and establish homes of their own. But she couldn't remember ever hearing of Noah pursuing anyone.

And why not? She couldn't say there was any good reason Noah hadn't settled down yet. He was certainly handsome. With his dark hair, warm green eyes, and strong jaw, there was nothing lacking in his appearance. He was known for working hard—though that was evident by his muscled physique as much as by word of mouth. Noah was solid, dependable, and trustworthy. And there were plenty of girls who were waiting around for just such a man to settle down with.

If Noah was interested in her, well, she was beyond flattered. She could certainly do worse. Problem was, she could not fathom doing any better. She couldn't possibly understand why he would want her out of all the girls.

⚜ ❦ ⚜

Sitting next to a man who was not related to her was something Sally had done less than a handful of times. Not a single one of those times had it been with someone who specifically wanted to spend time with her.

As Noah turned to take the long way back to her house, she felt her stomach tighten. Was this really happening? She could hardly dare hope.

"Are ya warm enough?" he asked as the horse clopped ahead of their covered buggy.

"*Jah*, I am. *Denki* for asking. This rain sure has made the chill in the air feel colder, hasn't it? I am awfully tired of the rain. But I like snow, though I know some people complain about it. I think the world looks wonderfully crisp and clean under a blanket of fresh snow. That and it's really good moisture for the ground. Something we need when the spring comes around," she answered.

Sally held back a wince. Was she really going to talk about the weather? Again?

"Farmers don't mind snow," Noah agreed easily.

"Two of yer *bruders* farm, *jah*?" she asked. He nodded. "But ya took a different path." She let the statement hang. If he wanted to talk about his work, he could. If not, that was okay. She could just...talk more about the weather.

"I like working with my hands," he replied.

And for the next many, many miles their conversation flowed easily from work, to family, to friends and even their hobbies.

Sally felt a pang of disappointment as the warm lights of home peeked over the hill ahead of them. All too soon Noah had the buggy pulled up close to her house. She only had a few steps before she would be under the shelter of the porch roof and out of the rain.

"*Denki* for the ride home," she said quietly.

"Any time," Noah answered. The way he said it gave her goosebumps.

Sally slid out of the buggy and quickly skipped up to the door. She turned to give him a wave just before she turned the knob and pushed the door open. In the dark, she could see him wave back at her before the buggy lurched into motion and pulled away.

⋅ᴏᴇ ᴊᴀ⋅

The many hours Sally spent wondering when she would see Noah again turned out to be a waste, she realized when he came by the market with yet another load of furniture. Over the next days, weeks, and months, it seemed Noah was often there. At every Singing she would sit and watch and wait with a strange tickling anticipation in her stomach. But then he would arrive, find her across the room, and smile at her. And nothing else would matter.

Being with Noah was both the easiest and most exhilarating thing. Butterflies would assail her at first, then as the time passed they would ease into something different. The nervousness would melt away into a peaceful, contented happiness.

Noah wasn't a big talker, but he was a wonderful listener. Sally could tell because he would so often remember something she had said a week or two before and then ask her about it. He never seemed distracted or bored by her chatter.

And when the snowstorm came that Tuesday morning, it was Noah who showed up at the market, ready to take her home. He must have remembered she would be working that day. He must have made some kind of note that Fletch had brought her to work and planned to pick her up later that afternoon. And he must have somehow known she might need a ride home earlier than planned. How it all happened, she didn't really understand. But when she found herself tucked in tight against his warm, solid body, she didn't particularly care. It felt familiar, comfortable, and entirely right to be snuggled in next to him—more so than any other person in the world.

"I'm glad ya came when ya did," Sally confessed. "I was getting worried watching the wind pick up and the snow fall. Nathaniel said the storm was going to be a doozy. I know he would have taken me home, but I am sure glad he didn't have to. I don't like it when he leaves Amy at the store alone. And I know he doesn't like it. Not after that attack. Thank goodness those men were caught and we don't have to worry about them anymore."

"I feel better with you home safe with this weather blowing in," Noah admitted. "Even if ya like a good snow."

"When I was a child, there was nothing better than a fresh snow. I loved snowstorms, too. Those days when it would snow so much that we didn't have school were such fun. *Maam* would get out board games and we would make wonderful snacks. We would make homemade hot chocolate and our own paper snowflakes. No one can cut a snowflake like *mei maam*. I hope that didn't sound prideful. It's just that she is so *gut* with a scissors after all her years of sewing. What would ya do on snow days?" She asked, turning her face to him.

Noah grinned. "Chores."

"Oh, that's no fun!" Sally argued.

Noah laughed then.

"Sometimes we would go sledding. *Mei bruders* would pull me up the hill in the sled."

"*Jah*, us older siblings get to do that a lot!" Sally agreed with wide eyes. "It's a lot of work to take little ones sledding. You should come over and help me out with my *familye* sometime."

"Maybe when the wind dies down," he offered.

"I'd like that," Sally said quietly.

Noah pulled the buggy up to her house. It appeared quiet from the outside, but Sally knew it would be a different story inside.

Sally turned to give Noah a warm smile and thank him for the ride, but she found him much closer than she expected.

"*Denki*, Noah," she said quietly.

He leaned closer.

"Any time," he said lowly. Slowly and gently, he pressed his lips against hers.

Sally sat frozen, blinking back at him.

"Aren't ya going to say something?" he asked after a long moment.

Sally's mouth opened and closed several times, but no words came out. She stared at Noah as he merely stared back at her.

Finally, her fingers softly touched her lips where his had just been. She had so many words, so many thoughts. And yet, there was nothing. Nothing she could say. None of the words would line up into sentences.

"I-I don't know what to say," she finally stuttered.

Noah frowned slightly but swallowed and eased back.

The silence was more than she could take. But she couldn't break it. A gust of wind blew hard against the buggy and she felt it sway. With a jerky movement, Sally opened the door and jumped out. After quickly closing the door, she ran inside the house.

Inside she leaned against the closed door, her heart pounding, her ears roaring, and her lips tingling. The voices of her siblings filled the house. But inside Sally's head, there was overwhelming silence.

⊷⊱❀⊰⊶

The small pile of sand and salt she had swept up was evidence of the type of week they had endured. Nathaniel went out multiple times each day to chip away at the layers of ice that coated the long deck that surrounded the market. He'd been sprinkling sand and salt over the steps as well. And of course the customers, few and far between, were tracking it in.

"Sure has been a quiet week," Amy observed as she watched Nathaniel scattering more of sand and salt.

"Mm," Sally hummed in agreement. She pulled the small pile over to her dustpan and bent to sweep it all up.

"You don't have to, but if ya want to *geh* home ya surely can," Amy offered.

Sally peered out the glass doors. The sky was gray but calm. Not stormy.

"*Nee*. Fletch is planning to pick me up at four o'clock."

"Maybe ya could call someone to pick ya up earlier," Amy suggested. Her voice was low and gentle.

Sally could only shake her head.

"Is everything all right, Sally? You don't seem…yerself," Amy asked, her brow furrowing as Sally moved to put the broom behind the counter.

"I'm fine," Sally insisted. Was she though? Noah had kissed her. Actually kissed her on the lips. She should be dancing on air, twirling around the store with a silly grin on her face. But instead of smiling at Noah and being sweet, she had stared at him mutely. Then, to make matters worse, she had run into the house without explanation or even saying goodbye. What he must think of her…

She'd never expected a *buwe* to like her. Then again, Noah was more of a man than a boy. It was thrilling and a little scary.

"Oh, here's Ira," Amy murmured as she stared out the glass. Sally's head whipped up to follow her gaze. Sure as she was breathing there was Ira, Noah's boss, with a buggy-load of furniture. Far more pieces than Noah typically brought over in one delivery. Nathaniel showed old Ira the seasonal storage room.

It took forever for Ira and his other young apprentice, Abe, to unload the whole wagon. It would have taken Noah far less time.

Why hadn't Noah made the delivery?

Guilt settled thick and uneasy in Sally's stomach.

ᴥᴥᴥ

Sally craned her neck to see past the rows and rows of older married women ahead of her. Somewhere, on the opposite side of the Glicks' house, Noah must be sitting. She hadn't seen him when she arrived, but then again most of the men had been in the barn, tending to the horses. Even now, with the second and final sermon well underway, she could not see him from where she sat.

If she could just catch his eye...

And apologize. She just wanted to explain and apologize. Her strange behavior the other night was rude and truly not how she had meant to treat him. He'd just...surprised her so.

This was certainly the longest church service of her entire life.

When the service at last ended, Sally nearly sagged in relief. But then the butterflies came raging back. It took far too many minutes for all the other members to file out of the house into the crisp winter air. By the time Sally's feet hit the wraparound front porch, the yard was filled with a swarm of black-coated and felt-hatted Amish men. With a hand up to shield her eyes, she searched for Noah.

Sally moved through the yard, peering at all the faces. None of them were Noah.

Where could he have gone? Had he even come to church?

She stared up and down the yard, until her eyes landed on a buggy making its way down the driveway to the road. It was Noah. She knew it. She ran a few steps and then stopped, feeling utterly foolish. She wasn't going to catch up to his horse. That much was obvious. And she didn't want to make more of a scene than she already was.

Something was wrong. Sally knew that, too. Noah never left so quickly after church. What was worse—she knew it was because of her.

.⊶⊷.

Noah looked out the window at the sound of a buggy pulling onto the yard. When he saw Caleb climbing out, he went for his coat.

"Just the guy I was looking for!" Caleb called as he climbed out of his buggy. He reached back in and pulled out the chainsaw he had borrowed last week.

"Did ya get them all down before the storm came?" Noah asked, taking the chainsaw from Caleb's large hands.

"*Jah*. Good thing, too. Those suckers would be frozen solid now," he laughed. "*Denki* for letting me borrow that," Caleb said with a nod at the chainsaw.

Noah nodded. "Any time."

"Speaking of being the guy I was looking for…" Caleb drawled as he leaned against his buggy, crossing his arms across his chest.

Noah studied him.

"Seems I'm not the only one looking for ya today." Caleb smirked.

Noah frowned. "I don't know what ya mean by that."

"Well…" Caleb quirked a brow. "I saw a certain chatty young lady running after yer buggy after church today."

Noah's eyes fixed on Caleb's face. But even though the young man was teasing him, he was obviously telling the truth. Noah's heart fell to his stomach. If he had seen her, he would have stopped. He never would have left if he'd known Sally wanted to talk. He had been so determined to escape before she noticed him, he never realized…Never thought…

"I'd better take care of this," Noah said, lifting the chainsaw and moving to put it away in the shop.

Caleb grinned. "What about Sally?"

"That too," Noah murmured.

.⊶⊷.

The house was blissfully quiet for once. Sally pulled in a deep breath and tried to let the quiet soak into her bones. But the peace didn't calm her heart.

With the rest of her family off at a friend's house for the evening, she needed the time alone to just sit, and think, and pray. She didn't feel sociable. There were certain words she wanted to say, but those words were only for Noah.

How could she explain? How could she tell him he was the dream she had never dared to have for herself? How could she explain she had never seen his kiss coming and it had frightened her? But in the very best way.

The sudden knock on the door startled her. She hadn't heard a buggy pull up, but then again she had been lost in her thoughts. She rushed to open it. With a tug, she yanked it open and stood staring at the one person she hadn't expected to see.

"Can I come in?" Noah asked, his eyes warm and gentle and fixed wholly on her face.

"*Jah*," Sally breathed.

"Someone told me you were looking for me after church today," he explained.

"S-someone?" she stammered.

Noah ignored the question but pulled the hat from his head. "I wouldn't have left so quickly if I had known."

"I—I did want to talk to ya."

Noah merely nodded and stood, waiting patiently.

Never in her whole life could Sally remember struggling to find words. There were always words—far too many words—just rattling around in her head. They always seemed to just come spilling out. Often almost uncontrollably. But not tonight. Not now.

Noah drew in a deep breath and slowly let it out. "Are ya upset that I kissed you?" he asked gently.

"*Nee*," Sally whispered.

"You don't talk anymore," Noah murmured.

"I have so many words that I just don't know what to say first," she said, pressing her cool hands against her warm cheeks.

Noah smiled then. "Doesn't matter what ya say first. Just say something."

"I talk too much," Sally said abruptly.

"Not lately." Noah quirked an eyebrow at her.

"*Nee*, I mean that's why people—*buwes*—avoid me. Because I talk too much."

"I don't think ya do," Noah said evenly.

"You don't?" Sally asked in quiet surprise.

"*Nee*."

"It doesn't…bother ya? That I never stop talking?" she asked. That was the real fear. That was what had driven her out of the buggy that night. That was what had bothered her all these days since. What if her constant chatter was something he just put up with or tolerated? She didn't want to be tolerated.

"Doesn't bother me at all."

Sally stared at him. Noah's face was calm, patient, and kind. He wasn't holding in laughter—some humor at her expense. He wasn't irritated by her questions or her awkwardness. He wasn't angry she had panicked and reacted badly.

"I like listening to ya," he said.

"You do?" Sally stared in amazement.

"*Jah*. Besides…" Noah smiled crookedly and took a step closer. "I think I may have found a way to quiet ya down every once in a while."

Sally blinked up at him.

Very slowly, Noah lowered his lips to hers and kissed her.

"I'm glad you kissed me," Sally whispered as he pulled away.

The warmth and love in Noah's eyes made her feel melty inside.

"You should do it again," Sally breathed.

Noah kissed her again, and this time Sally's fingers wrapped around his suspenders and pulled him closer.

"I never thought I would find someone who could love me," Sally admitted as she stood in his embrace.

"You're awfully easy to love," Noah murmured.

For the first time, Sally felt like he might be right. And there wasn't a thing she needed to say about it.